OCT 7 2010

D1272043

The Juniper Tree

AND OTHER BLUE ROSE STORIES

The Juniper Tree

AND OTHER BLUE ROSE STORIES

||||||||||||||||||||||||||||||||||||||||||||||||||||||||||||||||||||||||||||||||||||||||||||||||||||||||

PETER STRAUB

Subterranean Press 2010

First Edition

ISBN
978-1-59606-295-5

Subterranean Press
PO Box 190106
Burton, MI 48519

www.subterraneanpress.com

Table of Contents

Blue Rose

for Rosemary Clooney

1

ON A STIFLING SUMMER day the two youngest of the five Beevers children, Harry and Little Eddie, were sitting on cane backed chairs in the attic of their house on South Sixth Street in Palmyra, New York. Their father called it "the upstairs junk room," as this large irregular space was reserved for the boxes of tablecloths, stacks of diminishingly sized girls' winter coats, and musty old dresses Maryrose Beevers had mummified as testimony to the superiority of her past to her present.

A tall mirror that could be tilted in its frame, an artifact of their mother's onetime glory, now revealed to Harry the rear of Little Eddie's head. This object,

9

looking more malleable than a head should be, was just peeking above the back of the chair. Even the back of Little Eddie's head looked tense to Harry.

"Listen to me," Harry said. Little Eddie squirmed in his chair, and the wobbly chair squirmed with him. "You think I'm kidding you? I had her last year."

"Well, she didn't kill *you*," Little Eddie said.

"'Course not, she liked me, you little dummy. She only hit me a couple of times. She hit some of those kids every single day."

"But teachers can't *kill* people," Little Eddie said.

At nine, Little Eddie was only a year younger than he, but Harry knew that his undersized fretful brother saw him as much a part of the world of big people as their older brothers.

"Most teachers can't," Harry said. "But what if they live right in the same building as the principal? What if they won *teaching awards,* hey, and what if every other teacher in the place is scared stiff of them? Don't you think they can get away with murder? Do you think anybody really misses a snot-faced little brat—a little brat like you? Mrs. Franken took this kid, this runty little Tommy Golz, into the cloakroom, and she killed him right there. I heard him scream. At the end, it sounded just like bubbles. He was trying to yell, but there was too much blood in his throat. He never came back, and nobody ever said boo about it. She killed him, and next year she's going to be your teacher. I hope you're afraid, Little Eddie, because you ought to be." Harry leaned forward. "Tommy Golz even looked sort of like you, Little Eddie."

Little Eddie's entire face twitched as if a lightning bolt had crossed it.

In fact, the young Golz boy had suffered an epileptic fit and been removed from school, as Harry knew.

"Mrs. Franken especially hates selfish little brats that don't share their toys."

"I do share my toys," Little Eddie wailed, tears beginning to run down through the delicate smears of dust on his cheeks. "Everybody *takes* my toys, that's why."

"So give me your Ultraglide Roadster," Harry said. This had been Little Eddie's birthday present, given three days previous by a beaming father and a scowling mother. "Or I'll tell Mrs. Franken as soon as I get inside that school, this fall."

Under its layer of grime, Little Eddie's face went nearly the same white-gray shade as his hair.

An ominous slamming sound came up the stairs.

"Children? Are you messing around up there in the attic? Get down here!"

"We're just sitting in the chairs, Mom," Harry called out.

"Don't you bust those chairs! Get down here this minute!"

Little Eddie slid out of his chair and prepared to bolt.

"I want that car," Harry whispered. "And if you don't give it to me, I'll tell Mom you were foolin' around with her old clothes."

"I didn't do nothin'!" Little Eddie wailed, and broke for the stairs.

"Hey, Mom, we didn't break any stuff, honest!" Harry yelled. He bought a few minutes more by adding, "I'm coming right now," and stood up and went toward a cardboard box filled with interesting books he had noticed the day before his brother's birthday, and which had been his goal before he had remembered the Roadster and coaxed Little Eddie upstairs.

When, a short time later, Harry came through the door to the attic steps, he was carrying a tattered paperback book. Little Eddie stood quivering with misery and rage just outside the bedroom the two boys shared with their older brother Albert. He held out a small blue metal car, which Harry instantly took and eased into a front pocket of his jeans.

"When do I get it back?" Little Eddie asked.

"Never," Harry said. "Only selfish people want to get presents back. Don't you know anything at all?" When Eddie pursed his face up to wail, Harry tapped the book in his hands and said, "I got something here that's going to help you with Mrs. Franken, so don't complain."

||||||||||||||||||||||||||||||||||||||||||||||||||||||

HIS MOTHER INTERCEPTED him as he came down the stairs to the main floor of the little house—here were the kitchen and living room, both floored with faded linoleum, the actual "junk room" separated by a stiff brown woolen curtain from the little makeshift room where Edgar Beevers slept, and the larger bedroom reserved for Maryrose. Children were never permitted more than a few steps within this awful chamber, for they might disarrange Maryrose's mysterious "papers" or interfere with the rows of antique dolls on the window seat which was the sole, much-revered architectural distinction of the Beevers house.

Maryrose Beevers stood at the bottom of the stairs, glaring suspiciously up at her fourth son. She did not ever look like a woman who played with dolls, and she did not look that way now. Her hair was twisted into a knot at the back of her head. Smoke from her cigarette curled up past the big glasses like bird's wings, which magnified her eyes.

Harry thrust his hand into his pocket and curled his fingers protectively around the Ultraglide Roadster.

"'Those things up there are the possessions of my family," she said. "Show me what you took."

Harry shrugged and held out the paperback as he came down within striking range.

His mother snatched it from him, and tilted her head to see its cover through the cigarette smoke. "Oh. This is from that little box of books up there? Your father used to pretend to read books." She squinted at the print on the cover. *"Hypnosis Made Easy.* Some drugstore trash. You want to read this?"

Harry nodded.

"I don't suppose it can hurt you much." She negligently passed the book back to him. "People in society read books, you know—I used to read a lot, back before I got stuck here with a bunch of dummies. *My* father had a lot of books."

Maryrose nearly touched the top of Harry's head, then snatched back her hand. "You're my scholar, Harry. You're the one who's going places."

"I'm gonna do good in school next year," he said.

"*Well.* You're going to do well. As long as you don't ruin every chance you have by speaking like your father."

Harry felt that particular pain composed of scorn, shame, and terror that filled him when Maryrose spoke of his father in this way. He mumbled something that sounded like acquiescence, and moved a few steps sideways and around her.

2

THE PORCH OF the Beevers house extended six feet on either side of the front door, and was the repository for furniture either too large to be crammed into the junk room or too humble to be enshrined in the attic. A sagging porch swing sat beneath the living room window, to the left of an ancient couch whose imitation green leather had been repaired with black duct tape; on the other side of the front door through which Harry Beevers now emerged stood a useless icebox dating from the earliest days of the Beeverses' marriage and two unsteady camp chairs Edgar Beevers had won in a card game. These had never been allowed into the house. Unofficially, this side of the porch was Harry's father's, and thereby had an entirely different atmosphere—defeated, lawless, and shameful—from the side with the swing and couch.

Harry knelt down in neutral territory directly before the front door and fished the Ultraglide Roadster from his pocket. He placed the hypnotism book on the porch and rolled the little metal car across its top. Then he gave the car a hard shove and watched it clunk nosedown onto the wood. He repeated this several times before moving the book aside, flattening himself out on his stomach, and giving the little car a decisive push toward the swing and the couch.

The Roadster rolled a few feet before an irregular board tilted it over on its side and stopped it.

"You dumb car," Harry said, and retrieved it. He gave it another push deeper into his mother's realm. A stiff, brittle section of paint which had separated from its board cracked in half and rested atop the stalled Roadster like a miniature mattress.

Harry knocked off the chip of paint and sent the car backward down the porch, where it flipped over again and skidded into the side of the icebox. The boy ran down the porch and this time simply hurled the

15

little car back in the direction of the swing. It bounced off the swing's padding and fell heavily to the wood. Harry knelt before the icebox, panting.

His whole head felt funny, as if wet hot towels had been stuffed inside it. Harry picked himself up and walked across to where the car lay before the swing. He hated the way it looked, small and helpless. He experimentally stepped on the car and felt it pressing into the undersole of his moccasin. Harry raised his other foot and stood on the car, but nothing happened. He jumped on the car, but the moccasin was no better than his bare foot. Harry bent down to pick up the Roadster.

"You dumb little car," he said. "You're no good anyhow, you low-class little jerky thing." He turned it over in his hands. Then he inserted his thumbs between the frame and one of the little tires. When he pushed, the tire moved. His face heated. He mashed his thumbs against the tire, and the little black doughnut popped into the tall thick weeds in front of the porch. Breathing hard more from emotion than exertion, Harry popped the other front tire into the weeds. Harry whirled around, and ground the car into the wall beside his father's bedroom window. Long deep scratches appeared in the paint. When Harry peered at the top of the car, it too was scratched. He found a nail head which protruded a quarter of an inch out from the front of the house, and scraped a long paring of blue paint off the driver's side of the Roadster. Gray metal shone through. Harry slammed the car several times against the edge of the nail head, chipping off small quantities of paint. Panting, he popped off the two small rear tires and put them in his pocket because he liked the way they looked.

Without tires, well-scratched and dented, the Ultraglide Roadster had lost most of its power. Harry looked it over with a bitter, deep satisfaction and walked across the porch and shoved it far into the nest of weeds. Gray metal and blue paint shone at him from within the stalks and leaves. Harry thrust his hands into their midst and swept his arms back and forth. The car tumbled away and fell into invisibility.

When Maryrose appeared scowling on the porch, Harry was seated serenely on the squeaking swing, looking at the first few pages of the paperback book.

"What are you doing? What was all that banging?"

"I'm just reading, I didn't hear anything," Harry said.

3

"WELL, IF IT isn't the shitbird," Albert said, jumping up the porch steps thirty minutes later. His face and T-shirt bore broad black stripes of grease. A short, muscular thirteen-year-old, Albert spent every possible minute hanging around the gas station two blocks from their house. Harry knew that Albert despised him. Albert raised a fist and made a jerky, threatening motion toward Harry, who flinched. Albert had often beaten him bloody, as had their two older brothers, Sonny and George, now at Army bases in Oklahoma and Germany. Like Albert, his two oldest brothers had seriously disappointed their mother.

Albert laughed, and this time swung his fist within a couple of inches of Harry's face. On the backswing he knocked the book from Harry's hands.

"Thanks," Harry said.

Albert smirked and disappeared around the front door. Almost immediately Harry could hear his mother beginning to shout about the grease on Albert's face and clothes. Albert thumped up the stairs.

Harry opened his clenched fingers and spread them wide, closed his hands into fists, then spread them wide again. When he heard the bedroom door slam shut upstairs, he was able to get off the swing and pick up the book. Being around Albert made him feel like a spring coiled up in a box. From the upper rear of the house, Little Eddie emitted a ghostly wail. Maryrose screamed that she was going to start smacking him if he didn't shut up, and that was that. The three unhappy lives within the house fell back into silence. Harry sat down, found his page, and began reading again.

A man named Dr. Roland Mentaine had written *Hypnosis Made Easy,* and his vocabulary was much larger than Harry's. Dr. Mentaine used words like "orchestrate" and "ineffable" and "enhance," and some of his sentences wound their way through so many subordinate clauses that Harry lost his way. Yet Harry, who had begun the book only half-expecting that he would comprehend anything in it at all, found it a wonderful book. He had made it most of the way through the chapter call "Mind Power."

Harry thought it was neat that hypnosis could cure smoking, stuttering, and bed-wetting. (He himself had wet the bed almost nightly until months after his ninth birthday. The bed-wetting stopped the night a certain lovely dream came to Harry. In the dream he had to urinate terribly, and was hurrying down a stony castle corridor past suits of armor and torches guttering on the walls. At last Harry reached an open door, through which he saw the most splendid bathroom of his life. The floors were of polished marble, the walls white-tiled. As soon as he entered the gleaming bathroom, a uniformed butler waved him toward the rank of urinals. Harry began pulling down his zipper, fumbled with himself, and got his penis out of his underpants just in time. As the dream-urine gushed out of him, Harry had blessedly awakened.) Hypnotism could get you right inside someone's mind and let you do things there. You could make a person speak in any foreign language they'd ever heard, even if they'd only heard it once, and you could make them act like a baby. Harry considered how pleasurable it would be to make his brother Albert lie squalling and red-faced on the floor, unable to walk or speak as he pissed all over himself.

Also, and this was a new thought to Harry, you could take a person back to a whole row of lives they had led before they were born as the person they were now. This process of rebirth was called reincarnation. Some of Dr. Mentaine's patients had been kings in Egypt and pirates in the Caribbean, some had been murderers, novelists, and artists. They remembered the houses they'd lived in, the names of their mothers and servants and children, the locations of shops where they'd bought cake and wine. Neat stuff, Harry thought. He wondered if someone who had been a famous murderer a long time ago could remember pushing in the knife or bringing down the hammer. A lot of the books remaining in the little cardboard box upstairs, Harry had noticed, seemed to be about murderers. It would not be any use to take Albert back to a previous life, however. If Albert had any previous lives, he had spent them as inanimate objects on the order of boulders and anvils.

Maybe in another life Albert was a murder weapon, Harry thought.

"Hey, college boy! Joe College!"

Harry looked toward the sidewalk and saw the baseball cap and T-shirted gut of Mr. Petrosian, who lived in a tiny house next to the tavern on the corner of South Sixth and Livermore Street. Mr. Petrosian was always shouting genial things at kids, but Maryrose wouldn't let Harry or Little Eddie talk to him. She said Mr. Petrosian was common as dirt. He worked as a janitor in the telephone building and drank a case of beer every night while he sat on his porch.

"Me?" Harry said.

"Yeah! Keep reading books, and you could go to college, right?"

Harry smiled noncommittally. Mr. Petrosian lifted a wide arm and continued to toil down the street toward his house next to the Idle Hour.

In seconds Maryrose burst through the door, folding an old white dish towel in her hands. "Who was that? I heard a man's voice."

"Him," Harry said, pointing at the substantial back of Mr. Petrosian, now half of the way home.

"What did he say? As if it could possibly be interesting, coming from an Armenian janitor."

"He called me Joe College."

Maryrose startled him by smiling.

"Albert says he wants to go back to the station to-night, and I have to go to work soon." Maryrose worked the night shift as a secretary at St. Joseph's Hospital. "God knows when your father'll show up. Get something to eat for Little Eddie and yourself, will you, Harry? I've just got too many things to take care of, as usual."

"I'll get something at Big John's." This was a hamburger stand, a magical place to Harry, erected the summer before in a vacant lot on Livermore Street two blocks down from the Idle Hour.

His mother handed him two carefully folded dollar bills, and he pushed them into his pocket. "Don't let Little Eddie stay in the house alone," his mother said before going back inside. "Take him with you. You know how scared he gets."

"Sure," Harry said, and went back to his book. He finished the chapter on "Mind Power" while first Maryrose left to stand up at the bus stop on the corner, and then while Albert noisily departed. Little Eddie sat frozen before his soap operas in the living room. Harry turned a page and started reading "Techniques of Hypnosis."

4

AT EIGHT-THIRTY THAT night the two boys sat alone in the kitchen, on opposite sides of the table covered in yellow bamboo Formica. From the living room came the sound of Sid Caesar babbling in fake German to Imogene Coca on "Your Show of Shows." Little Eddie claimed to be scared of Sid Caesar, but when Harry had returned from the hamburger stand with a Big Johnburger (with "the works") for himself and a Mama Marydog for Eddie, double fries, and two chocolate shakes, he had been sitting in front of the television, his face moist with tears of moral outrage. Eddie usually liked Mama Marydogs, but he had taken only a couple of meager bites from the one before him now, and was disconsolately pushing a french fry through a blob of ketchup. Every now and then he wiped at his eyes, leaving nearly symmetrical smears of ketchup to dry on his cheeks.

"Mom *said* not to leave me alone in the house," said Little Eddie. "I heard. It was during 'The Edge of Night' and you were on the porch. I think I'm gonna tell on you." He peeped across at Harry, then quickly looked back at the french fry and drew it out of the puddle of ketchup. "I'm ascared to be alone in the house." Sometimes Eddie's voice was like a queer speeded-up mechanical version of Maryrose's.

"Don't be so dumb," Harry said, almost kindly. "How can you be scared in your own house? You live here, don't you?"

"I'm ascared of the attic," Eddie said. He held the dripping french fry before his mouth and pushed it in. "The attic makes noise." A little squirm of red appeared at the corner of his mouth. "You were supposed to take me with you."

"Oh, jeez, Eddie, you slow everything down. I wanted to just get the food and come back. I got you your dinner, didn't I? Didn't I get you what you like?"

In truth, Harry liked hanging around Big John's by himself because then he could talk to Big John and listen to his theories. Big John called himself a "renegade Papist" and considered Hitler the greatest man of the twentieth century, followed closely by Paul XI, Padre Pio who bled from the palms of his hands, and Elvis Presley.

The Juniper Tree
AND OTHER BLUE ROSE STORIES

All these events occurred in what is usually but wrongly called a simpler time, before Kennedy and feminism and ecology, before the Nixon presidency and Watergate, and before American soldiers, among them a twenty-one-year-old Harry Beevers, journeyed to Vietnam.

"I'm still going to tell," said Little Eddie. He pushed another french fry into the puddle of ketchup. "And that car was my birthday present." He began to snuffle. "Albert hit me, and you stole my car, and you left me alone, and I was scared. And I don't wanna have Mrs. Franken next year, cuz I think she's gonna hurt me."

Harry had nearly forgotten telling his brother about Mrs. Franken and Tommy Golz, and this reminder brought back very sharply the memory of destroying Eddie's birthday present.

Eddie twisted his head sideways and dared another quick look at his brother. "Can I have my Ultraglide Roadster back, Harry? You're going to give it back to me, aren'cha? I won't tell Mom you left me alone if you give it back."

"Your car is okay," Harry said. "It's in a sort of a secret place I know."

"You hurt my car!" Eddie squalled. "You did!"

"Shut up!" Harry shouted, and Little Eddie flinched. "You're driving me crazy!" Harry yelled. He realized that he was leaning over the table, and that Little Eddie was getting ready to cry again. He sat down. "Just don't scream at me like that, Eddie."

"You did something to my car," Eddie said with a stunned certainty. "I knew it."

"Look, I'll prove your car is okay," Harry said, and took the two rear tires from his pocket and displayed them on his palm.

Little Eddie stared. He blinked, then reached out tentatively for the tires.

Harry closed his fist around them. "Do they look like I did anything to them?"

"You took them *off!*"

"But don't they look okay, don't they look fine?" Harry opened his fist, closed it again, and returned the tires to his pocket. "I didn't want to show you the whole car, Eddie, because you'd get all worked up, and you gave it to me. Remember? I wanted to show you the tires so you'd see everything was all right. Okay? Got it?"

Eddie miserably shook his head.

"Anyway, I'm going to help you, just like I said."

"With Mrs. Franken?" A fraction of his misery left Little Eddie's smeary face.

"Sure. You ever hear of something called hypnotism?"

"I heard a hypmotism." Little Eddie was sulking. "Everybody in the whole world heard a that."

"Hypnotism, stupid, not hypmotism."

"Sure, hypmotism. I saw it on the TV. They did it on 'As the World Turns.' A man made a lady go to sleep and think she was going to have a baby."

Harry smiled. "That's just TV, Little Eddie. Real hypnotism is a lot better than that. I read all about it in one of the books from the attic."

Little Eddie was still sulky because of the car. "So what makes it better?"

"Because it lets you do amazing things," Harry said. He called on Dr. Mentaine. "Hypnosis unlocks your mind and lets you use all the power you really have. If you start now, you'll really knock those books when school starts up again. You'll pass every test Mrs. Franken gives you, just like the way I did." He reached across the table and grasped Little Eddie's wrist, stalling a fat brown french fry on its way to the puddle. "But it won't just make you good in school. If you let me try it on you, I'm pretty sure I can show you that you're a lot stronger than you think you are."

Eddie blinked.

"And I bet I can make you so you're not scared of anything anymore. Hypnotism is real good for that. I read in this book, there was this guy who was afraid of bridges. Whenever he even *thought* about crossing a bridge he got all dizzy and sweaty. Terrible stuff happened to him, like he lost his job and once he just had to ride in a car across a bridge and he dumped a load in his pants. He went to see Dr. Mentaine, and Dr. Mentaine hypnotized him and said he would never be afraid of bridges again, and he wasn't."

Harry pulled the paperback from his hip pocket. He opened it flat on the table and bent over the pages. "Here. Listen to this. 'Benefits of the course of treatment were found in all areas of the patient's life, and results were obtained for which he would have paid any price.'" Harry read these words haltingly, but with complete understanding.

"Hypmotism can make me strong?" Little Eddie asked, evidently having saved this point in his head.

"Strong as a bull."

"Strong as Albert?"

"A lot stronger than Albert. A lot stronger than me, too."

"And I can beat up on big guys that hurt me?"

"You just have to learn how."

Eddie sprang up from the chair, yelling nonsense. He flexed his stringlike biceps and for some time twisted his body into a series of muscleman poses.

"You want to do it?" Harry finally asked.

Little Eddie popped into his chair and stared at Harry. His T-shirt's neck band sagged all the way to his breastbone without ever actually touching his chest. "I wanna start."

"Okay, Eddie, good man." Harry stood up and put his hand on the book. "Up to the attic."

"Only, I don't wanna go in the attic," Eddie said. He was still staring at Harry, but his head was tilted over like a weird little echo of Maryrose, and his eyes had filled with suspicion.

"I'm not gonna *take* anything from you, Little Eddie," Harry said. "It's just, we should be out of everybody's way. The attic's real quiet."

Little Eddie stuck his hand inside his T-shirt and let his arm dangle from the wrist.

"You turned your shirt into an armrest," Harry said.

Eddie jerked his hand out of its sling.

"Albert might come waltzing in and wreck everything if we do it in the bedroom."

"If you go up first and turn on the lights," Eddie said.

5

HARRY HELD THE book open on his lap, and glanced from it to Little Eddie's tense smeary face. He had read these pages over many times while he sat on the porch. Hypnotism boiled down to a few simple steps, each of which led to the next. The first thing he had to do was get his brother started right, "relaxed and receptive," according to Dr. Mentaine.

Little Eddie stirred in his cane-backed chair and kneaded his hands together. His shadow, cast by the bulb dangling overhead, imitated him like a black little chair-bound monkey. "I wanna get started, I wanna get to be strong," he said.

"Right here in this book it says you have to be relaxed," Harry said. "Just put your hands on top of your legs, nice and easy, with your fingers pointing forward. Then close your eyes and breathe in and out a couple of times. Think about being nice and tired and ready to go to sleep."

"I don't wanna go to sleep!"

"It's not really sleep, Little Eddie, it's just sort of like it. You'll still really be awake, but nice and relaxed. Or else it won't work. You have to do everything I tell you. Otherwise everybody'll still be able to beat up on you, like they do now. I want you to pay attention to everything I say."

"Okay." Little Eddie made a visible effort to relax. He placed his hands on his thighs and twice inhaled and exhaled.

"Now close your eyes."

Eddie closed his eyes.

Harry suddenly knew that it was going to work—if he did everything the book said, he would really be able to hypnotize his brother.

"Little Eddie, I want you just to listen to the sound of my voice," he said, forcing himself to be calm. "You are already getting nice and relaxed, as easy and peaceful as if you were lying in bed, and the more you listen to my voice the more relaxed and tired you are going to get. Nothing can bother you. Everything bad is far away, and you're just sitting here, breathing in and out, getting nice and sleepy."

He checked his page to make sure he was doing it right, and then went on.

"It's like lying in bed, Eddie, and the more you hear my voice the more tired and sleepy you're getting, a little more sleepy the more you hear me. Everything else is sort of fading away, and all you can hear is my voice. You feel tired but good, just like the way you do right before you fall asleep. Everything is fine, and you're drifting a little bit, drifting and drifting, and you're getting ready to raise your right hand."

He leaned over and very lightly stroked the back of Little Eddie's grimy right hand. Eddie sat slumped in the chair with his eyes closed, breathing shallowly. Harry spoke very slowly.

"I'm going to count backward from ten, and every time I get to another number, your hand is going to get lighter and lighter. When I count, your right hand is going to get so light it floats up and finally touches your nose when you hear me say 'One.' And then you'll be in a deep sleep. Now I'm starting. Ten. Your hand is already feeling light. Nine. It wants to float up. Eight. Your hand really feels light now. It's going to start to go up now. Seven."

Little Eddie's hand obediently floated an inch up from his thigh.

"Six." The grimy little hand rose another few inches. "It's getting lighter and lighter now, and every time I say another number it gets closer and closer to your nose, and you get sleepier and sleepier. Five."

The hand ascended several inches nearer Eddie's face. "Four."

The hand now dangled like a sleeping bird half of the way between Eddies knee and his nose.

"Three."

It rose nearly to Eddies chin.

"Two."

Eddie's hand hung a few inches from his mouth.

"One. You are going to fall asleep now."

The gently curved, ketchup-streaked forefinger delicately brushed the tip of Little Eddies nose, and stayed there while Eddie sagged against the back of the chair.

Harry's heart beat so loudly that he feared the sound would bring Eddie out of his trance. Eddie remained motionless. Harry breathed quietly by himself for a moment. "Now you can lower your hand to your lap, Eddie. You are going deeper and deeper into sleep. Deeper and deeper and deeper."

Eddie's hand sank gracefully downward.

The attic seemed hot as the inside of a furnace to Harry. His fingers left blotches on the open pages of the book. He wiped his face on his sleeve and looked at his little brother. Little Eddie had slumped so far down in the chair that his head was no longer visible in the tilting mirror. Perfectly still and quiet, the attic stretched out on all sides of them, waiting (or so it seemed to Harry) for what would happen next. Maryrose's trunks sat in rows under the eaves far behind the mirror, her old dresses hung silently within the dusty wardrobe. Harry rubbed his hands on his jeans to dry them, and flicked a page over with the neatness of an old scholar who had spent half his life in libraries.

"You're going to sit up straight in your chair," he said.

Eddie pulled himself upright.

"Now I want to show you that you're really hypnotized, Little Eddie. It's like a test. I want you to hold your right arm straight out before you. Make it as rigid as you can. This is going to show you how strong you can be."

Eddie's pale arm rose and straightened to the wrist, leaving his fingers dangling.

Harry stood up and said, "That's pretty good." He walked the two steps to Eddie's side and grasped his brothers arm and ran his fingers down the length of it, gently straightening Eddie's hand. "Now I want you to imagine that your arm is getting harder and harder. It's getting as hard and rigid as an iron bar. Your whole arm is an iron bar, and nobody on earth could bend it. Eddie, it's stronger than Superman's arm." He removed his hands and stepped back.

"Now. This arm is so strong and rigid that you can't bend it no matter how hard you try. It's an iron bar, and nobody on earth could bend it. Try. Try to bend it."

Eddie's face tightened up, and his arm rose perhaps two degrees. Eddie grunted with invisible effort, unable to bend his arm.

"Okay, Eddie, you did real good. Now your arm is loosening up, and when I count backward from ten, it's going to get looser and looser. When I get to *one*, your arm'll be normal again." He began counting, and Eddie's fingers loosened and drooped, and finally the arm came to rest again on his leg.

Harry went back to his chair, sat down, and looked at Eddie with great satisfaction. Now he was certain that he would be able to do the next demonstration, which Dr. Mentaine called "The Chair Exercise."

"Now you know that this stuff really works, Eddie, so we're going to do something a little harder. I want you to stand up in front of your chair."

Eddie obeyed. Harry stood up too, and moved his chair forward and to the side so that its cane seat faced Eddie, about four feet away.

"I want you to stretch out between these chairs, with your head on your chair and your feet on mine. And I want you to keep your hands at your sides."

Eddie hunkered down uncomplainingly and settled his head hack on the seat of his chair. Supporting himself with his arms, he raised one leg and placed his foot on Harry's chair. Then he lifted the other foot. Difficulty immediately appeared in his face. He raised his arms and clamped them in so that he looked trussed.

"Now your whole body is slowly becoming as hard as iron, Eddie. Your entire body is one of the strongest things on earth. Nothing can make it bend. You could hold yourself there forever and never feel the slightest pain or discomfort. It's like you're lying on a mattress, you're so strong."

The expression of strain left Eddies face. Slowly his arms extended and relaxed. He lay propped string-straight between the two chairs, so at ease that he did not even appear to be breathing.

"While I talk to you, you're getting stronger and stronger. You could hold up anything. You could hold up an elephant. I'm going to sit down on your stomach to prove it."

Cautiously, Harry seated himself down on his brother's midriff. He raised his legs. Nothing happened. After he had counted slowly to fifteen, Harry lowered his legs and stood. "I'm going to take my shoes off now, Eddie, and stand on you."

He hurried over to a piano stool embroidered with fulsome roses and carried it back; then he slipped off his moccasins and stepped on top of the stool. As Harry stepped on top of Eddies exposed thin belly, the chair supporting his brother's head wobbled. Harry stood stock-still for a moment, but the chair held. He lifted the other foot from the stool. No movement from the chair. He set the other foot on his brother. Little Eddie effortlessly held him up.

Harry lifted himself experimentally up on his toes and came back down on his heels. Eddie seemed entirely unaffected. Then Harry jumped perhaps half an inch into the air, and since Eddie did not even grunt when he landed, he kept jumping, five, six, seven, right times, until he was breathing hard. "You're amazing, Little Eddie," he said, and stepped off onto the stool.

"Now you can begin to relax. You can put your feet on the floor. Then I want you to sit back up in your chair. Your body doesn't feel stiff anymore."

Little Eddie had been rather tentatively lowering one foot, but as soon as Harry finished speaking he buckled in the middle and thumbed his bottom on the floor. Harry's chair (Maryrose's chair) sickeningly tipped over, but landed soundlessly on a neat woolen stack of layered winter coats.

Moving like a robot, Little Eddie slowly sat upright on the floor. His eyes were open but unfocused.

"You can stand up now and get back in your chair," Harry said. He did not remember leaving the stool, but he had left it. Sweat ran into his eyes. He pressed his face into his shirtsleeve. For a second, panic had brightly beckoned. Little Eddie was sleepwalking back to his chair. When he sat down, Harry said, "Close your eyes. You're going deeper and deeper into sleep. Deeper and deeper, Little Eddie."

Eddie settled into the chair as if nothing had happened, and Harry reverently set his own chair upright again. Then he picked up the book and opened it. The print swam before his eyes. Harry shook his head and looked again, but still the lines of print snaked across the page. He pressed the palms of his hands against his eyes, and red patterns exploded across his vision.

He removed his hands from his eyes, blinked, and found that although the lines of print were now behaving themselves, he no longer wanted to go on. The attic was too hot, he was too tired, and the toppling of the chair had been too close a brush with actual disaster. But for a time he leafed purposefully through the book while Eddie tranced on, and then found the subheading "Posthypnotic Suggestion."

"Little Eddie, we're just going to do one more thing. If we ever do this again, it'll help us go faster." Harry shut the book. He knew exactly how this went; he would even use the same phrase Dr. Mentaine used with his patients. *Blue rose*—Harry did not quite know why, but he liked the sound of that.

"I'm going to tell you a phrase, Eddie, and from now on whenever you hear me say this phrase, you will instantly go back to sleep and be hypnotized again. The phrase is 'Blue rose.' Blue Rose. When you hear me say 'Blue rose,' you will go right to sleep, just the way you are now, and we can make you stronger again. 'Blue rose' is our secret, Eddie, because nobody else knows it. What is it?"

"Blue rose," Eddie said in a muffled voice.

"Okay. I'm going to count backward from ten, and when I get to 'one' you will be wide awake again. You will not remember anything we did, but you will feel happy and strong. Ten."

As Harry counted backward, Little Eddie twitched and stirred, let his arms fall to his sides, thumped one foot carelessly on the floor, and at "one" opened his eyes.

"Did it work? What'd I do? Am I strong?"

"You're a bull," Harry said. "It's getting late, Eddie—time to go downstairs."

Harry's timing was accurate enough to be uncomfortable. As soon as the two boys closed the attic door behind them they heard the front door slide open in a cacophony of harsh coughs and subdued mutterings followed by the sound of unsteady footsteps proceeding to the bathroom. Edgar Beevers was home.

6

LATE THAT NIGHT the three homebound Beevers sons lay in their separate beds in the good-sized second-floor room next to the attic stairs. Directly above Maryrose's bedroom, its dimensions were nearly identical to it except that the boys' room, the "dorm," had no window seat and the attic stairs shaved a couple of feet from Harry's end. When the other two boys had lived at home, Harry and Little Eddie had slept together, Albert had slept in a bed with Sonny, and only George, who at the time of his induction into the Army had been six feet tall and weighed two hundred and one pounds, had slept alone. In those days, Sonny had often managed to make Albert cry out in the middle of the night. The very idea of George could still make Harry's stomach freeze.

Though it was now very late, enough light from the street came in through the thin white net curtains to give complex shadows to the bunched muscles of Albert's upper arms as he lay stretched out atop his sheets. The voices of Maryrose and Edgar Beevers, one approximately sober and the other unmistakably drunk, came clearly up the stairs and through the open door.

"*Who* says I waste my time? I don't say that. I don't waste my time."

"I suppose you think you've done a good day's work when you spell a bartender for a couple of hours—and then drink up your wages! That's the story of your life, Edgar Beevers, and it's a sad sad story of W-A-S-T-E. If my father could have seen what would become of you..."

"I ain't so damn bad."

"You ain't so damn good, either."

"Albert," Eddie said softly from his bed between his two brothers.

As if galvanized by Little Eddie's voice, Albert suddenly sat up in bed, leaned forward, and reached out to try to smack Eddie with his fist.

"I didn't do nothin'!" Harry said, and moved to the edge of his mattress. The blow had been for him, he knew, not Eddie, except that Albert was too lazy to get up.

"I hate your lousy guts," Albert said. "If I wasn't too tired to get out of this here bed, I'd pound your face in."

"Harry stole my birthday car, Albert," Eddie said. "Makum gimme it back."

"One day," Maryrose said from downstairs, "at the end of the summer when I was seventeen, late in the afternoon, my father said to my mother, 'Honey, I believe I'm going to take out our pretty little Maryrose and get her something special,' and he called up to me from the drawing room to make myself pretty and get set to go, and because my father was a gentleman and a Man of His Word, I got ready in two shakes. My father was wearing a very handsome brown suit and a red bow tie and his boater. I remember just like I can see it now. He stood at the bottom of the staircase, waiting for me, and when I came down he took my arm and we just went out that front door like a courting couple. Down the stone walk, which my father put in all by himself even though he was a white-collar worker, down Majeski Street, arm in arm down to South Palmyra Avenue. In those days all the best people, all the people who counted, did their shopping on South Palmyra Avenue."

"I'd like to knock your teeth down your throat," Albert said to Harry.

"Albert, he took my birthday car, he really did, and I want it back. I'm ascared he busted it. I want it back so much I'm gonna die."

Albert propped himself up on an elbow and for the first time really looked at Little Eddie. Eddie whimpered. "You're such a twerp," Albert said. "I wish you *would* die, Eddie, I wish you'd just drop dead so we could stick you in the ground and forget about you. I wouldn't even cry at your funeral. Prob'ly I wouldn't even be able to remember your name. I'd just say, 'Oh, yeah, he was that little creepy kid used to hang around cryin' all the time, glad he's dead, whatever his name was.'"

Eddie had turned his back on Albert and was weeping softly, his unwashed face distorted by the shadows into an uncanny image of the mask of tragedy.

"You know, I really wouldn't mind if you dropped dead," Albert mused. "You neither, shitbird."

"...realized he was taking me to Allouette's. I'm sure you used to look in their windows when you were a little boy. You remember Allouette's, don't you? There's never been anything so beautiful as that store. When I was a little girl and lived in the big house, all the best people used to go there. My father marched me right inside, with his arm around me, and took me up in the elevator and we went straight to the lady who managed the dress department. 'Give my little girl the best,' he said. Price was no object. Quality was all he cared about. 'Give my little girl the best.' *Are you listening to me, Edgar?*"

ⅢⅢⅢⅢⅢⅢⅢⅢⅢⅢⅢⅢⅢⅢⅢⅢⅢⅢⅢⅢⅢ

ALBERT SNORED FACE-DOWN into his pillow; Little Eddie twitched and snuffled. Harry lay awake for so long he thought he would never get to sleep. Before him he kept seeing Little Eddie's face all slack and dopey under hypnosis—Little Eddie's face made him feel hot and uncomfortable. Now that Harry was lying down in bed, it seemed to him that everything he had done since returning from Big John's seemed really to have been done by someone else, or to have been done in a dream. Then he realized that he had to use the bathroom.

Harry slid out of bed, quietly crossed the room, went out onto the dark landing, and felt his way downstairs to the bathroom.

When he emerged, the bathroom light showed him the squat black shape of the telephone atop the Palmyra directory. Harry moved to the low telephone table beside the stairs. He lifted the phone from the directory and opened the book, the width of a Big 5 tablet, with his other hand. As he had done on many other nights which his bladder forced him downstairs, Harry leaned over the page and selected a number. He kept the number in his head as he closed the directory and replaced the telephone. He dialed. The number rang so often Harry lost count. At last a hoarse voice answered. Harry said, "I'm watching you, and you're a dead man." He softly replaced the receiver in the cradle.

7

HARRY CAUGHT UP with his father the next afternoon just as Edgar Beevers had begun to move up South

Sixth Street toward the corner of Livermore. His father wore his usual costume of baggy gray trousers cinched far above his waist by a belt with a double buckle, a red-and-white plaid shirt, and a brown felt hat stationed low over his eyes. His long fleshy nose swam before him, cut in half by the shadow of the hat brim.

"Dad!"

His father glanced incuriously at him, then put his hands back in his pockets. He turned sideways and kept walking down the street, though perhaps a shade more slowly. "What's up, kid? No school?"

"It's summer, there isn't any school. I just thought I'd come with you for a little."

"Well, I ain't doing much. Your ma asked me to pick up some hamburg on Livermore, and I thought I'd slip into the Idle Hour for a quick belt. You won't turn me in, will you?"

"No."

"You ain't a bad kid, Harry. Your ma's just got a lot of worries. I worry about Little Eddie too, sometimes."

"Sure."

"What's with the books? You read when you walk?"

"I was just sort of looking at them," Harry said.

His father insinuated his hand beneath Harry's left elbow and extracted two luridly jacketed paperback books. They were titled *Murder, Incorporated* and *Hitler's Death Camps*. Harry already loved both of these books. His father grunted and handed *Murder,*

Incorporated back to him. He raised the other book nearly to the top of his nose and peered at the cover, which depicted a naked woman pressing herself against a wall of barbed wire while a uniformed Nazi aimed a rifle at her back.

Looking up at his father, Harry saw that beneath the harsh line of shadow cast by the hat brim, his father's whiskers grew in different colors and patterns. Black and brown, red and orange, the glistening spikes swirled across his father's cheek.

"I bought this book, but it didn't look nothing like that," his father said, and returned the book.

"What didn't?"

"That place. Dachau. That death camp."

"How do you know?"

"I was there, wasn't I? You wasn't even born then. It didn't look anything like that picture on that book. It just looked like a piece a shit to me, like most of the places I saw when I was in the Army."

This was the first time Harry had heard that his father had been in the service.

"You mean, you were in World War II?"

"Yeah, I was in the Big One. They made me corporal over there. Had me a nickname, too. 'Beans.' 'Beans' Beevers. And I got a Purple Heart from the time I got a infection."

"You saw Dachau with your own eyes?"

"Damn straight I did." He bent down suddenly. "Hey—don't let your ma catch you readin' that book."

Secretly pleased, Harry shook his head. Now the book and the death camp were a bond between himself and his father.

"Did you ever kill anybody?"

His father wiped his mouth and both cheeks with one long hand. Harry saw a considering eye far back in the shadow of the brim.

"I killed a guy once."

A long pause.

"I shot him in the back."

His father wiped his mouth again, and then motioned forward with his head. He had to get to the bar, the butcher, and back again in a very carefully defined period of time. "You really want to hear this?"

Harry nodded. He swallowed.

"I guess you do, at that. Okay—we was sent into this camp, Dachau, at the end of the war to process the prisoners and arrest the guards and the commandant. Everything was all arranged. A bunch of brass hats from Division were going to come on an inspection, so we had to wait there a couple days. We had these guards lined up, see, and these skinny old wrecks would come up and give 'em hell. We wasn't supposed to let 'em get too near."

They were passing Mr. Petrosian's little tar-paper house, and Harry felt a spasm of relief that Mr. Petrosian was not out on his tiny porch, working on his case of beer. The Idle Hour was only a few paces ahead.

"Anyhow, one of these guards, one of the worst ones, suddenly decided he's going to run for it. He takes off, runnin' like crazy toward the woods. What do I do? I ask. Nobody knows what the hell to do. Shoot him, somebody says. So I shot him in the back. That was all she wrote."

Now they had reached the screen door that led into the Idle Hour, and the smells of malt and hops filled the air. "See you back at the house," his father said, and disappeared through the screen door like a magician.

8

AFTER HARRY HAD read a hundred pages of *Murder, Incorporated,* his favorite murderers were Louis "Lepke" Buchalter and Abe "Kid Twist" Reles. They were dependable professionals. A kind of black light surrounded them and made them glitter. Lepke Buchalter and Abe Reles looked out at the world from the shadows of their hat brims. They lived in shadowy rooms and peered out through the curtains. They appeared on a dark corner before their terrified victim, did their work, and walked away, turning up their coat collars.

Suppose you had some kind of job that took you around the country, like a salesman's job, Harry thought as he read away the afternoon in the porch swing; suppose you had a job that took you from one town to another. Suppose you killed someone in each one of those towns, carefully and quietly, and hid the bodies so it would take people a long time to find them. Your work would never be done.

9

"BLUE ROSE," HARRY said.

Little Eddie sagged openmouthed against the cane of his chair, his hands loose in his lap.

It had worked. Harry looked around as if he expected applause, and did feel that all the things in the attic looked back at him with warm approval. It was nine-thirty at night; he and Eddie, alone in the house, occupied the attic in perfect safety. Harry wanted to see if he could put other people under and make them do things, but for now, for tonight, he was content to experiment with Eddie.

"You're going deeper and deeper asleep, Eddie, deeper and deeper, and you're listening to every word I say. You're just sinking down and down, hearing my voice come to you, going deeper and deeper with every word, and now you are real deep asleep and ready to begin."

Little Eddie sat sprawled over Maryrose's cane-backed chair, his chin touching his chest and his little pink mouth drooping open. He looked like a slightly undersized seven-year-old, like a second-grader instead of the fourth-grader he would be when he joined Mrs. Franken's class in the fall. Suddenly he reminded Harry of the Ultraglide Roadster, scratched and dented and stripped of its tires.

"Tonight you're going to see how strong you really are. Sit up, Eddie."

Eddie pulled himself upright and closed his mouth, almost comically obedient.

Harry thought it would be fun to make Little Eddie believe he was a dog and trot around the attic on all fours, barking and lifting his leg. Then he saw Little Eddie staggering across the attic, his tongue bulging out of his mouth, his own hands squeezing and squeezing his throat. Maybe he would try that too, after he had done several other exercises he had discovered in Dr. Mentaine's book. He checked the underside of his collar for maybe the fifth time that evening, and felt the long thin shaft of the pearl-headed hat pin he had stopped reading *Murder, Incorporated* long enough to smuggle out of Maryrose's bedroom after she had left for work.

"Eddie," he said, "now you are very deeply asleep, and you will be able to do everything I say. I want you to hold your right arm straight out in front of you."

Eddie stuck his arm out like a poker.

"'That's good, Eddie. Now I want you to notice that all the feeling is leaving that arm. It's getting number and number. It doesn't even feel like flesh and blood anymore. It feels like it's made out of steel or something. It's so numb that you can't feel anything there anymore. You can't even feel pain in it."

Harry stood up, went toward Eddie, and brushed his fingers along his arm. "You didn't feel anything, did you?"

"No," Eddie said in a slow gravel-filled voice.

"Do you feel anything now?" Harry pinched the underside of Eddie's forearm.

"No."

"Now?" Harry used his nails to pinch the side of Eddie's bicep, hard, and left purple dents in the skin.

"No," Eddie repeated.

"How about this?" He slapped his hand against Eddie's forearm as hard as he could. There was a sharp loud smacking sound, and his fingers tingled. If Little Eddie had not been hypnotized, he would have tried to screech down the walls.

"No," Eddie said.

Harry pulled the hat pin out of his collar and inspected his brother's arm. "You're doing great, Little Eddie. You're stronger than anybody in your whole class—you're probably stronger than the whole rest of the school." He turned Eddie's arm so that the palm was up and the white forearm, lightly traced by small blue veins, faced him.

Harry delicately ran the point of the hat pin down Eddie's pale, veined forearm. The pinpoint left a narrow chalk-white scratch in its wake. For a moment

Harry felt the floor of the attic sway beneath his feet; then he closed his eyes and jabbed the hat pin into Little Eddie's skin as hard as he could.

He opened his eyes. The floor was still swaying beneath him. From Little Eddie's lower arm protruded six inches of the eight-inch hat pin, the mother-of-pearl head glistening softly in the light from the overhead bulb. A drop of blood the size of a watermelon seed stood on Eddie's skin. Harry moved back to his chair and sat down heavily. "Do you feel anything?"

"No," Eddie said again in that surprisingly deep voice.

Harry stared at the hat pin embedded in Eddie's arm. The oval drop of blood lengthened itself out against the white skin and began slowly to ooze toward Eddie's wrist. Harry watched it advance across the pale underside of Eddie's forearm. Finally he stood up and returned to Eddie's side. The elongated drop of blood had ceased moving. Harry bent over and twanged the hat pin. Eddie could feel nothing. Harry put his thumb and forefinger on the glistening head of the pin. His face was so hot he might have been standing before an open fire. He pushed the pin a further half-inch into Eddie's arm, and another small quantity of blood welled up from the base. The pin seemed to be moving in Harry's grasp, pulsing back and forth as if it were breathing.

"Okay," Harry said. "Okay."

He tightened his hold on the pin and pulled. It slipped easily from the wound. Harry held the hat pin

before his face just as a doctor holds up a thermom-
eter to read a temperature. He had imagined that the
entire bottom section of the shaft would be painted
with red, but saw that only a single winding glutinous
streak of blood adhered to the pin. For a dizzy second
he thought of slipping the end of the pin in his mouth
and sucking it clean.

He thought: Maybe in another life I was Lepke
Buchalter.

He pulled his handkerchief, a filthy square of red
paisley, from his front pocket and wiped the streak of
blood from the shaft of the pin. Then he leaned over
and gently wiped the red smear from Little Eddie's un-
derarm. Harry refolded the handkerchief so the blood
would not show, wiped sweat from his face, and shoved
the grubby cloth back into his pocket.

"That was good, Eddie. Now we're going to do
something a little bit different."

He knelt down beside his brother and lifted Eddie's
nearly weightless, delicately veined arm. "You still
can't feel a thing in this arm, Eddie, it's completely
numb. It's sound asleep and it won't wake up until I tell
it to." Harry repositioned himself in order to hold himself steady while he knelt, and put the point of the hat
pin nearly flat against Eddie's arm. He pushed it forward far enough to raise a wrinkle of flesh. The point
of the hat pin dug into Eddie's skin but did not break
it. Harry pushed harder, and the hat pin raised the little
bulge of skin by a small but appreciable amount.

Skin was a lot tougher to break through than anyone imagined.

The pin was beginning to hurt his fingers, so Harry opened his hand and positioned the head against the base of his middle finger. Grimacing, he pushed his hand against the pin. The point of the pin popped through the raised wrinkle.

"Eddie, you're made out of beer cans," Harry said, and tugged the head of the pin backward. The wrinkle flattened out. Now Harry could shove the pin forward again, sliding the shaft deeper and deeper under the surface of Little Eddie's skin. He could see the raised line of the hat pin marching down his brother's arm, looking as prominent as the damage done to a cartoon lawn by a cartoon rabbit. When the mother-of-pearl head was perhaps three inches from the entry hole, Harry pushed it down into Little Eddie's flesh, thus raising the point of the pin. He gave the head a sharp jab, and the point appeared at the end of the ridge in Eddie's skin, poking through a tiny smear of blood. Harry shoved the pin in further. Now it showed about an inch and a half of gray metal at either end.

"Feel anything?"

"Nothing."

Harry jiggled the head of the pin, and a bubble of blood walked out of the entry wound and began to slide down Eddie's arm. Harry sat down on the attic floor beside Eddie and regarded his work. His mind seemed pleasantly empty of thought, filled only with a variety of sensations. He *felt* but could not hear a buzzing in his head, and a blurry film seemed to cover his eyes. He breathed through his mouth. The long pin stuck through Little Eddie's arm looked monstrous seen one way; seen another, it was sheerly beautiful. Skin, blood, and metal. Harry had never seen anything like it before. He reached out and twisted the pin, causing another little blood-snail to crawl from the exit wound. Harry saw all this as if through smudgy glasses, but he did not mind. He knew the blurriness was only mental. He touched the head of the pin again and moved it from side to side. A little more blood leaked from both punctures. Then Harry shoved the pin in, partially withdrew it so that the point nearly disappeared back into Eddie's arm, moved it forward again; and went on like this, back and forth, back and forth as if he were sewing his brother up, for some time.

Finally he withdrew the pin from Eddie's arm. Two long streaks of blood had nearly reached his brother's wrist. Harry ground the heels of his hands into his eyes, blinked, and discovered that his vision had cleared.

He wondered how long he and Eddie had been in the attic. It could have been hours. He could not quite remember what had happened before he had slid the hat pin into Eddie's skin. Now his blurriness really was mental, not visual. A loud uncomfortable pulse beat in his temples. Again he wiped the blood from Eddie's arm. Then he stood on wobbling knees and returned to his chair.

"How's your arm feel, Eddie?"

"Numb," Eddie said in his gravelly sleepy voice.

"The numbness is going away now. Very very slowly. You are beginning to feel your arm again, and it feels very good. There is no pain. It feels like the sun was shining on it all afternoon. It's strong and healthy. Feeling is coming back into your arm, and you can move your fingers and everything."

When he had finished speaking Harry leaned back against the chair and closed his eyes. He rubbed his forehead with his hand and wiped the moisture off on his shirt.

"How does your arm feel?" he said without opening his eyes.

"Good."

"That's great, Little Eddie." Harry flattened his palms against his flushed face, wiped his cheeks, and opened his eyes.

I can do this every night, he thought. I can bring Little Eddie up here every single night, at least until school starts.

"Eddie, you're getting stronger and stronger every day. This is really helping you. And the more we do it the stronger you'll get. Do you understand me?"

"I understand you," Eddie said.

"We're almost done for tonight. There's just one more thing I want to try. But you have to be really deep asleep for this to work. So I want you to go deeper and deeper, as deep as you can go. Relax, and now you are

really deep asleep, deep deep, and relaxed and ready
and feeling good."

Little Eddie sat sprawled in his chair with his head
tilted back and his eyes closed. Two tiny dark spots
of blood stood out like mosquito bites on his lower
right forearm.

"When I talk to you, Eddie, you're slowly getting
younger and younger, you're going backward in time,
so now you're not nine years old anymore, you're eight,
it's last year and you're in the third grade, and now
you're seven, and now you're six years old...and now
you're five, Eddie, and it's the day of your fifth birthday. You're five years old today, Little Eddie. How old
are you?"

"I'm five." To Harry's surprised pleasure, Little
Eddies voice actually seemed younger, as did his
hunched posture in the chair.

"How do you feel?"

"Not good. I hate my present. It's terrible. Dad
got it, and Mom says it should never be allowed in the
house because it's just junk. I wish I wouldn't ever have
to have birthdays, they're so terrible. I'm gonna cry."

His face contracted. Harry tried to remember what
Eddie had gotten for his fifth birthday, but could not—
he caught only a dim memory of shame and disappointment. "What's your present, Eddie?"

In a teary voice, Eddie said, "A radio. But it's busted
and Mom says it looks like it came from the junkyard. I
don't want it anymore. I don't even wanna see it."

Yes, Harry thought, yes, yes, yes. He could remember. On Little Eddie's fifth birthday, Edgar Beevers had produced a yellow plastic radio which even Harry had seen was astoundingly ugly. The dial was cracked, and it was marked here and there with brown circular scablike marks where someone had mashed out cigarettes on it.

The radio had long since been buried in the junk room, where it now lay beneath several geological layers of trash.

"Okay, Eddie, you can forget the radio now, because you're going backward again, you're getting younger, you're going backward through being four years old, and now you're three."

He looked with interest at Little Eddie, whose entire demeanor had changed. From being tearfully unhappy, Eddie now demonstrated a self-sufficient good cheer Harry could not ever remember seeing in him. His arms were folded over his chest. He was smiling, and his eyes were bright and clear and childish.

"What do you see?" Harry asked.

"Mommy-ommy-om."

"What's she doing?"

"Mommy's at her desk. She's smoking and looking through her papers." Eddie giggled. "Mommy looks funny. It looks like smoke is coming out of the top of her head." Eddie ducked his chin and hid his smile behind a hand. "Mommy doesn't see me. I can see her, but she doesn't see me. Oh! Mommy works hard! She works hard at her desk!"

Eddie's smile abruptly left his face. His face froze for a second in a comic rubbery absence of expression; then his eyes widened in terror and his mouth went loose and wobbly.

"What happened?" Harry's mouth had gone dry.

"No, Mommy!" Eddie wailed. "Don't, Mommy! I wasn't spying, I wasn't, I promise—" His words broke off into a screech. "NO, MOMMY! DON'T! DON'T, MOMMY!" Eddie jumped upward, sending his chair flying back, and ran blindly toward the rear of the attic. Harry's head rang with Eddie's screeches. He heard a sharp *crack!* of wood breaking, but only as a small part of all the noise Eddie was making as he charged around the attic. Eddie had run into a tangle of hanging dresses, spun around, enmeshing himself deeper in the dresses, and was now tearing himself away from the web of dresses, pulling some of them off the rack. A long-sleeved purple dress with an enormous lace collar had draped itself around Eddie like a ghostly dance partner, and another dress, of dull red velvet, snaked around his right leg. Eddie screamed again and yanked himself away from the tangle. The entire rack of clothes wobbled and then went over in a mad jangle of sound.

"NO!" he screeched. "HELP!" Eddie ran straight into a big wooden beam marking off one of the eaves, bounced off, and came windmilling toward Harry. Harry knew his brother could not see him.

"Eddie, stop," he said, but Eddie was past hearing him. Harry tried to make Eddie stop by wrapping his arms around him, but Eddie slammed right into him, hitting Harry's chest with a shoulder and knocking his head painfully against Harry's chin; Harry's arms closed on nothing and his eyes lost focus, and Eddie went crashing into the tilting mirror. The mirror yawned over sideways. Harry saw it tilt with dreamlike slowness toward the floor, then in an eyeblink drop and crash. Broken glass sprayed across the attic floor.

"STOP!" Harry yelled. "STAND STILL, EDDIE!"

Eddie came to rest. A ripped and dirty dress of dull red velvet still clung to his right leg. Blood oozed down his temple from an ugly cut above his eye. He was breathing hard, releasing air in little whimpering exhalations.

"Holy shit," Harry said, looking around at the attic. In only a few seconds Eddie had managed to create what looked at first like absolute devastation. Maryrose's ancient dresses lay tangled in a heap of dusty fabrics from which wire hangers skeletally protruded; gray Eddie-sized footprints lay like a pattern over the muted explosion of colors the dresses now created. When the rack had gone over, it had knocked a section the size of a dinner plate out of a round wooden coffee table Maryrose had particularly prized for its being made from a single section of teak—"a single piece of *teak*, the rarest wood in all the world, all the way from Ceylon!" The much-prized mirror lay in hundreds of glittering pieces across the attic floor. With growing horror, Harry saw that the wooden frame had

57

cracked like a bone, showing a bone-pale, shockingly white fracture in the expanse of dark stain.

Harry's blood tipped within his body, nearly tipping him with it, like the mirror. "Oh God oh God oh God."

He turned slowly around. Eddie stood blinking two feet to his side, wiping ineffectually at the blood running from his forehead and now covering most of his left cheek. He looked like an Indian in war paint— a defeated, lost Indian, for his eyes were dim and his head turned aimlessly from side to side.

A few feet from Eddie lay the chair in which he had been sitting. One of its thin curved wooden arms lay beside it, crudely severed. It looked like an insect's leg, Harry thought, like a toy gun.

For a moment Harry thought that his face too was red with blood. He wiped his hand over his forehead and looked at his glistening palm. It was only sweat. His heart beat like a bell. Beside him Eddie said, "Aaah...what...?" The injury to his head had brought him out of the trance.

The dresses were ruined, stepped-on, tangled, torn. The mirror was broken. The table had been mutilated. Maryrose's chair lay on its side like a murder victim, its severed arm ending in a bristle of snapped ligaments.

"My head *hurts*," Eddie said in a weak, trembling voice. "What happened? Aaah! I'm all blood! I'm all blood, Harry!"

"You're all blood, you're all blood?" Harry shouted at him. "Everything's *all blood,* you dummy! Look around!" He did not recognize his own voice, which sounded high and tinny and seemed to be coming from somewhere else. Little Eddie took an aimless step away from him, and Harry wanted to fly at him, to pound his bloody head into a pancake, to destroy him, smash him....

Eddie held up his bloodstained palm and stared at it. He wiped it vaguely across the front of his T-shirt and took another wandering step. "I'm ascared, Harry," his tiny voice uttered.

"Look what you did!" Harry screamed. "You wrecked everything! Damn it! What do you think is going to happen to us?"

"What's Mom going to do?" Eddie asked in a voice only slightly above a whisper.

"You don't know?" Harry yelled. "You're dead!"

Eddie started to weep.

Harry bunched his hands into fists and clamped his eyes shut. They were both dead, that was the real truth. Harry opened his eyes, which felt hot and oddly heavy, and stared at his sobbing, red-smeared, useless little brother. "Blue rose," he said.

10

LITTLE EDDIE'S HANDS fell to his sides. His chin dropped, and his mouth fell open. Blood ran in a smooth wide band down the left side of his face, dipped under the line of his jaw, and continued on down his neck and into his T-shirt. Pooled blood in his left eyebrow dripped steadily onto the floor, as if from a faucet.

"You are going deep *asleep,*" Harry said. Where was the hat pin? He looked back to the single standing chair and saw the mother-of-pearl head glistening on the floor near it. "Your whole body is *numb.*" He moved over to the pin, bent down, and picked it up. The metal shaft felt warm in his fingers. "You can feel no *pain.*" He went back to Little Eddie. "Nothing can *hurt* you." Harry's breath seemed to be breathing itself, forcing itself into his throat in hot harsh shallow pants, then expelling itself out.

"Did you *hear* me, Little Eddie?"

In his gravelly, slow-moving hypnotized voice, Little Eddie said, "I heard you."

"And you can feel no *pain?*"

"I can feel no pain."

Harry drew his arm back, the point of the hat pin extending forward from his fist, and then jerked his hand forward as hard as he could and stuck the pin into Eddie's abdomen right through the blood-soaked T-shirt. He exhaled sharply, and tasted a sour misery on his breath.

"You don't feel a thing."

"I don't feel a thing."

Harry opened his right hand and drove his palm against the head of the pin, hammering it in another few inches. Little Eddie looked like a voodoo doll. A kind of sparkling light surrounded him. Harry gripped the head of the pin with his thumb and forefinger and yanked it out. He held it up and inspected it. Glittering light surrounded the pin too. The long shaft was painted with blood. Harry slipped the point into his mouth and closed his lips around the warm metal.

He saw himself, a man in another life, standing in a row with men like himself in a bleak gray landscape defined by barbed wire. Emaciated people in rags shuffled up toward them and spat on their clothes. The smells of dead flesh and of burning flesh hung in the air. Then the vision was gone, and Little Eddie stood before him again, surrounded by layers of glittering light.

Harry grimaced or grinned, he could not have told the difference, and drove his long spike deep into Eddies stomach.

Eddie uttered a small *Oof.*

"You don't feel anything, Eddie," Harry whispered. "You feel good all over. You never felt better in your life."

"Never felt better in my life."

Harry slowly pulled out the pin and cleaned it with his fingers.

He was able to remember every single thing anyone had ever told him about Tommy Golz.

"Now you're going to play a funny, funny game," he said. "This is called the Tommy Golz game because it's going to keep you safe from Mrs. Franken. Are you ready?" Harry carefully slid the pin into the fabric of his shirt collar, all the while watching Eddie's slack blood-streaked person. Vibrating bands of light beat rhythmically and steadily about Eddie's face.

"Ready," Eddie said.

"I'm going to give you your instructions now, Little Eddie. Pay attention to everything I say and it's all going to be okay. Everything's going to be okay—as long as you play the game exactly the way I tell you. You understand, don't you?"

"I understand."

"Tell me what I just said."

"Everything's gonna be okay as long as I play the game exactly the way you tell me." A dollop of blood slid off Eddie's eyebrow and splashed onto his already soaked T-shirt.

"Good, Eddie. Now the first thing you do is fall down—not now, when I tell you. I'm going to give you all the instructions, and then I'm going to count backward from ten, and when I get to *one*, you'll start playing the game. Okay?"

"Okay."

"So first you fall down, Little Eddie. You fall down real hard. Then comes the fun part of the game. You bang your head on the floor. You start to go crazy. You twitch, and you bang your hands and feet on the floor. You do that for a long time. I guess you do that until you count to about a hundred. You foam at the mouth, you twist all over the place. You get real stiff, and then you get real loose, and then you get real stiff, and then real loose again, and all this time you're banging your head and your hands and feet on the floor, and you're twisting all over the place. Then when you finish counting to a hundred in your head, you do the last thing. You swallow your tongue. And that's the game. When you swallow your tongue you're the winner. And then nothing bad can happen to you, and Mrs. Franken won't be able to hurt you ever ever ever."

Harry stopped talking. His hands were shaking. After a second he realized that his insides were shaking too. He raised his trembling fingers to his shirt collar and felt the hat pin.

"Tell me how you win the game, Little Eddie. What's the last thing you do?"

"I swallow my tongue."

"Right. And then Mrs. Franken and Mom will never be able to hurt you, because you won the game."

"Good," said Little Eddie. The glittering light shimmered about him.

"Okay, we'll start playing right now," Harry said. "Ten." He went toward the attic steps. "Nine." He reached the steps. "Eight."

He went down one step. "Seven." Harry descended another two steps. "Six." When he went down another two steps, he called up in a slightly louder voice, "Five."

Now his head was beneath the level of the attic floor, and he could not see Little Eddie anymore. All he could hear was the soft, occasional plop of liquid hitting the floor.

"Four."

"Three."

"Two." He was now at the door to the attic steps. Harry opened the door, stepped through it, breathed hard, and shouted "One!" up the stairs.

He heard a thud, and then quickly closed the door behind him.

Harry went across the hall and into the "dormitory" bedroom. There seemed to be a strange absence of light in the hallway. For a second he saw—was sure he saw— a line of dark trees across a wall of barbed wire. Harry closed this door behind him too, and went to his narrow bed and sat down. He could feel blood beating in his face; his eyes seemed oddly warm, as if they were heated by filaments. Harry slowly, almost reverently, extracted the hat pin from his collar and set it on his pillow. "A hundred," he said. "Ninety-nine, ninety-eight, ninety-seven, ninety-six, ninety-five, ninety-four..."

When he had counted down to *one,* he stood up and left the bedroom. He went quickly downstairs without looking at the door behind which lay the attic steps. On the ground floor he slipped into Maryrose's bedroom, crossed over to her desk, and slid open the bottom right-hand drawer. From the drawer he took a velvet-covered box. This he opened, and jabbed the hat pin in the ball of material, studded with pins of all sizes and descriptions, from which he had taken it. He replaced the box in the drawer, pushed the drawer into the desk, and quickly left the room and went upstairs. Back in his own bedroom, Harry took off his clothes and climbed into his bed. His face still burned.

HE MUST HAVE fallen asleep very quickly, because the next thing he knew Albert was slamming his way into the bedroom and tossing Ins clothes and boots all over the place. "You asleep?" Albert asked. "You left the attic light on, you fuckin' dummies, but if you think I'm gonna save your fuckin' asses and go up and turn it off, you're even stupider than you look."

Harry was careful not to move a finger, not to move even a hair.

He held his breath while Albert threw himself onto his bed, and when Albert's breathing relaxed and slowed, Harry followed his big brother into sleep. He did not awaken again until he heard his father half-screeching, half-sobbing up in the attic, and that was very late at night.

11

SONNY CAME FROM Fort Sill, George all the way from Germany. Between them, they held up a sodden Edgar

Beevers at the grave site while a minister Harry had never seen before read from a Bible as cracked and rubbed as an old brown shoe. Between his two older sons, Harry's father looked bent and ancient, a skinny old man only steps from the grave himself. Sonny and George despised their father, Harry saw—they held him up on sufferance, in part because they had chipped in thirty dollars apiece to buy him a suit and did not want to see it collapse with its owner inside onto the lumpy clay of the graveyard. His whiskers glistened in the sun, and moisture shone beneath his eyes and at the corners of his mouth. He had been shaking too severely for either Sonny or George to shave him, and had been capable of moving in a straight line only after George let him take a couple of long swallows from a leather-covered flask he took out of his duffel bag.

The minister uttered a few sage words on the subject of epilepsy.

Sonny and George looked as solid as brick walls in their uniforms, like prison guards or actual prisons themselves. Next to them, Albert looked shrunken and unfinished. Albert wore the green plaid sport jacket in which he had graduated from the eighth grade, and his wrists hung prominent and red four inches below the bottoms of the sleeves. His motorcycle boots were visible beneath his light gray trousers, but they, like the green jacket, had lost their flash. Like Albert, too: ever since the discovery of Eddie's body, Albert had gone around the house looking as if he'd just bitten off the end of his tongue and was trying to decide whether or not to spit it out. He never looked anybody in the eye, and he rarely spoke. Albert acted as though a gigantic padlock had been fixed to the middle of his chest and *he* was damned if he'd ever take if off. He had not asked Sonny or George a single question about the Army. Every now and then he would utter a remark about the gas station so toneless that it suffocated any reply.

Harry looked at Albert standing beside their mother, kneading his hands together and keeping his eyes fixed as if by decree on the square foot of ground before him. Albert glanced over at Harry, knew he was being looked at, and did what to Harry was an extraordinary thing. Albert *froze*. All expression drained out of his face, and his hands locked immovably together. He looked as little able to see or hear as a statue. *He's that way because he told Little Eddie that he wished he would die,* Harry thought for the tenth or eleventh time since he had realized this, and with undiminished awe. Then was he lying? Harry wondered. And if he really did wish that Little Eddie would drop dead, why isn't he happy now? Didn't he get what he wanted? Albert would never spit out that piece of his tongue, Harry thought, watching his brother blink slowly and sightlessly toward the ground.

Harry shifted his gaze uneasily to his father, still propped up between George and Sonny, heard that the minister was finally reaching the end of his speech, and took a fast look at his mother. Maryrose was standing very straight in a black dress and black sunglasses, holding the straps of her bag in front of her with both hands. Except for the color of her clothes, she could have been a spectator at a tennis match. Harry knew by the way she was holding her face that she was wishing she could smoke. Dying for a cigarette, he thought, ha ha, the Monster Mash, it's a graveyard smash.

The minister finished speaking, and made a rhetorical gesture with his hands. The coffin sank on ropes into the rough earth. Harry's father began to weep loudly. First George, then Sonny, picked up large damp shovel-marked pieces of the clay and dropped them on the coffin. Edgar Beevers nearly fell in after his own tiny clod, but George contemptuously swung him back. Maryrose marched forward, bent and picked up a random piece of clay with thumb and forefinger as if using tweezers, dropped it, and turned away before it struck. Albert fixed his eyes on Harry—his own clod had split apart in his hand and crumbled away between his fingers. Harry shook his head *no*. He did not want to drop dirt on Eddie's coffin mid make that noise. He did not want to look at Eddie's coffin again. There was enough dirt around to do the job without him hitting that metal box like he was trying to ring Eddie's doorbell. He stepped back.

"Mom says we have to get back to the house," Albert said.

Maryrose lit up as soon as they got into the single black car they had rented through the funeral parlor, and breathed out acrid smoke over everybody crowded into the backseat. The car backed into a narrow grave-yard lane, and turned down the main road toward the front gates.

In the front seat, next to the driver, Edgar Beevers drooped sideways and leaned his head against the window, leaving a blurred streak on the glass.

"How in the name of hell could Little Eddie have epilepsy without anybody knowing about it?" George asked.

Albert stiffened and stared out the window.

"Well, that's epilepsy," Maryrose said. "Eddie could have gone on for years without having an attack." That she worked in a hospital always gave her remarks of this sort a unique gravity, almost as if she were a doctor.

"Must have been some fit," Sonny said, squeezed into place between Harry and Albert.

"*Grand mal*," Maryrose said, and took another hungry drag on her cigarette.

"Poor little bastard," George said. "Sorry, Mom."

"I know you're in the Armed Forces, and Armed Forces people speak very freely, but I wish you would not use that kind of language."

Harry, jammed into Sonny's rock-hard side, felt his brother's body twitch with a hidden laugh, though Sonny's face did not alter.

"I said I was sorry, Mom," George said.

"Yes. Driver! Driver!" Maryrose was leaning forward, reaching out one claw to tap the chauffeur's shoulder. "Livermore is the next right. Do you know South Sixth Street?"

"I'll get you there," the driver said.

This is not my family, Harry thought. I came from somewhere else and my rules are different from theirs.

IIIIIIIIIIIIIIIIIIIIIIIIIIIIIIIIIIIIIIIIIIIIIII

HIS FATHER MUMBLED something inaudible as soon as they got in the door and disappeared into his curtained-off cubicle. Maryrose put her sunglasses in her purse and marched into the kitchen to warm the coffeecake and the macaroni casserole, both made that morning, in the oven. Sonny and George wandered into the living room and sat down on opposite ends of the couch. They did not look at each other—George picked up a *Reader's Digest* from the table and began leafing through it backward, and Sonny folded his hands in his lap and stared at his thumbs. Albert's footsteps plodded up the stairs, crossed the landing, and went into the dormitory bedroom.

"What's she in the kitchen for?" Sonny asked, speaking to his hands. "Nobody's going to come. Nobody ever comes here, because she never wanted them to."

"Albert's taking this kind of hard, Harry," George said. He propped the magazine against the stiff folds of his uniform and looked across the room at his little brother. Harry had seated himself beside the door, as out of the way as possible. George's attentions rather frightened him, though George had behaved with consistent kindness ever since his arrival two days after Eddie's death. His crew cut still bristled and he could still break rocks with his chin, but some violent demon seemed to have left him. "You think he'll be okay?"

"Him? Sure." Harry tilted his head, grimaced.

"He didn't see Little Eddie first, did he?"

"No, Dad did," Harry said. "He saw the light on in the attic when he came home, I guess. Albert went up there, though. I guess there was so much blood Dad thought somebody broke in and killed Eddie. But he just bumped his head, and that's where the blood came from."

"Head wounds bleed like bastards," Sonny said. "A guy hit me with a bottle once in Tokyo, I thought I was gonna bleed to death right there."

"And Mom's stuff got all messed up?" George asked quietly.

This time Sonny looked up.

"Pretty much, I guess. The dress rack got knocked down. Dad cleaned up what he could, the next day. One of the cane-back chairs got broke, and a hunk got knocked out of the teak table. And the mirror got broken into a million pieces."

Sonny shook his head, and made a soft whistling sound through his pursed lips.

"She's a tough old gal," George said. "I hear her coming though, so we have to stop, Harry. But we can talk tonight."

Harry nodded.

12

AFTER DINNER THAT night, when Maryrose had gone to bed—the hospital had given her two nights off— Harry sat across the kitchen table from a George who clearly had something to say. Sonny had polished off a six-pack by himself in front of the television and gone up to the dormitory bedroom by himself. Albert had disappeared shortly after dinner, and their father had never emerged from his cubicle beside the junk room.

"I'm glad Pete Petrosian came over," George said. "He's a good old boy. Ate two helpings, too."

Harry was startled by George's use of their neighbor's first name—he was not even sure that he had ever heard it before.

Mr. Petrosian had been their only caller that afternoon. Harry had seen that his mother was grateful that someone had come, and despite her preparations wanted no more company after Mr. Petrosian had left.

"Think I'll get a beer, that is if Sonny didn't drink it all," George said, and stood up and opened the fridge. His uniform looked as if it had been painted on his body, and his muscles bulged and moved like a horse's. "Two left," he said. "Good thing you're underage." George popped the caps off both bottles and came back to the table. He winked at Harry, then tilted the first bottle to his lips and took a good swallow. "So what the devil was Little Eddie doing up there, any-how? Trying on dresses?"

"I don't know," Harry said. "I was asleep."

"Hell, I know I kind of lost touch with Little Eddie, but I got the impression he was scared of his own shad-ow. I'm surprised he had the nerve to go up there and mess around with Mom's precious stuff."

"Yeah," Harry said. "Me too."

"You didn't happen to go with him, did you?" George tilted the bottle to his mouth and winked at Harry again.

Harry just looked back. He could feel his face getting hot.

"I just was thinking maybe you saw it happen to Little Eddie, and got too scared to tell anybody. Nobody would be mad at you, Harry. Nobody would blame you for anything. You couldn't know how to help someone who's having an epileptic fit. Little Eddie swallowed his tongue. Even if you'd been standing next to him when he did it and had the presence of mind to call an ambulance, he would have died be-fore it got there. Unless you knew what was wrong and how to correct it. Which nobody would expect you to know, not in a million years. Nobody'd blame you for anything, Harry, not even Mom."

"I was asleep," Harry said.

"Okay, okay. I just wanted you to know."

They sat in silence for a time, then both spoke at once.

"Did you know—"

"We had this—"

"Sorry," George said. "Go on."

"Did you know that Dad used to be in the Army? In World War II?"

"Yeah, I knew that. Of course I knew that."

"Did you know that he committed the perfect murder once?"

"*What?*"

"Dad committed the perfect murder. When he was at Dachau, that death camp."

"Oh, Christ, is that what you're talking about? You got a funny way of seeing things, Harry. He shot an enemy who was trying to escape. That's not murder, it's war. There's one hell of a big difference."

"I'd like to see war someday," Harry said. "I'd like to be in the Army, like you and Dad."

"Hold your horses, hold your horses," George said, smiling now. "That's sort of one of the things I wanted to talk to you about." He set down his beer bottle, cradled his hands around it, and tilted his head to look at Harry. This was obviously going to be serious. "You know, I used to be crazy and stupid, that's the only way to put it. I used to look for fights. I had a chip on my shoulder the size of a house, and pounding some dipshit into a coma was my idea of a great time. The Army did me a lot of good. It made me grow up. But I don't think you need that, Harry. You're too smart for that—if you have to go, you go, but out of all of us, you're the one who could really amount to something in this world. You could be a doctor. Or a lawyer. You ought to get the best education you can, Harry. What you have to do is stay out of trouble and get to college."

"Oh, college," Harry said.

"Listen to me, Harry. I make pretty good money, and I got nothing to spend it on. I'm not going to get married and have kids, that's for sure. So I want to make you a proposition. If you keep your nose clean and make it through high school, I'll help you out with college. Maybe you can get a scholarship—I think you're smart enough, Harry, and a scholarship would be great. But either way, I'll see you make it through." George emptied the first bottle, set it down, and gave Harry a quizzical look. "Let's get one person in this family off on the right track. What do you say?"

"I guess I better keep reading," Harry said.

"I hope you'll read your ass off, little buddy," George said, and picked up the second bottle of beer.

13

THE DAY AFTER Sonny left, George put all of Eddie's toys and clothes into a box and squeezed the box into the junk room; two days later, George took a bus to New York so he could get his flight to Munich from Idlewild. An hour before he caught his bus, George walked Harry up to Big John's and stuffed him full of hamburgers and french fries and said, "You'll probably miss Eddie a lot, won't you?" "I guess," Harry said, but the truth was that Eddie was now only a vacancy, a blank space. Sometimes a door would close and Harry would know that Little Eddie had just come in; but when he turned to look, he saw only emptiness. George's question, asked a week ago, was the last time Harry had heard anyone pronounce his brother's name.

In the seven days since the charmed afternoon at Big John's and the departure on a southbound bus of George Beevers, everything seemed to have gone back to the way it was before, but Harry knew that really everything had changed. They had been a loose, divided family of five, two parents and three sons. Now they seemed to be a family of three, and Harry thought that the actual truth was that the family had shrunk down to two, himself and his mother.

Edgar Beevers had left home—he too was an absence. After two visits from policemen who parked their cars right outside the house, after listening to his mother's muttered expressions of disgust, after the spectacle of his pale, bleary, but sober and clean-shaven father trying over and over to knot a necktie in front of the bathroom mirror, Harry finally accepted that his father had been caught shoplifting. His father had to go to court, and he was scared. His hands shook so uncontrollably that he could not shave himself, and in the end Maryrose had to knot his tie—doing it in one, two, three quick movements as brutal as the descent of a knife, never removing the cigarette from her mouth.

GRIEF-STRICKEN AREA MAN FORGIVEN OF SHOP-LIFTING CHARGE, read the headline over the little story in the evening newspaper which at last explained his father's crime. Edgar Beevers had been stopped on the sidewalk outside the Livermore Avenue National Tea, T-bone steaks hidden inside his shirt and a bottle of Rhinegold beer in each of his front pockets. He had stolen two steaks! He had put beer bottles in his pockets! This made Harry feel like he was sweating inside. The judge had sent him home, but home was not where he went. For a short time, Harry thought, his father had hung out on Oldtown Road, Palmyra's skid row, and slept in vacant lots with winos and bums. (Then a woman was supposed to have taken him in.)

Albert was another mystery. It was as though a creature from outer space had taken him over and was using his body, like *Invasion of the Body Snatchers*. Albert looked like he thought somebody was always standing behind him, watching every move he made. He was still carrying around that piece of his tongue, and pretty soon, Harry thought, he'd get so used to it that he would forget he had it.

Three days after George left Palmyra, Albert actually tagged along after Harry on the way to Big John's. Harry turned around on the sidewalk and saw Albert in his black jeans and grease-blackened T-shirt halfway down the block, shoving his hands in his pockets and looking hard at the ground. That was Albert's way of pretending to be invisible. The next time he turned around, Albert growled, "Keep walking."

Harry went to work on the pinball machine as soon as he got inside Big John's. Albert slunk in a few minutes later and went straight to the counter. He took one of the stained paper menus from a stack squeezed in beside a napkin dispenser and inspected it as if he had never seen it before.

"Hey, let me introduce you guys," said Big John, leaning against the far side of the counter. Like Albert, he wore black jeans and motorcycle boots but his dark hair, daringly for the nineteen fifties, fell over his ears. Beneath his stained white apron he wore a long-sleeved black shirt with a pattern of tiny azure palm trees. "You two are the Beevers boys, Harry and Bucky. Say hello to each other, fellows."

Bucky Beaver was a toothy rodent in an Ipana television commercial. Albert blushed, still grimly staring at his menu sheet.

"Call me 'Beans,'" Harry said, and felt Albert's gaze shift wonderingly to him.

"Beans and Bucky, the Beevers boys," Big John said. "Well, Buck, what'll you have?"

"Hamburger, fries, shake," Albert said.

Big John half-turned and yelled the order through the hatch to Mama Mary's kitchen. For a time the three of them stood in uneasy silence. Then Big John said, "Heard your old man found a new place to hang his hat. His new girlfriend is a real pistol, I heard. Spent some time in County Hospital. On account of she picked up little messages from outer space on the good old Philco. You hear that?"

"He's gonna come home real soon," Harry said. "He doesn't have any new girlfriend. He's staying with an old friend. She's a rich lady and she wants to help him out because she knows he had a lot of trouble and she's going to get him a real good job, and then he'll come home, and we'll be able to move to a better house and everything."

He never even saw Albert move, but Albert had materialized beside him. Fury, rage, and misery distorted his face. Harry had time to cry out only once, and then Albert slammed a fist into his chest and knocked him backward into the pinball machine.

"I bet that felt real good," Harry said, unable to keep down his own rage. "I bet you'd like to kill me, huh? Huh, Albert? How about that?"

Albert moved backward two paces and lowered his hands, already looking impassive, locked into himself.

For a second in which his breath failed and dazzling light filled his eyes, Harry saw Little Eddie's slack, trusting face before him. Then Big John came up from nowhere with a big hamburger and a mound of french fries on a plate and said, "Down, boys. Time for Rocky here to tackle his dinner."

That night Albert said nothing at all to Harry as they lay in their beds. Neither did he fall asleep. Harry knew that for most of the night Albert just closed his eyes and faked it, like a possum in trouble. Harry tried to stay awake long enough to see when Albert's fake sleep melted into the real thing, but he sank into dreams long before that.

||||||||||||||||||||||||||||||||||||||||||||||||

HE WAS RUSHING down the stony corridor of a castle past suits of armor and torches guttering in sconces. His bladder was bursting, he had to let go, he could not hold it more than another few seconds.... At last he came to the open bathroom door and ran into that splendid gleaming place. He began to tug at his zipper, and looked around for the butler and the row of marble urinals. Then he froze. Little Eddie was standing before him, not the uniformed butler. Blood ran in a gaudy streak from a gash high on his forehead over his cheek and right down his neck, neat as paint. Little Eddie was waving frantically at Harry, his eyes bright and hysterical, his mouth working soundlessly because he had swallowed his tongue.

Harry sat up straight in bed, about to scream, then realized that the bedroom was all around him and Little Eddie was gone. He hurried downstairs to the bathroom.

14

AT TWO O'CLOCK the next afternoon Harry Beevers had to pee again, and just as badly, but this time he was a long way from the bathroom across from the junk room and his father's old cubicle. Harry was standing in the humid sunlight across the street from 45 Oldtown Way. This short street connected the bums, transient hotels, bars, and seedy movie theaters of Oldtown Road with the more respectable hotels, department stores, and restaurants of Palmyra Avenue—the real downtown. Forty-five Oldtown Way was a four-story brick tenement with an exoskeleton of fire escapes. Black iron bars covered the ground-floor windows. On one side of 45 Oldtown Way were the large soap-smeared windows of a bankrupted shoe store, on the other a vacant lot where loose bricks and broken bottles nestled amongst dandelions and tall Queen Anne's Lace. Harry's father lived in that building now. Everybody else knew it, and since Big John had told him, now Harry knew it too.

He jigged from leg to leg, waiting for a woman to come out through the front door. It was as chipped and peeling as his own, and a broken fanlight sat drunkenly atop it. Harry had checked the row of dented mailboxes on the brick wall just outside the door for his father's name, but none bore any names at all. Big John hadn't known the name of the woman who had taken Harry's father in, but he said that she was large, black-haired, and crazy, and that she had two children in foster care. About half an hour ago a dark-haired woman had come through the door, but Harry had not followed her because she had not looked especially large to him. Now he was beginning to have doubts. What did Big John mean by "large," anyhow? As big as he was? And how could you tell if someone was crazy? Did it show? Maybe he should have followed that woman. This thought made him even more anxious, and he squeezed his legs together.

His father was in that building now, he thought. Harry thought of his father lying on an unmade bed, his brown winter coat around him, his hat pulled low on his forehead like Lepke Buchalter's, drawing on a cigarette, looking moodily out the window.

Then he had to pee so urgently that he could not have held it in for more than a few seconds, and trotted across the street and into the vacant lot. Near the back fence the tall weeds gave him some shelter from the street. He frantically unzipped and let the braided yellow stream splash into a nest of broken bricks. Harry looked up at the side of the building beside him. It looked very tall, and seemed to be tilting slightly toward him. The four blank windows on each floor looked back down at him. Just as he was tugging at his zipper, he heard the front door of the building slam shut.

His heart slammed too. Harry hunkered down behind the tall white weeds. Anxiety that she might walk the other way, toward downtown, made him twine his fingers together and bend his fingers back. If he waited about five seconds, he figured, he'd know she was going toward Palmyra Avenue and would be able to get across the lot in time to see which way she turned. His knuckles cracked. He felt like a soldier hiding in a forest, like a murder weapon.

He raised up on his toes and got ready to dash back across the street, because an empty grocery cart closely followed by a moving belly with a tiny head and basketball shoes, a cigar tilted in its mouth like a flag, appeared past the front of the building. He could go back and wait across the street. Harry settled down and watched the stomach go down the sidewalk past him. Then a shadow separated itself from the street side of the fat man, and the shadow became a black-haired woman in a long loose dress now striding past the grocery cart. She shook back her head, and Harry saw that she was tall as a queen and that her skin was darker than olive. Deep lines cut through her cheeks. It had to be the woman who had taken his father in. Her long rapid strides had taken her well past the fat man's grocery cart. Harry ran across the rubble of the lot and began to follow her up the sidewalk.

His father's woman walked in a hard, determined way. She stepped down into the street to get around groups too slow for her. At the Oldtown Road corner she wove her way through a group of saggy-bottomed men passing around a bottle in a paper bag and cut in front of two black children dribbling a basketball up the street. She was on the move, and Harry had to hurry along to keep her in sight.

"I bet you don't believe me," he said to himself, practicing, and skirted the group of winos on the corner. He picked up his speed until he was nearly trotting. The two black kids with the basketball ignored him as he kept pace with them, then went on ahead. Far up the block, the tall woman with bouncing black hair marched right past a flashing neon sign in a bar window. Her bottom moved back and forth in the loose dress, surprisingly big whenever it bulged out the fabric of the dress; her back seemed as long as a lion's. "What would you say if I told you," Harry said to himself.

A block and a half ahead, the woman turned on her heel and went through the door of the A & P store. Harry sprinted the rest of the way, pushed the yellow wooden door marked ENTER, and walked into the dense, humid air of the grocery store. Other A & P stores may have been air-conditioned, but not the little shop on Oldtown Road.

What was foster care, anyway? Did you get money if you gave away your children?

A good person's children would never be in foster care, Harry thought. He saw the woman turning into the third aisle past the cash register. He took in with a small shock that she was taller than his father. If I told you, you might not believe me. He went slowly around the corner of the aisle. She was standing on the pale wooden floor about fifteen feet in front of him, carrying a wire basket in one hand. He stepped forward. What I have to say might seem. For good luck, he touched the hat pin inserted into the bottom of his collar. She was staring at a row of brightly colored bags of potato chips. Harry cleared his throat. The woman reached down and picked up a big bag and put it in the basket.

"Excuse me," Harry said.

She turned her head to look at him. Her face was as wide as it was long, and in the mellow light from the store's low-wattage bulbs her skin seemed a very light shade of brown. Harry knew he was meeting an equal. She looked like she could do magic, as if she could shoot fire and sparks out of her fierce black eyes.

"I bet you don't believe me," he said, "but a kid can hypnotize people just as good as an adult."

"What's that?"

His rehearsed words now sounded crazy to him, but he stuck to his script.

"A kid can hypnotize people. I can hypnotize people. Do you believe that?"

"I don't think I even care," she said, and wheeled away toward the rear of the aisle.

"I bet you don't think I could hypnotize you," Harry said.

"Kid, get lost."

Harry suddenly knew that if he kept talking about hypnotism the woman would turn down the next aisle and ignore him no matter what he said, or else begin to speak in a very loud voice about seeing the manager. "My name is Harry Beevers," he said to her back. "Edgar Beevers is my dad."

She stopped and turned around and looked expressionlessly into his face.

"I wonder if you maybe you call him Beans," Harry said.

"Oh, great," she said. "That's just great. So you're one of his boys. Terrific. *Beans* wants potato chips, what do you want?"

"I want you to fall down and bang your head and swallow your tongue and *die* and get buried and have people drop dirt on you," Harry said. The woman's mouth fell open. "Then I want you to puff up with *gas*. I want you to *rot*. I want you to turn green and *black*. I want your *skin* to slide off your bones."

"You're crazy!" the woman shouted at him. "Your whole family's crazy! Do you think your mother wants him anymore?"

"My father shot us in the back," Harry said, and turned and bolted down the aisle for the door.

Outside, he began to trot down seedy Oldtown Road. At Oldtown Way he turned left. When he ran past number 45, he looked at every blank window. His face, his hands, his whole body felt hot and wet. Soon he had a stitch in his side. Harry blinked, and saw a dark line of trees, a wall of barbed wire before him. At the top of Oldtown Way he turned into Palmyra

Avenue. From there he could continue running past Allouette's boarded-up windows, past all the stores old and new, to the corner of Livermore, and from there, he only now realized, to the little house that belonged to Mr. Petrosian.

15

ON A SWELTERING mid-afternoon eleven years later at a camp in the central highlands of Vietnam, Lieutenant Harry Beevers closed the flap of his tent against the mosquitos and sat on the edge of his temporary bunk to write a long-delayed letter back to Pat Caldwell, the young woman he wanted to marry—and to whom he would be married for a time, after his return from the war to New York State.

This is what he wrote, after frequent crossings-out and hesitations. Harry later destroyed this letter.

> Dear Pat:
> *First of all I want you to know how much I miss you, my darling, and that if I ever get out of this beautiful and terrible country, which I am going to do, that I am going to chase you mercilessly and unrelentingly until you say that you'll marry me. Maybe in the euphoria of re-lief (YES!!!), I have the future all worked out,*

Pat, and you're a big part of it. I have eighty-six days until DEROS, when they pat me on the head and put me on that big bird out of here. Now that my record is clear again, I have no doubts that Columbia Law School will take me in. As you know, my law board scores were pretty respectable (modest me!) when I took them at Adelphi. I'm pretty sure I could even get into Harvard Law, but I settled on Columbia because then we could both be in New York.

My brother George has already told me that he will help out with whatever money I— you and I—will need. George put me through Adelphi. I don't think you knew this. In fact, nobody knew this. When I look back, in college I was such a jerk. I wanted everybody to think my family was well-to-do, or at least middle-class. The truth is, we were damn poor, which I think makes my accomplishments all the more noteworthy, all the more loveworthy!

You see, this experience, even with all the ugly and self-doubting and humiliating moments, has done me a lot of good. I was right to come here, even though I had no idea what it was really like. I think I needed the experience of war to complete me, and I tell you this even though I know that you will detest any such idea. In fact, I have to tell you that a big part of me loves being here, and that in some way, even with all this trouble, this year will always be one of the high points of my life. Pat, as you see I'm determined to be honest—to be an honest man. If I'm going to be a lawyer, I ought to be honest, don't you think? (Or maybe the reverse is the reality!) One thing that has meant a lot to me here has been what I can only call the close comradeship of my friends and my men—I actually like the grunts more than the usual officer types, which of course means that I get more loyalty and better performance from my men than the usual lieutenant. Someday I'd like you to meet Mike Poole and Tim Underhill and Pumo the Puma and the most amazing of all, M.O. Dengler, who of course was involved with me in the Ia Thuc cave incident. These guys stuck by me. I even have a nickname, "Beans. " They call me "Beans" Beevers, and I like it.

There was no way my court-martial could have really put me in any trouble, because all the facts, and my own men, were on my side. Besides, could you see me actually killing children? This is Vietnam and you kill people, that's what we're doing here—we kill Charlies. But we don't kill babies and children. Not even in the heat of wartime—and Ia Thuc was pretty hot!

Well, this is my way of letting you know that at the court-martial of course I received a complete and utter vindication. Dengler did too. There were even unofficial mutterings about giving us medals for all the BS we put up with for the past six weeks—including that amazing story in Time *magazine. Before people start yelling about atrocities, they ought to have all the facts straight. Fortunately, last week's magazines go out with the rest of the trash.*

Besides, I already knew too much about what death does to people.

I never told you that I once had a little brother named Edward. When I was ten, my little brother wandered up into the top floor of our house one night and suffered a fatal epileptic fit. This event virtually destroyed my family. It led directly to my father's leaving home. (He had been a hero in WWII, something else I never told you.) It deeply changed, I would say even damaged, my older brother Albert. Albert tried to enlist in 1964, but they wouldn't take him because they said he was psychologically unfit. My mom too almost came apart for a while. She used to go up in the attic and cry and wouldn't come down. So you could say that my family was pretty well destroyed, or ruined, or whatever you want to call it, by a sudden death. I took it, and my dad's desertion, pretty hard myself. You don't get over these things easily.

The court-martial lasted exactly four hours. Big deal, hey?, as we used to say back in Palmyra.

We used to have a neighbor named Pete Petrosian who said things like that, and against what must have been million-to-one odds, died exactly the same way my brother did, about two weeks after—lightning really did strike twice. I guess it's dumb to think about him now, but maybe one thing war does is to make you conversant with death. How it happens, what it does to people, what it means, how all the dead in your life are somehow united, joined, part of your eternal family. This is a profound feeling, Pat, and no damn whipped-up failed court-martial can touch it. If there were any innocent children in that cave, then they are in my family forever, like little Edward and Pete Petrosian, and the rest of my life is a poem to them. But the Army says there weren't, and so do I.

I love you and love you and love you. You can stop worrying now and start thinking about being married to a Columbia Law student with one hell of a good future. I won't tell you any more war stories than you want to hear. And that's a promise, whether the stories are about Nam or Palmyra.

Always yours,
Harry
(aka "Beans!")

The Juniper Tree

I T IS A SCHOOL yard in my Midwest of empty lots, waving green and brilliant with tiger lilies, of ugly new "ranch" houses set down in rows in glistening clay, of treeless avenues cooking in the sun. Our school yard is black asphalt—on June days, patches of the asphalt loosen and stick like gum to the soles of our high-top basketball shoes.

Most of the playground is black empty space from which heat radiates up like the wavery images on the screen of a faulty television set. Tall wire mesh surrounds it. A new boy named Paul is standing beside me.

Though it is now nearly the final month of the semester, Paul came to us, carroty-haired, pale-eyed, too shy to ask even the whereabouts of the lavatory, only six weeks ago. The lessons baffle him, and his Southern accent is a fatal error of style. The popular students broadcast in hushed, giggling whispers the terrible news that Paul "talks like a nigger." Their voices are *almost* awed—they are conscious of the enormity of what they are saying, of the enormity of its consequences.

The Juniper Tree

AND OTHER BLUE ROSE STORIES

Paul is wearing a brilliant red shirt too heavy, too enveloping, for the weather. He and I stand in the shade at the rear of the school, before the cream-colored brick wall in which is placed at eye level a newly broken window of pebbly green glass reinforced with strands of copper wire. At our feet is a little scatter of green, edible-looking pebbles. The pebbles dig into the soles of our shoes, too hard to shatter against the softer asphalt. Paul is singing to me in his slow, lilting voice that he will never have friends in this school. I put my foot down on one of the green candy pebbles and feel it push up, hard as a bullet, against my foot. "Children are so cruel," Paul casually sings. I think of sliding the pebble of broken glass across my throat, slicing myself wide open to let death in.

Paul did not return to school in the fall. His father, who had beaten a man to death down in Mississippi, had been arrested while leaving a movie theater near my house named the Orpheum-Oriental. Paul's father had taken his family to see an Esther Williams movie costarring Fernando Lamas, and when they came out, their mouths raw from salty popcorn, the baby's hands sticky with spilled Coca-Cola, the police were waiting for them. They were Mississippi people, and I think of Paul now, seated at a desk on a floor of an office building in Jackson filled with men like him at desks: his tie perfectly knotted, a good shine on his cordovan shoes, a necessary but unconscious restraint in the set of his mouth.

94

In those days I used to spend whole days in the Orpheum-Oriental.

I was seven. I held within me the idea of a disappearance like Paul's, of never having to be seen again. Of being an absence, a shadow, a place where something no longer visible used to be.

Before I met that young-old man whose name was "Frank" or "Stan" or "Jimmy," when I sat in the rapture of education before the movies at the Orpheum-Oriental, I watched Alan Ladd and Richard Widmark and Glenn Ford and Dane Clark. *Chicago Deadline*. Martin and Lewis, tangled up in the same parachute in *At War With the Army*. William Boyd and Roy Rogers. Openmouthed, I drank down movies about spies and criminals, wanting the passionate and shadowy ones to fulfill themselves, to gorge themselves on what they needed.

The feverish gale of Richard Widmark, the anger of Alan Ladd, Berry Kroeger's sneaky eyes, girlish and watchful—vivid, total elegance.

When I was seven, my father walked into the bathroom and saw me looking at my face in the mirror. He slapped me, not with his whole strength, but hard, raging instantly. "What do you think you're looking at?" His hand cocked and ready. "What do you think you see?"

"Nothing," I said.

"Nothing is right."

A carpenter, he worked furiously, already defeated, and never had enough money—as if, permanently beyond reach, some quantity of money existed that would have satisfied him. In the mornings he went to the job site hardened like cement into anger he barely knew he had. Sometimes he brought men from the taverns home with him at night. They carried transparent bottles of Miller High Life in paper bags and set them down on the table with a bang that said: Men are here! My mother, who had returned from her secretary's job a few hours earlier, fed my brothers and me, washed the dishes, and put the three of us to bed while the men shouted and laughed in the kitchen.

He was considered an excellent carpenter. He worked slowly, patiently; and I see now that he spent whatever love he had in the rented garage that was his workshop. In his spare time he listened to baseball games on the radio. He had professional, but not personal, vanity, and he thought that a face like mine should not be examined.

Because I saw "Jimmy" in the mirror, I thought my father, too, hold seen him.

One Saturday my mother took the twins and me on the ferry across Lake Michigan to Saginaw—the point of the journey was the journey, and at Saginaw the boat docked for twenty minutes before wallowing back out into the lake and returning. With us were women like my mother, her friends, freed by the weekend from their jobs, some of them accompanied by men like my father, with their felt hats and baggy weekend trousers flaring over their weekend shoes. The women wore blood-bright lipstick that printed itself onto their cigarettes and smeared across their front teeth. They laughed a great deal and repeated the words that had made them laugh. "Hot dog," "slippin' 'n' slidin'," "opera singer." Thirty minutes after departure, the men disappeared into the enclosed deck bar; the women, my mother among them, arranged deck chairs into a long oval tied together by laughter, attention, gossip. They waved their cigarettes in the air. My brothers raced around the deck, their shirts flapping, their hair glued to their skulls with sweat—when they squabbled, my mother ordered them into empty deck chairs. I sat on the deck, leaning against the railings, quiet. If someone had asked me: What do you want to do this afternoon, what do you want to do for the rest of your life? I would have said, I want to stay right here, I want to stay here forever.

After a while I stood up and left the women. I went across the deck and stepped through a hatch into the bar. Dark, deeply grained imitation wood covered the walls. The odors of beer and cigarettes and the sound of men's voices filled the enclosed space. About twenty men stood at the bar, talking and gesturing with half-filled glasses. Then one man broke away from the others with a flash of dirty-blond hair. I saw his shoulders move, and my scalp tingled and my stomach froze and

The Juniper Tree
AND OTHER BLUE ROSE STORIES

I thought: Jimmy. "Jimmy." But he turned all the way around, dipping his shoulders in some ecstasy of beer and male company, and I saw that he was a stranger, not "Jimmy," after all.

I WAS THINKING: Someday when I am free, when I am out of this body and in some city whose name I do not even know now, I will remember this from beginning to end and then I will be free of it.

The women floated over the empty lake, laughing out clouds of cigarette smoke, the men, too, as boisterous as the children on the sticky asphalt playground with its small green spray of glass like candy.

IN THOSE DAYS I knew I was set apart from the rest of my family, an island between my parents and the twins. Those pairs that bracketed me slept in double beds in adjacent rooms at the back of the ground floor of the duplex owned by the blind man who lived above us. My bed, a cot coveted by the twins, stood in their room. An invisible line of great authority divided my territory and possessions from theirs.

THIS IS WHAT happened in the mornings in our half of the duplex. My mother got up first—we heard her showering, heard drawers closing, the sounds of bowls and milk being set out on the table. The smell of bacon frying for my father, who banged on the door and called out my brothers' names. "Don't you make me come in there, now!" The noisy, puppyish turmoil of my brothers getting out of bed. All three of us scramble into the bathroom as soon as my father leaves it. The bathroom was steamy, heavy with the odor of shit and the more piercing, almost palpable smell of shaving— lather and amputated whiskers. We all pee into the toilet at the same time. My mother frets and frets, pulling the twins into their clothes so that she can take them down the street to Mrs. Candee, who is given a five-dollar bill every week for taking care of them. I am supposed to be running back and forth on the playground in Summer Play School, supervised by two teenage girls who live a block away from us. (I went to Play School only twice.) After I dress myself in clean underwear and socks and put on my everyday shirt and pants, I come into the kitchen while my father finishes his breakfast. He is eating strips of bacon and golden-brown pieces of toast shiny with butter. A cigarette smolders in the ashtray before him. Everybody else has already left the house. My father and I can hear the blind man banging on the piano in his living room. I sit down before a bowl of cereal. My father looks at me, looks away. Angry at the blind man for banging at the piano this early in

99

the morning, he is sweating already. His cheeks and forehead shine like the golden toast. My father glances at me, knowing he can postpone this no longer, and reaches wearily into his pocket and drops two quarters on the table. The high-school girls charge twenty-five cents a day, and the other quarter is for my lunch. "Don't lose that money," he says as I take the coins. My father dumps coffee into his mouth, puts the cup and his plate into the crowded sink, looks at me again, pats his pockets for his keys, and says, "Close the door behind you." I tell him that I will close the door. He picks up his gray toolbox and his black lunch pail, claps his hat on his head, and goes out, banging his toolbox against the door frame. It leaves a broad gray mark like a smear left by the passing of some angry creature's hide.

Then I am alone in the: house. I go back to the bedroom, close the door and push a chair beneath the knob, and read *Blackhawk* and *Henry* and *Captain Marvel* comic books until at last it is time to go to the theater.

While I read, everything in the house seems alive and dangerous. I can hear the telephone in the hall rattling on its hook, the radio clicking as it tries to turn itself on and talk to me. The dishes stir and chime in the sink. At these times all objects, even the heavy chairs and sofa, become their true selves, violent as the fire that fills the sky I cannot see, and races through the secret ways and passages beneath the streets. At these times other people vanish like smoke.

When I pull the chair away from the door, the house immediately goes quiet, like a wild animal feigning sleep. Everything inside and out slips cunningly back into place, the fires bank, men and women reappear on the sidewalks. I must open the door and I do. I walk swiftly through the kitchen and the living room to the front door, knowing that if I look too carefully at any one thing, I will wake it up again. My mouth is so dry, my tongue feels fat. "I'm leaving," I say to no one. Everything in the house hears me.

THE QUARTER GOES through the slot at the bottom of the window, the ticket leaps from its slot. For a long time, before "Jimmy," I thought that unless you kept your stub unfolded and safe in a shirt pocket, the usher could rush down the aisle in the middle of the movie, seize you, and throw you out. So into the pocket it goes, and I slip through the big doors into the cool, cross the lobby, and pass through a swinging door with a porthole window.

Most of the regular daytime patrons of the Orpheum-Oriental sit in the same seats every day—I am one of those who comes here every day. A small, talkative gathering of bums sits far to the right of the theater, in the rows beneath the sconces fastened like bronze torches to the walls. The bums choose these seats so that they can examine their bits of paper, their "documents," and show them to each other during the movies. Always on their minds is the possibility that they might have lost one of these documents, and they frequently consult the tattered envelopes in which they are kept.

I take the end seat, left side of the central block of seats, just before the broad horizontal middle aisle. There I can stretch out. At other times I sit in the middle of the last row, or the first; sometimes when the balcony is open I go up and sit in its first row. From the first row of the balcony, seeing a movie is like being a bird and flying down into the movie from above. To be alone in the theater is delicious. The curtains hang heavy, red, anticipatory; the mock torches glow on the walls. Swirls of gilt wind through the red paint. On days when I sit near a wall, I reach out toward the red, which seems warm and soft, and find my fingers resting on a chill dampness. The carpet of the Orpheum-Oriental must once have been a bottomlessly rich brown; now it is a dark noncolor, mottled with the pink and gray smears, like melted Band-Aids, of chewing gum. From about a third of the seats dirty gray wool foams from slashes in the worn plush.

On an ideal day I sit through a cartoon, a travelogue, a sequence of previews, a movie, another cartoon, and another movie before anyone else enters the theater. This whole cycle is as satisfying as a meal. On other mornings, old women in odd hats and young women wearing scarves over their rollers, a few teenage couples

are scattered throughout the theater when I come in.
None of these people ever pays attention to anything but
the screen and, in the case of the teenagers, each other.

Once, a man in his early twenties, hair like a hay-
stack, sat up in the wide middle aisle when I took
my seat. He groaned. Rusty-looking dried blood was
spattered over his chin and his dirty white shirt. He
groaned again and then got to his hands and knees.
The carpet beneath him was spotted with what looked
like a thousand red dots. The young man stumbled
to his feet and began reeling up the aisle. A bright,
depthless pane of sunlight surrounded him before he
vanished into it.

At the beginning of July, I told my mother that
the high-school girls had increased the hours of the
Play School because I wanted to be sure of seeing both
features twice before I had to go home. After that I
could learn the rhythms of the theater itself, which
did not impress themselves upon me all at once but
revealed themselves gradually, so that by the middle
of the first week, I knew when the bums would begin
to move toward the seats beneath the sconces—they
usually arrived on Tuesdays and Fridays shortly after
eleven o'clock, when the liquor store down the block
opened up to provide them with the pints and half-
pints that nourished them. By the end of the second
week, I knew when the ushers left the interior of the

theater to sit on padded benches in the lobby and light up their Luckies and Chesterfields, when the old men and women would begin to appear. By the end of the third week, I felt like the merest part of a great, orderly machine. Before the beginning of the second showing of *Beautiful Hawaii* or *Curiosities Down Under,* I went out to the counter and with my second quarter purchased a box of popcorn or a packet of Good & Plenty candy.

In a movie theater nothing is random except the customers and hitches in the machine. Filmstrips break and lights fail; the projectionist gets drunk or falls asleep; and the screen presents a blank yellow face to the stamping, whistling audience. These inconsistencies are summer squalls, forgotten as soon as they have ended.

The occasion for the lights, the projectionist, the boxes of popcorn and packets of candy, the movies, enlarged when seen over and over. The truth gradually came to me that this deepening and widening out, this enlarging, was why movies were shown over and over all day long. The machine revealed itself most surely in the exact, limpid repetitions of the actors' words and gestures as they moved through the story. When Alan Ladd asked "Blackie Franchot," the dying gangster, "Who did it, Blackie?" his voice widened like a river, grew sandier with an almost unconcealed tenderness I had to learn to hear—the voice within the speaking voice.

CHICAGO DEADLINE WAS the exploration by a newspaper reporter named "Ed Adams" (Alan Ladd) of the tragedy of a mysterious young woman, "Rosita Jandreau," who had died alone of tuberculosis in a shabby hotel room. The reporter soon learns that she had many names, many identities. She had been in love with an architect, a gangster, a crippled professor, a boxer, a millionaire, and had given a different facet of her being to each of them. Far too predictably, the adult me complains, the obsessed "Ed" falls in love with "Rosita." When I was seven, little was predictable—I had not yet seen *Laura*—and I saw a man driven by the need to understand, which became identical to the need to protect. "Rosita Jandreau" was the embodiment of memory, which was mystery.

Through the sequences of her identities, the various selves shown to brother, boxer, millionaire, gangster, all the others, her memory kept her whole. I saw, twice a day, for two weeks, before and during "Jimmy," the machine deep within the machine. Love and memory were the same. Both love and memory accommodated us to death. (I did not understand this, but I saw it.) The reporter, Alan Ladd, with his dirty-blond hair, his perfect jawline, and brilliant, wounded smile, gave her life by making her memory his own.

"I think you're the only one who ever understood her," Arthur Kennedy—"Rosita's" brother—tells Alan Ladd.

The Juniper Tree ⅢⅢⅢⅢⅢⅢⅢⅢⅢⅢⅢⅢⅢⅢⅢⅢⅢⅢⅢⅢⅢⅢⅢⅢⅢⅢⅢⅢ
AND OTHER BLUE ROSE STORIES

Most of the world demands the kick of sensation, most of the world must gather and spend money, hunt for easier and more temporary forms of love, must feed itself, sell newspapers, destroy the enemy's plots with plots of its own....

"I don't know what you want," "Ed Adams" says to the editor of *The Journal.* "You got two murders..."

ⅢⅢⅢⅢⅢⅢⅢⅢⅢⅢⅢⅢⅢⅢⅢⅢⅢⅢⅢⅢⅢ

"...AND A MYSTERY woman," I say along with him. His voice is tough and detached, the voice of a wounded man acting. The man beside me laughs. Unlike his normal voice, his laughter is breathless and high-pitched. It is the second showing today of *Chicago Deadline,* early afternoon—after the next showing of *At War With the Army* I will have to walk up the aisle and out of the theater. It will be twenty minutes to five, and the sun will still burn high over the cream-colored buildings across wide, empty Sherman Boulevard.

I met the man, or he met me, at the candy counter. He was at first only a tall presence, blond, dressed in dark clothing. I cared nothing for him, he did not matter. He was vague even when he spoke. "Good popcorn." I looked up at him—narrow blue eyes, bad teeth smiling at me. Stubble on his face. I looked away and the uniformed man behind the counter handed me popcorn.

"Good for you, I mean. Good stuff in popcorn—comes right out of the ground. Grows on big plants tall as I am, just like other corn. You know that?"

When I said nothing, he laughed and spoke to the man behind the counter. "*He* didn't know that—the kid thought popcorn grew inside poppers." The counterman turned away. "You come here a lot?" the man asked me.

I put a few kernels of popcorn in my mouth and turned toward him. He was showing me his bad teeth.

"You do," he said. "You come here a lot."

I nodded.

"Every day?"

I nodded again.

"And we tell little fibs at home about what we've been doing all day, don't we?" he asked, and pursed his lips and raised his eyes like a comic butler in a movie. Then his mood shifted and everything about him became serious. He was looking at me, but he did not see me. "You got a favorite actor? I got a favorite actor. Alan Ladd."

And I saw—both saw and understood—that he thought he looked like Alan Ladd. He did, too, at least a little bit. When I saw the resemblance, he seemed like a different person, more glamorous. Glamour surrounded him, as though he were acting, impersonating a shabby young man with stained, irregular teeth.

"The name's Frank," he said, and stuck out his hand. "Shake?"

I took his hand.

"Real good popcorn," he said, and stuck his hand into the box. "Want to hear a secret?"

A secret.

"I was born twice. The first time, I died. It was on an Army base. Everybody told me I should have joined the Navy, and everybody was right. So I just had myself get born somewhere else. Hey—the Army's not for everybody, you know?" He grinned down at me. "Now I *told* you my secret. Let's go in—I'll sit with you. Everybody needs company, and I like you. You look like a good kid."

He followed me back to my seat and sat down beside me. When I quoted the lines along with the actors, he laughed.

Then he said—

Then he leaned toward me and said—

He leaned toward me, breathing sour wine over me, and took—

"No."

"I was just kidding out there," he said. "Frank ain't my real name. Well, it was my name. Before. See? Frank *used* to be my name for a while. But now my good friends call me Stan. I like that. Stanley the Steamer. Big Stan. Stan the Man. See? It works real good."

‖‖‖‖‖‖‖‖‖‖‖‖‖‖‖‖‖‖‖‖‖‖‖‖‖‖‖‖‖‖‖‖‖‖‖‖

YOU'LL NEVER BE a carpenter, he told me. You'll never be anything like that—because you got that look. *I* used to have that look, okay? So I know. I know about you just by looking at you.

He said he had been a clerk at Sears; after that he had worked as the custodian for a couple of apartment buildings owned by a guy who used to be a friend of his but was no longer. Then he had been the janitor at the high school where my grade school sent its graduates. "Good old booze got me fired, story of my life," he said. "Tight-ass bitches caught me drinking down in the basement, in a room I used there, and threw me out without a fare-thee-well. Hey, that was my *room*. My *place*. The best things in the world can do the worst things to you; you'll find that out someday. And when you go to that school, I hope you'll remember what they done to me there."

These days he was resting. He hung around, he went to the movies.

He said: You got something special in you. Guys like me, we're funny, we can tell.

We sat together through the second feature, Dean Martin and Jerry Lewis, comfortable and laughing. "Those guys are bigger bums than us," he said. I thought of Paul backed up against the school in his enveloping red shirt, imprisoned within his inability to be like anyone around him.

You coming back tomorrow? If I get here, I'll check around for you.

Hey. Trust me. I know who you are.

You know that little thing you pee with? Leaning sideways and whispering into my ear. That's the best thing a man's got. Trust me.

ⅢⅢⅢⅢⅢⅢⅢⅢⅢⅢⅢⅢⅢⅢⅢⅢⅢⅢⅢⅢⅢⅢⅢⅢ

THE BIG PROVIDENTIAL park near our house, two streets past the Orpheum-Oriental, is separated into three different areas. Nearest the wide iron gates on Sherman Boulevard through which we enter was a wading pool divided by a low green hedge, so rubbery it seemed artificial, from a playground with a climbing frame, swings, and a row of seesaws. When I was a child of two and three, I splashed in the warm pool and clung to the chains of the swings, making myself go higher and higher, terror and joy and grim duty so woven together that no one could pull them apart.

Beyond the children's pool and playground was the zoo. My mother walked my brothers and me to the playground and wading pool and sat smoking on a bench while we played; both of my parents took us into the zoo. An elephant extended his trunk to my father's palm and delicately lipped peanuts toward his maw. The giraffe stretched toward the constantly diminishing supply of leaves, ever fewer and higher, above his cage. The lions drowsed on amputated branches and paced behind the bars, staring out not at what was there but at the long, grassy plains imprinted on their memories. I knew the lions had the power not to see us, to look straight through us to Africa. But when they saw you instead of Africa, they looked right into your bones, they saw the blood traveling through your body. The lions were golden-brown, patient, green-eyed. They recognized me and could read thoughts. The lions neither liked nor disliked me, they did not miss me during their long weekdays, but they took me into the circle of known beings.

("You shouldn't have looked at me like that," June Havoc—"Leona"—tells "Ed Adams." She does not mean it, not at all.)

Past the zoo and across a narrow park road down which khaki-clothed park attendants pushed barrows heavy with flowers stood a wide, unexpected lawn bordered with flower beds and tall elms—open space hidden like a secret between the caged animals and the elm trees. Only my father brought me to this section of the park. Here he tried to make a baseball player of me.

"Get the bat off your shoulders," he says. "For God's sake, will you try to hit the ball, anyhow?"

When I fail once again to swing at his slow, perfect pitch, he spins around, raises his arm, and theatrically asks everyone in sight, "Whose kid is this, anyway? Can you answer me that?"

He has never asked me about the Play School I am supposed to be attending, and I have never told him about the Orpheum-Oriental—I will never come any closer to talking to him than now, for "Stan," "Stanley the Steamer," has told me things that cannot be true, that must be inventions and fables, part of the world of children wandering lost in the forest, of talking cats and silver boots filled with blood. In this world, dismembered children buried beneath juniper trees can rise and speak, made whole once again. Fables boil with underground explosions and hidden fires, and for this reason, memory rejects them, thrusts them out of its sight, and they must be repeated over and over. I cannot remember "Stan's" face—cannot even be sure I remember what he said. Dean Martin and Jerry Lewis are bums like us. I am certain of only one thing: tomorrow I am again going to see my newest, scariest, most interesting friend.

"When I was your age," my father says, "I had my heart set on playing pro ball when I grew up. And you're too damned scared or lazy to even take the bat off your shoulder. Kee-rist! I can't stand looking at you anymore."

He turns around and begins to move quickly toward the narrow park road and the zoo, going home, and I run after him. I retrieve the softball when he tosses it into the bushes.

"What the hell do you think you're going to do when you grow up?" my father asks, his eyes still fixed ahead of him. "I wonder what you think life is all *about*. I wouldn't give you a job, I wouldn't trust you around carpenter tools, I wouldn't trust you to blow your nose right—to tell you the truth, I wonder if the hospital mixed up the goddamn babies."

I follow him, dragging the bat with one hand, in the other cradling the softball in the pouch of my mitt.

At dinner my mother asks if Summer Play School is fun, and I say yes. I have already taken from my father's dresser drawer what "Stan" asked me to get for him, and it burns in my pocket as if it were alight. I want to ask: Is it actually true and not a story? Does the worst thing always have to be the true thing? Of course, I cannot ask this. My father does not know about worse things—he sees what he wants to see, or he tries so hard, he thinks he does see it.

"I guess he'll hit a long ball someday. The boy just needs more work on his swing." He tries to smile at me, a boy who will someday learn to hit a long ball. The knife is upended in his fist—he is about to smear a pat of butter on his steak. He does not see me at all. My father is not a lion, he cannot make the switch to seeing what is really there in front of him.

Late at night Alan Ladd knelt beside my bed. He was wearing a neat gray suit, and his breath smelled like cloves. "You okay, son?" I nodded. "I just wanted to tell you that I like seeing you out there every day. That means a lot to me."

ⅢⅢⅢⅢⅢⅢⅢⅢⅢⅢⅢⅢⅢⅢⅢⅢⅢⅢⅢⅢⅢⅢⅢⅢⅢ

"DO YOU REMEMBER what I was telling you about?"

And I knew: it was true. He had said those things, and he would repeat them like a fairy tale, and the world was going to change because it would be seen through changed eyes. I felt sick—trapped in the theater as if in a cage.

"You think about what I told you?"

"Sure," I said.

"That's good. Hey, you know what? I feel like changing seats. You want to change seats too?"

"Where to?"

He tilted his head back, and I knew he wanted to move to the last row. "Come on. I want to show you something."

We changed seats.

For a long time we sat watching the movie from the last row, nearly alone in the theater. Just after eleven, three of the bums filed in and proceeded to their customary seats on the other side of the theater—a rumpled graybeard I had seen many times before; a fat man with a stubby, squashed face, also familiar; and one of the shaggy, wild-looking young men who hung

114

around the bums until they became indistinguishable from them. They began passing a flat brown bottle back and forth. After a second I remembered the young man—I had surprised him awake one morning, passed out and spattered with blood, in the middle aisle.

Then I wondered if "Stan" was not the young man I had surprised that morning; they looked as alike as twins, though I knew they were not.

"Want a sip?" "Stan" said, showing me his own pint bottle. "Do you good."

Bravely, feeling privileged and adult, I took the bottle of Thunderbird and raised it to my mouth. I wanted to like it, to share the pleasure of it with "Stan," but it tasted horrible, like garbage, and the little bit I swallowed burned all the way down my throat.

I made a face, and he said, "This stuff's really not so bad. Only one thing in the world can make you feel better than this stuff."

He placed his hand on my thigh and squeezed. "I'm giving you a head start, you know. Just because I liked you the first time I saw you." He leaned over and stared at me. "You believe me? You believe the things I tell you?"

I said I guessed so.

"I got proof. I'll show you it's true. Want to see my proof?"

When I said nothing, "Stan" leaned closer to me, inundating me with the stench of Thunderbird. "You know that little thing you pee with? Remember how

I told you how it gets real big when you're about thirteen? Remember I told you about how incredible that feels? Well, you have to trust Stan now, because Stan's going to trust you." He put his face right beside my ear. "Then I'll tell you another secret."

He lifted his hand from my thigh and closed it around mine, and pulled my hand down onto his crotch. "Feel anything?"

I nodded, but I could not have described what I felt any more than the blind men could describe the elephant.

"Stan" smiled tightly and tugged at his zipper in a way even I could tell was nervous. He reached inside his pants, fumbled, and pulled out a thick, pale club that looked like nothing human. I was so frightened I thought I would throw up, and I looked back up at the screen. Invisible chains held me to my seat.

"See? Now you understand me."

Then he noticed that I was not looking at him. "Kid. Look. I said, look. It's not going to hurt you."

I could not look down at him. I saw nothing.

"Come on. Touch it, see what it feels like."

I shook my head.

"Let me tell you something. I like you a lot. I think the two of us are friends. This thing we're doing, it's unusual to you because this is the first time, but people do this all the time. Your mommy and daddy do it all the time, but they just don't tell you about it. We're pals, aren't we?"

I nodded dumbly. On the screen, Berry Kroeger was telling Alan Ladd, "Drop it, forget it, she's poison."

"Well, this is what friends do when they really like each other, like your mommy and daddy. Look at this thing, will you? Come on."

Did my mommy and daddy like each other? He squeezed my shoulder, and I looked.

Now the thing had folded up into itself and was drooping sideways against the fabric of his trousers. Almost as soon as I looked, it twitched and began to push itself out like the slide of a trombone.

"There," he said. "He likes you, you got him going. Tell me you like him too."

Terror would not let me speak. My brains had turned to powder.

"I know what—let's call him Jimmy. We'll say his name is Jimmy. Now that you've been introduced, say hi to Jimmy."

"Hi, Jimmy," I said, and, despite my terror, could not keep myself from giggling.

"Now go on, touch him."

I slowly extended my hand and put the tips of my fingers on "Jimmy."

"Pet him. Jimmy wants you to pet him."

I tapped my fingertips against "Jimmy" two or three times, and he twitched up another few degrees, as rigid as a surfboard.

"Slide your fingers up and down on him."

If I run, I thought, he'll catch me and kill me. If I don't do what he says, he'll kill me.

I rubbed my fingertips back and forth, moving the thin skin over the veins.

"Can't you imagine Jimmy going in a woman? Now you can see what you'll be like when you're a man. Keep on, but hold him with your whole hand. And give me what I asked you for."

I immediately took my hand from "Jimmy" and pulled my father's clean white handkerchief from my back pocket.

He took the handkerchief with his left hand and with his right guided mine back to "Jimmy." "You're doing really great," he whispered.

In my hand "Jimmy" felt warm and slightly gummy. I could not join my fingers around its width. My head was buzzing. "Is Jimmy your secret?" I was able to say.

"My secret comes later."

"Can I stop now?"

"I'll cut you into little pieces if you do," he said, and when I froze, he stroked my hair and whispered, "Hey, can't you tell when a guy's kidding around? I'm really happy with you right now. You're the best kid in the world. You'd want this, too, if you knew how good it felt."

After what seemed an endless time, while Alan Ladd was climbing out of a taxicab, "Stan" abruptly arched his back, grimaced, and whispered, "Look!"

His entire body jerked, and too startled to let go, I held "Jimmy" and watched thick, ivory-colored milk spurt and drool almost unendingly onto the handkerchief. An odor utterly foreign but as familiar as the toilet or the lakeshore rose from the thick milk. "Stan" sighed, folded the handkerchief, and pushed the softening "Jimmy" back into his trousers. He leaned over and kissed the top of my head. I think I nearly fainted. I felt lightly, pointlessly dead. I could still feel him pulsing in my palm and fingers.

When it was time for me to go home, he told me his secret—his own real name was Jimmy, not Stan. He had been saving his real name until he knew he could trust me.

"Tomorrow," he said, touching my cheek with his fingers. "We'll see each other again tomorrow. But you don't have anything to worry about. I trust you enough to give you my real name. You trusted me not to hurt you, and I didn't. We have to trust each other not to say anything about this, or both you and me'll be in a lot of trouble."

"I won't say anything," I said.

I love you.

I love you, yes I do.

Now *we're* a secret, he said, folding the handkerchief into quarters and putting it back in my pocket. A lot of love has to be secret. Especially when a boy and a man are getting to know each other and learning how to make each other happy and be good, loving friends—not many people can understand that, so the friendship has to be protected. When you walk out of here, he said, you have to forget that this happened. Otherwise people will try to hurt us both.

Afterward I remembered only the confusion of *Chicago Deadline,* how the story had abruptly surged forward, skipping over whole characters and entire scenes, how for long stretches the actors had moved their lips without speaking. I could see Alan Ladd stepping out of the taxicab, looking straight through the screen into my eyes, knowing me.

My mother said that I looked pale, and my father said that I didn't get enough exercise. The twins looked up from their plates, then went back to spooning macaroni and cheese into their mouths. "Were you ever in Chicago?" I asked my father, who asked what was it to me. "Did you ever meet a movie actor?" I asked, and he said, "This kid must have a fever." The twins giggled.

Alan Ladd and Donna Reed came into my bedroom together late that night, moving with brisk, cool theatricality, and kneeled down beside my cot. They smiled at me. Their voices were very soothing. I saw you missed a few things today, Alan said. Nothing to worry about. I'll take care of you. I know, I said, I'm your number-one fan.

Then the door cracked open, and my mother put her head inside the room. Alan and Donna smiled and stood up to let her pass between them and the cot. I missed them the second they stepped back. "Still awake?" I nodded. "Are you feeling all right, honey?" I nodded again, afraid that Alan and Donna would leave if she stayed too long. "I have a surprise for you," she said. "The Saturday after this, I'm taking you and the twins all the way across Lake Michigan on the ferry. There's a whole bunch of us. It'll be a lot of fun." Good, that's nice, I'll like that.

▏▎▎▎▎▎▎▎▎▎▎▎▎▎▎▎▎▎▎▎▎▎▎▎▎▎▎▎▎▎▎▎▎

"I THOUGHT ABOUT you all last night and all this morning."

When I came into the lobby, he was leaning forward on one of the padded benches where the ushers sat and smoked, his elbows on his knees and his chin in his hand, watching the door. The metal tip of a flat bottle protruded from his side pocket. Beside him was a package rolled up in brown paper. He winked at me, jerked his head toward the door into the theater, stood up, and went inside in an elaborate charade of not being with me. I knew he would be just inside the door, sitting in the middle of the last row, waiting for me. I gave my ticket to the bored usher, who tore it in half and handed over the stub. I knew exactly what had happened yesterday, just as if I had never forgotten any of it, and my insides began shaking. All the colors of the lobby, the red and the shabby gilt, seemed much brighter than I remembered them. I could smell the popcorn in the case and the oily butter heating in the machine. My legs moved me over a mile of sizzling brown carpet and past the candy counter.

Jimmy's hair gleamed in the empty, darkening theater. When I took the seat next to him, he ruffled my hair and grinned down and said he had been thinking about me all night and all morning. The package in brown paper was a sandwich for my lunch—a kid had to eat more than popcorn.

The lights went all the way down as the series of curtains opened over the screen. Loud music, beginning in the middle of a note, suddenly jumped from the speakers, and the Tom and Jerry cartoon "Bull Dozing" began. When I leaned back, Jimmy put his arm around me. I felt sweaty and cold at the same time, and my insides were still shaking. I suddenly realized that part of me was glad to be in this place, and I shocked myself with the knowledge that all morning I had been looking forward to this moment as much as I had been dreading it.

"You want your sandwich now? It's liver sausage, because that's my personal favorite." I said no, thanks,

I'd wait until the first movie was over. Okay, he said, just as long as you eat it. Then he said, Look at me. His face was right above mine, and he looked like Alan Ladd's twin brother. You have to know something, he said. You're the best kid I ever met. Ever. The man squeezed me up against his chest and into a dizzying funk of sweat and dirt and wine, along with a trace (imagined?) of that other, more animal odor that had come from him yesterday. Then he released me.

You want me to play with your little "Jimmy" today? No.

Too small, anyhow, he said with a laugh. He was in perfect good humor.

Bet you wish it was the same size as mine.

That wish terrified me, and I shook my head.

Today we're just going to watch the movies together, he said. I'm not greedy.

Except for when one of the ushers came up the aisle, we sat like that all day, his arm around my shoulders, the back of my neck resting in the hollow of his elbow. When the credits for *At War With the Army* rolled up the screen, I felt as though I had fallen asleep and missed everything. I couldn't believe that it was time to go home. Jimmy tightened his arm around me and in a voice full of amusement said, *Touch me*. I looked up into his face. Go on, he said, I want you to do that little thing for me. I prodded his fly with my index finger. "Jimmy" wobbled under the pressure of my

123

fingers, seeming as long as my arm, and for a second of absolute wretchedness I saw the other children running up and down the school playground behind the girls from the next block.

"Go on," he said.

||||||||||||||||||||||||||||||||||||||||||||||

TRUST ME, HE said, investing "Jimmy" with an identity more concentrated, more focused, than his own. "Jimmy" wanted "to talk," "to speak his piece," "was hungry," "was dying for a kiss." All these words meant the same thing. *Trust me:* I trust you, so you must trust me. Have I ever hurt you? No. Didn't I give you a sandwich? Yes. Don't I love you? You know I won't tell your parents what you do—as long as you keep coming here, I won't tell your parents anything because I won't *have* to, see? And you love me too, don't you?

There. You see how much I love you?

I dreamed that I lived underground in a wooden room. I dreamed that my parents roamed the upper world, calling out my name and weeping because the animals had captured and eaten me. I dreamed that I was buried beneath a juniper tree, and the cut-off pieces of my body called out to each other and wept because they were separate. I dreamed that I ran down a dark forest path toward my parents, and when I finally reached the small clearing where they sat before a bright fire, my mother was Donna and Alan was my father. I dreamed that I could remember everything that was happening to me, every second of it, and that when the teacher called on me in class, when my mother came into my room at night, when the policeman went past me as I walked down Sherman Boulevard, I had to spill it out. But when I tried to speak, I could not remember what it was that I remembered, *only that there was something to remember,* and so I walked again and again toward my beautiful parents in the clearing, repeating myself like a fable, like the jokes of the women on the ferry.

Don't I love you? Don't I show you, can't you tell, that I love you? Yes. Don't you, can't you, love me too?

He stares at me as I stare at the movie. He could see me, the way I could see him, with his eyes closed. He has me memorized. He has stroked my hair, my face, my body into his memory, stroke after stroke, stealing me from myself. Eventually he took me in his mouth and his mouth memorized me too, and I knew he wanted me to place my hands on that dirty-blond head resting so hugely in my lap, but I could not touch his head.

I thought: I have already forgotten this, I want to die, I am dead already, only death can make this not have happened.

When you grow up, I bet you'll be in the movies and I'll be your number-one fan.

The Juniper Tree IIIIIIIIIIIIIIIIIIIIIIIIIIIIIIIIIIIIIIIIIIIIIIIIIIIIIIIIII
AND OTHER BLUE ROSE STORIES

IIIIIIIIIIIIIIIIIIIIIIIIIIIIIIIIIIIIIIIIII

BY THE WEEKEND, those days at the Orpheum-Oriental seemed to have been spent underwater; or underground. The spiny anteater, the lyrebird, the kangaroo, the Tasmanian devil, the nun bat, and the frilled lizard were creatures found only in Australia. Australia was the world's smallest continent, its largest island. It was cut off from the earth's great landmasses. Beautiful girls with blond hair strutted across Australian beaches, and Australian Christmases were hot and sunbaked—everybody went outside and waved at the camera, exchanging presents from lawn chairs. The middle of Australia, its heart and gut, was a desert. Australian boys excelled at sports. Tom Cat loved Jerry Mouse, though he plotted again and again to murder him, and Jerry Mouse loved Tom Cat, though to save his life he had to run so fast, he burned a track through the carpet. Jimmy loved me and he would be gone someday, and then I would miss him a lot. Wouldn't I? *Say you'll miss me.*

I'll—

I'll miss—

I think I'd go crazy without you.

When you're all grown-up, will you remember me?

Each time I walked back out past the usher, who stood tearing in half the tickets of the people just

126

entering, handing them the stubs, every time I pushed open the door and walked out onto the heat-filled sidewalk of Sherman Boulevard and saw the sun on the buildings across the street, I lost my hold on what had happened inside the darkness of the theater. I didn't know what I wanted. I had two murders and a...My right hand felt as though I had been holding a smaller child's sticky hand very tightly between my palm and fingers. If I lived in Australia, I would have blond hair like Alan Ladd and run forever across tan beaches on Christmas Day.

I WALKED THROUGH high school in my sleep, reading novels, daydreaming in classes I did not like but earning spuriously good grades; in the middle of my senior year Brown University gave me a full scholarship. Two years later I amazed and disappointed all my old teachers and my parents and my parents' friends by dropping out of school shortly before I would have failed all my courses but English and history, in which I was getting A's. I was certain that no one could teach anyone else how to write. I knew exactly what I was going to do, and all I would miss of college was the social life.

For five years I lived inexpensively in Providence, supporting myself by stacking books in the school library and by petty thievery. I wrote when I was not working or listening to the local bands; then I destroyed what I had written and wrote it again. In this way I saw myself to the end of a novel, like walking through a park one way and then walking backward and forward through the same park, over and over, until every nick on every swing, every tawny hair on every lion's hide, had been witnessed and made to gleam or allowed to sink back into the importunate field of details from which it had been lifted. When this novel was rejected by the publisher to whom I sent it, I moved to New York City and began another novel while I rewrote the first all over again at night. During this period an almost impersonal happiness, like the happiness of a stranger, lay beneath everything I did. I wrapped parcels of books at the Strand Book Store. For a short time, no more than a few months, I lived on shredded wheat and peanut butter. When my first book was accepted, I moved from a single room on the Lower East Side into another, larger single room, a "studio apartment," on Ninth Avenue in Chelsea, where I continue to live. My apartment is just large enough for my wooden desk, a convertible couch, two large crowded bookshelves, a shelf of stereo equipment, and dozens of cardboard boxes of records. In this apartment everything has its place and is in it.

My parents have never been to this enclosed, tidy space, though I speak to my father on the phone every two or three months. In the past ten years I have returned to the city where I grew up only once, to visit my mother in the hospital after her stroke. During the four days I stayed in my father's house I slept in my old room; my father slept upstairs. After the blind man's death my father bought the duplex—on my first night home he told me that we were both successes. Now when we speak on the telephone he tells me of the fortunes of the local baseball and basketball teams and respectfully inquires about my progress on "the new book." I think: This is not my Father, he is not the same man.

My old cot disappeared long ago, and late at night I lay on the twins' double bed. Like the house as a whole, like everything in my old neighborhood, the bedroom was larger than I remembered it. I brushed the wallpaper with my fingers, then looked up to the ceiling. The image of two men tangled up in the ropes of the same parachute, comically berating each other as they fell, came to me, and I wondered if the image had a place in the novel I was writing, or if it was a gift from the as yet unseen novel that would follow it. I could hear the floor creak as my father paced upstairs in the blind man's former territory. My inner weather changed, and I began brooding about Mei-Mei Levitt, whom fifteen years earlier at Brown I had known as Mei-Mei Cheung.

Divorced, an editor at a paperback firm, she had called to congratulate me after my second novel was favorably reviewed in the *Times,* and on this slim but well-intentioned foundation we began to construct a long and troubled love affair. Back in the surroundings of my childhood, I felt profoundly uneasy, having spent the day beside my mother's hospital bed without knowing if she understood or even recognized me, and I thought of Mei-Mei with sudden longing. I wanted her in my arms, and I yearned for my purposeful, orderly, dreaming, adult life in New York. I wanted to call Mei-Mei, but it was past midnight in the Midwest, an hour later in New York, and Mei-Mei, no owl, would have gone to bed hours earlier. Then I remembered my mother lying stricken in the narrow hospital bed, and suffered a spasm of guilt for thinking about my lover. For a deluded moment I imagined that it was my duty to move back into the house. and see if I could bring my mother back to life while I did what I could for my retired father. At that moment I remembered, as I often did, an orange-haired boy enveloped in a red wool shirt. Sweat poured from my forehead, my chest.

Then a terrifying thing happened to me. I tried to get out of bed to go to the bathroom and found that I could not move. My arms and legs were cast in cement; they were lifeless and *would not move*. I thought that I was having a stroke, like my mother. I could not even cry out—my throat, too, was paralyzed. I strained to push myself up off the double bed and smelled that someone very near, someone just out of sight or around the corner, was making popcorn and heating butter. Another wave of sweat gouted out of my inert body, turning the sheet and the pillowcase slick and cold.

I saw—as if I were writing it—my seven-year-old self hesitating before the entrance of a theater a few blocks from this house. Hot, flat, yellow sunlight fell over everything, cooking the life from the wide boulevard. I saw myself turn away, felt my stomach churn with the smoke of underground fires, saw myself begin to run. Vomit backed up in my throat. My arms and legs convulsed, and I fell out of bed and managed to crawl out of the room and down the hall to throw up in the toilet behind the closed door of the bathroom.

MY AGE, AS I write these words, is forty-three. I have written five novels over a period of nearly twenty years, "only" five, each of them more difficult, harder to write than the one before. To maintain this hobbled pace of a novel every four years, I must sit at my desk at least six hours every day; I must consume hundreds of boxes of typing paper, scores of yellow legal pads, forests of pencils, miles of black ribbon. It is a fierce, voracious activity. Every sentence must be tested three or four ways, made to clear fences like a horse. The purpose of every sentence is to be an arrow into the secret center of the book. To find my way into the secret center I must hold the entire book, every detail and rhythm, in my memory. This comprehensive act of memory is the most crucial task of my life.

My books get flattering reviews, which usually seem to describe other, more linear novels, and they win occasional awards—I am one of those writers whose advances are funded by the torrents of money spun off by best-sellers. Lately I have had the impression that the general perception of me, to the extent that such a thing exists, is that of a hermetic painter inscribing hundreds of tiny, grotesque, fantastical details over every inch of a large canvas. (My books are unfashionably long.) I teach writing at various colleges, give occasional lectures, am modestly enriched by grants. This is enough, more than enough. Now and then I am both dismayed and amused to discover that a young writer I have met at a PEN reception or a workshop regards my life with envy. Envy misses the point completely.

"If you were going to give me one piece of advice," a young woman at a conference asked me, "I mean, real advice, not just the obvious stuff about keeping on writing, what would it be? What would you tell me to do?"

I won't tell you, but I'll write it out, I said, and picked up one of the conference flyers and printed a few words on its back. Don't read this until you are out of the room, I said, and watched while she folded the flyer into her bag.

What I had printed on the back of the flyer was: Go to a lot of movies.

|||||||||||||||||||||||||||||||||||||||||||||||||||

ON THE SUNDAY after the ferry trip I could not hit a single ball in the park. My eyes kept closing, and as soon as my eyelids came down, visions started up like movies—quick, automatic dreams. My arms seemed too heavy to lift. After I had trudged home behind my dispirited father, I collapsed on the sofa and slept straight through to dinner. In a dream a spacious box confined me, and I drew colored pictures of elm trees, the sun, wide fields, mountains, and rivers on its walls. At dinner loud noises, never scarce around the twins, made me jump. That kid's not right, I swear to you, my father said. When my mother asked if I wanted to go to Play School on Monday, my stomach closed up like a fist. I have to, I said, I'm really fine, I have to go. Sentences rolled from my mouth, meaning nothing, or meaning the wrong thing. For a moment of confusion I thought that I really was going to the playground, and saw black asphalt, deep as a field, where a few children, diminished by perspective, clustered at the far end. I went to bed right after dinner. My mother pulled down the shades, turned off the light, and finally left me alone. From above came the sound, like a beast's approximation of music, of random notes struck on a piano. I knew only that I was scared, not why. The next day I had to go to a certain place, but I could not think where until my fingers recalled the velvety plush of the end seat on the middle aisle. Then black-and-white images, full of intentional menace, came to me from the previews I had seen for two weeks—*The Hitch-Hiker,* starring Edmund O'Brien. The spiny anteater and nun bat were animals found only in Australia.

I longed for Alan Ladd, "Ed Adams," to walk into the room with his reporter's notebook and pencil, and knew that I had *something to remember* without knowing what it was.

After a long time the twins cascaded into the bedroom, undressed, put on pajamas, brushed their teeth. The front door slammed—my father had gone out to the taverns. In the kitchen, my mother ironed shirts and talked to herself in a familiar, rancorous voice. The twins went to sleep. I heard my mother put away the ironing board and walk down the hall to the living room.

I saw "Ed Adams" calmly walking up and down on the sidewalk outside our house, as handsome as a god in his neat gray suit. "Ed" went all the way to the end of the block, put a cigarette in his mouth, and leaned into a sudden, round flare of brightness before exhaling smoke and walking away. I knew I had fallen asleep only when the front door slammed for the second time that night and woke me up.

In the morning my father struck his fist against the bedroom door and the twins jumped out of bed and began yelling around the bedroom, instantly filled with energy. As in a cartoon, into the bedroom drifted tendrils of the odor of frying bacon. My brothers jostled toward the bathroom. Water rushed into the sink and the toilet bowl, and my mother hurried in, her face tightened down over her cigarette, and began yanking the twins into their clothes. "You made your decision," she said to me, "now I hope you're going to make it to the playground on time." Doors opened, doors slammed shut. My father shouted from the kitchen, and I got out of bed. Eventually I sat down before the bowl of cereal. My father smoked and did not meet my eyes. The cereal tasted of dead leaves. "You look the way that asshole upstairs plays piano," my father said. He dropped quarters on the table and told me not to lose that money.

After he left, I locked myself in the bedroom. The piano dully resounded overhead like a sound track. I heard the cups and dishes rattle in the sink, the furniture moving by itself, looking for something to hunt down and kill. *Love me, love me,* the radio called from beside a family of brown-and-white porcelain spaniels. I heard some light, whispery thing, a lamp or a magazine, begin to slide around the living room. *I am imagining all this,* I said to myself, and tried to concentrate on a *Blackhawk* comic book. The pictures jigged and melted in their panels. *Love me,* Blackhawk cried out from the cockpit of his fighter as he swooped down to exterminate a nest of yellow, slant-eyed villains. Outside, fire raged beneath the streets, trying to pull the world apart. When I dropped the comic book and closed my eyes, the noises ceased and I could hear the hovering stillness of perfect attention. Even Blackhawk, belted into his airplane within the comic book, was listening to what I was doing.

‖‖‖‖‖‖‖‖‖‖‖‖‖‖‖‖‖‖‖‖‖‖‖‖‖‖‖‖‖‖‖‖‖

IN THICK, HAZY sunlight I went down Sherman Boulevard toward the Orpheum-Oriental. Around me the world was motionless, frozen like a frame in a comic strip. After a time I noticed that the cars on the boulevard and the few people on the sidewalk had not actually frozen into place but instead were moving with great slowness. I could see men's legs advancing within their trousers, the knee coming forward to strike the crease, the cuff slowly lifting off the shoe, the shoe drifting up like Tom Cat's paw when he crept toward Jerry Mouse. The warm, patched skin of Sherman Boulevard...I thought of walking along Sherman Boulevard forever, moving past the nearly immobile cars and people, past the theater, past the liquor store, through the gates and past the wading pool and swings, past the elephants and lions reaching out to be fed, past the secret park where my father flailed in a rage of disappointment, past the elms and out the opposite gate, past the big houses on the opposite side of the park, past picture windows and past lawns with bikes and plastic pools, past slanting driveways and basketball hoops, past men getting out of cars, past playgrounds where children raced back and forth on a surface shining black. Then past fields and crowded markets, past high yellow tractors with mud dried like old wool inside the enormous hubs, past eloquent cats and fearful lions on wagons piled high with hay, past deep woods where lost children followed trails of bread crumbs to a gingerbread door, past other cities where nobody would see me because nobody knew my name, past everything, past everybody.

At the Orpheum-Oriental, I stopped still. My mouth was dry and my eyes would not focus. Everything around me, so quiet and still a moment earlier, jumped into life as soon as I stopped walking. Horns blared, cars roared down the boulevard. Beneath these sounds I heard the pounding of great machines, and the fires gobbling up oxygen beneath the street. As if I had eaten them from the air, fire and smoke poured into my stomach. Flame slipped up my throat and sealed the back of my mouth. In my mind I saw myself taking the first quarter from my pocket, exchanging it for a ticket, pushing through the door, and moving into the cool air. I saw myself holding out the ticket to be torn in half, going over an endless brown carpet toward the inner door. From the last row of seats on the other side of the inner door, inside the shadowy but not yet dark theater, a shapeless monster whose wet black mouth said *Love me, love me* stretched yearning arms toward me. Shock froze my shoes to the sidewalk, then shoved me firmly in the small of the back, and I was running down the block, unable to scream because I had to clamp my lips against the smoke and fire trying to explode from my mouth.

The rest of that afternoon remains vague. I wandered through the streets, not in the clean, hollow way I had imagined but almost blindly, hot and uncertain. I remember the taste of fire in my mouth and the loudness of my heart. After a time I found myself before the elephant enclosure in the zoo. A newspaper reporter in a neat gray suit passed through the space before me, and I followed him, knowing that he carried a notebook in his pocket, and that he had been beaten by gangsters, that he could locate the speaking secret that hid beneath the disconnected and dismembered pieces of the world. He would fire his pistol on an empty chamber and trick evil "Sully Wellman," Berry Kroeger, with his girlish, watchful eyes. And when "Solly Wellman" came gloating out of the shadow, the reporter would shoot him dead.

Dead.

Donna Reed smiled down from an upstairs window: has there ever been a smile like that? Ever? I was in Chicago, and behind a closed door "Blackie Franchot" bled onto a brown carpet. "Sully Wellman," something like "Sully Wellman," called and called to me from the decorated grave where he lay like a secret. The man in the gray suit finally carried his notebook and his gun through a front door, and I saw that I was only a few blocks from home.

Paul leans against the wire fence surrounding the playground, looking out, looking backward. Alan Ladd brushes off "Leona," for she has no history that matters and exists only in the world of work and pleasure, of cigarettes and cocktail bars. Beneath this world is another, and "Leona's" life is a blind, strenuous denial of that other world.

My mother held her hand to my forehead and declared that I not only had a fever but had been building up to it all week. I was not to go to the playground that next day; I had to spend the day lying down on Mrs. Candee's couch. When she lifted the telephone to call one of the high-school girls, I said not to bother, other kids were gone all the time, and she put down the receiver.

I LAY ON Mrs. Candee's couch staring up at the ceiling of her darkened living room. The twins squabbled outside, and maternal, slow-witted Mrs. Candee brought me orange juice. The twins ran toward the sandbox, and Mrs. Candee groaned as she let herself fall into a wobbly lawn chair. The morning newspaper folded beneath the lawn chair said that *The Hitch-Hiker* and *Double Cross* had begun playing at the Orpheum-Oriental. *Chicago Deadline* had done its work and traveled on. It had broken the world in half and sealed the monster deep within. Nobody but me knew this. Up and down the block, sprinklers whirred, whipping loops of water onto the dry lawns. Men driving slowly up and down the street hung their elbows out of their windows. For a moment free of regret and nearly without emotion of any kind, I understood that I belonged utterly to myself. Like everything else, I had been torn asunder and glued back together with shock, vomit, and orange juice. The knowledge sifted into me that I was all alone. "Stan," "Jimmy," whatever his name was, would never come back to the theater. He would be afraid that I had told my parents and the police about him. I knew that I had killed him by forgetting him, and then I forgot him again.

The next day I went back to the theater and went through the inner door and saw row after row of empty seats falling toward the curtained screen. I was all alone. The size and grandeur of the theater surprised me. I went down the long, descending aisle and took the last seat, left side, on the broad middle aisle. The next row seemed nearly a playground's distance away. The lights dimmed and the curtains rippled slowly away from the screen. Anticipatory music filled the air, and the first letters appeared on the screen.

What I am, what I do, why I do it. I am simultaneously a man in his early forties, that treacherous time, and a boy of seven before whose bravery I shall forever fall short. I live underground in a wooden room and patiently, in joyful concentration, decorate the walls.

Before me, half unseen, hangs a large and appallingly complicated vision I must explore and memorize, must witness again and again in order to locate its hidden center. Around me, everything is in its proper place. My typewriter sits on the sturdy table. Beside the typewriter a cigarette smolders, raising a gray stream of smoke. A record revolves on the turntable, and my small apartment is dense with music. ("Bird of Prey Blues," with Coleman Hawkins, Buck Clayton, and Hank Jones.) Beyond my walls and windows is a world toward which I reach with outstretched arms and an ambitious and divided heart. As if "Bird of Prey Blues" has evoked them, the voices of sentences to be written this afternoon, tomorrow, or next month stir and whisper, beginning to speak, and I lean over the typewriter toward them, getting as close as I can.

Bunny is Good Bread

for Stephen King

PART ONE

1

FEE'S FIRST MEMORY WAS of a vision of fire, not an actual fire but an imagined fire leaping upward at an enormous grate upon which lay a naked man. Attached to this image was the accompanying memory of his father gripping the telephone. For a moment his father, Bob Bandolier, the one and only king of this realm, seemed rubbery, almost boneless with shock. He repeated the word, and a second time five-year-old Fielding Bandolier, little blond Fee, saw the flames jumping at the blackening figure on the grate. "I'm fired? This has got to be a joke."

The flames engulfed the tiny man on the slanting grate. The man opened his mouth to screech. This was hell, it was interesting. Fee was scorched, too, by those flames. His father saw the child looking up at him, and the child saw his father take in his presence. A fire of pain and anger flashed out of his father's face, and Fee's insides froze. His father waved him away with a back-paddling gesture of his left hand. In the murk of their apartment, Bob Bandolier's crisp white shirt gleamed like an apparition. The creases from the laundry jutted up from the shirt's starched surface.

"You *know* why I haven't been coming in," he said. "This is not a matter where I have a choice. You will never, ever find a man who is as devoted—"

He listened, bowing over as if crushing down a spring in his chest. Fee crept backward across the room, hoping to make no noise at all. When he backed into the chaise against the far wall, he instinctively dropped to his knees and crawled beneath it, still looking at the way his father was bending over the telephone. Fee bumped into a dark furry lump, Jude the cat, and clamped it to his chest until it stopped struggling.

"No, sir," his father said. "If you think about the way I work, you will have to—"

He blew air out of his mouth, still pushing down that coiled spring in his chest. Fee knew that his father hated to be interrupted.

"I see that, sir, but a person on my salary can't hire a nurse or a housekeeper, and—"

Another loud exhalation.

"Do I have to tell you what goes on in hospitals? The infections, the sheer sloppiness, the...I have to keep her at home. I don't know if you're aware of this, sir, but there have been very few nights when I have not been able to spend most of my time at the hotel."

Slowly, as if he had become aware of the oddness of his posture, Fee's father began straightening up. He pressed his hand into the small of his back. "Sometimes we pray."

Fee saw the air around his father darken and fill with little white sparkling swirling things that winked and dazzled before they disappeared. Jude saw them too, and moved deeper beneath the chaise.

"Well, I suppose you are entitled to your own opinion about that ," said his father, "but you are very much mistaken if you feel that my religious beliefs did in any way—"

"I dispute that absolutely," his father said.

"I have already explained that," his father said. "Almost every night since my wife fell ill, I managed to get to the hotel. I bring an attitude to work with me, sir, of absolute dedication—"

"I'm sorry you feel that way, sir," his father said, "but you are making a very great mistake."

"I mean, you are making a *mistake*," his father said. The little white dancing lines spun and winked out in the air like fireworks.

Both Fee and Jude stared raptly from beneath the chaise.

His father gently replaced the receiver, and then set the telephone down on the table. His face was set in the cement of prayer.

Fee looked at the black telephone on its little table between the big chair and the streaky window: the headset like a pair of droopy ears, the round dial. On the matching table, a porcelain fawn nuzzled a porcelain doe.

Heavy footsteps strode toward him. Jude searched warmth against his side. His father came striding in his gleaming shirt with the boxy lines from the dry cleaner's, his dark trousers, his tacked down necktie, his shiny shoes. His mustache, two fat commas, seemed like another detachable ornament.

Bob Bandolier bent down, settled his thick white hands beneath Fee's arms, and pulled him up like a toy. He set him on his feet and frowned down at the child.

Then his father slapped his face and sent him backward against the chaise. Fee was too stunned to cry. When his father struck the other side of his face, his knees went away and he began to slip toward the rug. His cheeks burned. Bob Bandolier leaned down again. Silver light from the window painted a glowing white line on his dark hair. Fee's breath burned its way past the hot ball in his throat, and he closed his eyes and wailed.

"Do you know why I did that?"

His father's voice was still as low and reasonable as it had been when he was on the telephone.

Fee shook his head.

"Two reasons. Listen to me, son. Reason number one." He raised his index finger. "You disobeyed me and I will always punish disobedience."

"No," Fee said.

"I sent you from the room, didn't I? Did you go out?"

Fee shook his head again, and his father gripped him tightly between his two hands and waited for him to stop sobbing. "I will not be contradicted, is that clear?"

Fee nodded miserably. His father gave a cool kiss to his burning cheek.

"I said there were two reasons, remember?"

Fee nodded.

"Sin is the second reason." Bob Bandolier's face moved hugely through the space between them, and his eyes, deep brown with luminous eggshell whites, searched Fee and found his crime. Fee began to cry again. His father held him upright. "The Lord Jesus is very, very angry today, Fielding. He will demand payment, and we must pay."

When his father talked like this, Fee saw a page from *Life* magazine, a torn battlefield covered with shell craters, trees burned to charred stumps, and huddled corpses.

147

"We will pray together," his father said, and hitched up the legs of his trousers and went down on his knees. "Then we will go in to see your mother." His father touched one of his shoulders with an index finger and pressed down, trying to push Fee all the way through the floor to the regions of eternal flame. Fee finally realized that his father was telling him to kneel, and he too went to his knees.

His father had closed his eyes, and his forehead was full of vertical lines. "Are you going to talk?" Fee said.

"Pray *silently,* Fee—say the words to yourself."

He put his hands together before his face and began moving his lips. Fee closed his own eyes and heard Jude dragging her tongue over and over the same spot of fur.

His father said, "Let's get in there. She's our job, you know."

Inside the bedroom, he opened the clothing press and took his suit jacket from a hanger, replaced the hanger, and closed the door of the press. He shoved his arms into the jacket's sleeves and transformed himself into the more formal and forbidding man Fee knew best. He dipped his knees in front of the bedroom mirror to check the knot in his tie. He swept his hands over the smooth hair at the sides of his head. His eyes in the mirror found Fee's. "Go to your mother, Fee."

Until two weeks ago, the double bed had stood on the far end of the rag rug, his mother's perfume and lotion bottles had stood on the left side of what she called her "vanity table," her blond wooden chair in front of it. His father now stood there, watching him in the mirror. Up until two weeks ago, the curtains had been open all day, and the bedroom had always seemed full of a warm magic. Fat black Jude spent all day lying in the pool of sunlight that collected in the middle of the rug. Now the curtains stayed shut, and the room smelled of sickness—it reminded Fee of the time his father had brought him to work with him and, giddy with moral outrage, thrust him into a ruined, stinking room. *You want to see what people are really like?* Slivers of broken glass had covered the floor, and the stuffing foamed out of the slashed sofa, but the worst part had been the smell of the lumps and puddles on the floor. The walls had been streaked with brown. *This is their idea of fun,* his father had said. *Of a good time.* Now the rag rug was covered by the old mattress his father had placed on the floor beside the bed. The blond chair in front of the vanity had disappeared, as had the row of little bottles his mother had cherished. Two weeks ago, when everything had changed, Fee had heard his father smashing these bottles, roaring, smashing the chair against the wall. It was as if a monster had burst from his father's skin to rage back and forth in the bedroom. The next morning, his father said that Mom was sick. Pieces of the chair lay all over the room, and the walls were covered with explosions. The whole room smelled overpoweringly sweet, like heaven with its flowers. *Your mother needs to rest. She needs to get better.*

Fee had dared one glance at her tumbled hair and open mouth. A tiny curl of blood crept from her nose. *She's sick but we'll take care of her.*

She had not gotten any better. As the perfume explosions had dried on the wall, his father's shirts and socks and underwear had gradually covered the floor between the old mattress and the bare vanity table, and Fee now walked over the litter of clothing to step on the mattress and approach the bed. The sickroom smell intensified as he came closer to his mother. He was not sure that he could look at his mother's face— the bruised, puffy mask he had seen the last time his father had let him into the bedroom. He stood on the thin mattress beside the bed, looking at the wisps of brown hair that hung down over the side of the bed. They reached all the way to the black letters stamped on the sheet that read *St. Alwyn Hotel.* Maybe her hair was still growing. Maybe she was waiting for him to look at her. Maybe she was better—the way she used to be. Fee touched the letters, and let his fingers drift upward so that his mother's hair brushed his hand. He could hear breath moving almost soundlessly in his mother's throat.

"See how good she looks now? She's looking real good, aren't you, honey?"

Fee moved his eyes upward. It felt as though his chest and his stomach, everything inside him, swung out of his body and swayed in the air a moment before corning back inside him. Except for a fading yellow bruise that extended from her eye to her hairline, she looked like his mother again. Flecks of dried oatmeal clung to her chin and the sides of her mouth. The fine lines in her cheeks looked like pencil marks. Her mouth hung a little bit open, as if to sip the air, or to beg for more oatmeal.

Fee is five, and he is looking at his mother for the first time since he saw her covered with bruises. His conscious life—the extraordinary life of Fee's consciousness—has just begun.

He thought for a second that his mother was going to answer. Then he realized that his father had spoken to her as he would speak to Jude, or to a dog in the street. He let his fingertips touch her skin. Unlike her face, his mother's hands were rough, with enlarged knuckles like knots and callused fingertips that widened out at their ends. The skin on the back of her hand felt cool and peculiarly coarse.

"Sure you are, honey," said his father behind him. "You're looking better every day."

Fee clutched her hand and tried to squeeze some of his own life into her. His mother lay on her bed like a princess frozen by a curse in a fairy tale. A blue vein pulsed in her eyelid. All she could see was black night.

For a second Fee saw night too, a deep swooning blackness that called to him.

Yes, he thought. *Okay. That's okay.*

"We're here, honey," his father said.

Fee wondered if he had ever before heard his father call his mother *honey*.

"That's your little Fee holding your hand, honey, can't you feel his love?"

A startling sense of negation—of revulsion—caused Fee to pull back his hands. If his father saw, he did not mind, for he said nothing. Fee saw his mother floating away into the immense sea of blackness inside her.

For a second he forgot to breathe through his mouth, and the stench that rose from the bed assaulted him.

"Didn't have time to clean her up yet today. I'll get to it before long—but you know, she could be lying on a bed of silk, it'd be all the same to her."

Fee wanted to lean forward and put his arms around his mother but he stepped back.

"We're none of us doctors and nurses here, Fee."

For a moment Fee thought there must be more people in the room. Then he realized that his father meant the two of them, and that put into his head an idea of great simplicity and truth.

"Mommy ought to have a doctor," he said, and risked looking up at his father.

His father leaned over and pulled him by the shoulders, making him move awkwardly backward over the mattress on the floor. Fee braced himself to be struck again, but his father turned him around and faced him with neither the deepening of feeling nor the sparkling of violence that usually preceded a blow.

"If I was three nurses instead of just one man, I could give her a change of sheets twice a day—hell, I could probably wash her hair and brush her teeth for her. But, Fee—" His father's grip tightened, and the wedges of his fingers drove into Fee's skin. "Do you think your mother would be happy, away from us?"

The person lying on the bed no longer had anything to do with happiness and unhappiness.

"She could only be happy being here with us, that's right, Fee, you're *right*. She knew you were holding her hand—that's why she's going to get better." He looked up. "Pretty soon, you're going to be sitting up and sassing back, isn't that right?"

He wouldn't allow anybody to sass him back, not ever.

"Let's pray for her now."

His father pushed him down to his knees again, then joined him on the blanket. "Our Father who art in heaven," he said. "Your servant, Anna Bandolier, my wife and this boy's mother, needs Your help. And so do we. Help us to care for her in her weakness, and we ask you to help her to overcome this weakness. Not a single person on earth is perfect, this poor sick woman included, and maybe we all have strayed in thought and deed from Your ways. Mercy is the best we can hope for, and we sinners know we do not deserve it, amen."

He lowered his hands and got to his feet. "Now leave the room, Fee." He removed his jacket and hung it on one of the bedposts and rolled up his sleeves. He tucked his necktie into his shirt. He stopped to give his son a disturbingly concentrated look. "We're going to take care of her by ourselves, and we don't want anybody else knowing our business."

"Yes, sir," Fee said.

His father jerked his head toward the bedroom door. "You remember what I said."

2

HIS FATHER NEVER asked if he wanted to kiss his mom, and he never thought to ask if he could—the pale woman lying on the bed with her eyes closed was not someone you could kiss. She was sailing out into the vast darkness within her a little more every day. She was like a radio station growing fainter and fainter as you drove into the country.

The yellow bruise faded away, and one morning Fee realized that it had vanished altogether. Her cheeks sank inward toward her teeth, drawing a new set of faint pencil lines across her face. One day, five or six days after the bruise had disappeared, Fee saw that the round blue shadows of her temples had collapsed some fraction of an inch inward, like soft ground sinking after a rain.

Fee's father kept saying that she was getting better, and Fee knew that this was true in a way that his father could not understand and he himself could only barely see. She was getting better because her little boat had sailed a long way into the darkness.

Sometimes Fee held a half-filled glass of water to her lips and let teaspoon-sized sips slide, one after another, into the dry cavern of her mouth. His mother never seemed to swallow these tiny drinks, for the moisture slipped down her throat by itself. He could see it move, quick as a living thing, shining and shivering as it darted into her throat.

Sometimes when his father prayed, Fee found himself examining the nails on his mother's hand, which grew longer by themselves. At first her fingernails were pink, but in a week, they turned an odd yellowish-white. The moons disappeared. Oddest of all, her long fingernails grew a yellow-brown rind of dirt.

He watched the colors alter in her face. Her lips darkened to brown, and a white fur appeared in the corner of her mouth.

Lord, this woman needs Your mercy. We're counting on You here, Lord.

When Fee left the bedroom each evening, he could hear his father go about the business of cleaning her up. When his father came out of the room, he carried the reeking ball of dirty sheets downstairs into the basement, his face frozen with distaste.

Mrs. Sunchana from the upstairs apartment washed her family's things twice a week, on Monday and Wednesday mornings, and never came downstairs at night. Fee's father put the clean sheets through the wringer and then took the heavy sheets outside to hang them on the two washing lines that were the Bandoliers'.

One night, his father slapped him awake and leaned over him in the dark. Fee, too startled to cry, saw his father's enormous eyes and the glossy commas of the mustache glaring down at him. His teeth shone. Heat and the odor of alcohol poured from him.

—You think I was put on earth to be your servant. I was not put on earth to be your servant. I could close the door and walk out of here tomorrow and never look back. Don't kid yourself—I'd be a lot happier if I did.

3

ONE DAY BOB Bandolier got a temporary job as desk man at the Hotel Hepton. Fee buffed his father's black shoes and got the onyx cufflinks from the top of the dresser. He pulled on his own clothes and watched his father pop the dry cleaner's hand from around a beautiful stiff white shirt, settle the shirt like armor around his body and squeeze the buttons through the holes, coax the cuff link into place, tug his sleeves, knot a lustrous and silvery tie, button his dark suit. His father dipped his knees before the bedroom mirror, brushed back the smooth hair at the sides of his head, used his little finger to rub wax into his perfect mustache, a comb no larger than a thumbnail to coax it through the whiskers.

His father pulled his neat dark topcoat on over the suit, patted his pockets, and gave Fee a dollar. He was to sit on the steps until noon, when he could walk to the Beldame Oriental Theater. A quarter bought him admission, and fifty cents would get him a hot dog, popcorn, and a soft drink; he could see *From Dangerous Depths,* starring Robert Ryan and Ida Lupino, along with a second feature, the travelogue, previews, and a cartoon; then he was to walk back down Livermore without talking to anybody and wait on the steps until his father came back home to let him in. The movies ended at twenty-five minutes past five, and his father said he would be home before six, so it would not be a long wait.

"We have to make it snappy," his father said. "You can't be late for the Hepton, you know."

Fee went dutifully to the closet just inside the front door, where his jacket and his winter coat hung from hooks screwed in halfway down the door. He reached up dreamily, and his father ripped the jacket off the hook and pushed it into his chest.

Before Fee could figure out the jacket, his father had opened the front door and shoved him out onto the landing. Fee got an arm into a sleeve while his father locked the door. Then he pulled at the jacket, but his other arm would not go into its sleeve.

"Fee, you're deliberately trying to louse me up," his father said. He ripped the jacket off his arm, turned it around, and jammed his arms into the sleeves. Then he fought the zipper for a couple of seconds. "You zip it. I have to go. You got your money?"

He was going down the steps and past the rosebushes to the path that went to the sidewalk.

Fee nodded.

Bob Bandolier walked away without looking back. He was tall and almost slim in his tight black coat. Nobody else on the street looked like him—all the other men wore plaid caps and old army jackets.

In a little while, smiling Mrs. Sunchana came up the walk carrying a bag of groceries. "Fee, you are enjoying the sunshine? You don't feel the cold today?" Her slight foreign accent made her speech sound musical, and her creamy round face, with its dark eyes and black eyebrows beneath her black bangs, could seem either witchlike or guilelessly pretty. Mrs. Sunchana looked nothing at all like Fee's mother—short, compact, and energetic where his mother was tall, thin, and weary; dark and cheerful where she was sorrowing and fair.

"I'm not cold," he said, though the chill licked in under the collar of his jacket, and his ears had begun to tingle. Mrs. Sunchana smiled at him again, said, "Hold this for me, Fee," and thrust the grocery bag onto his lap. He gripped the heavy bag as she opened her purse and searched for her key. There were no lines in her face at all. Both her cheeks and her lips were plump with health and life—for a second, bending over her black plastic purse and frowning with concentration, she seemed almost volcanic to Fee, and he wondered what it would be like to have this woman for his mother. He thought of her plump strong arms closing around him. Her face expanded above him. A rapture that was half terror filled his body.

For a second he was her child.

Mrs. Sunchana unlocked the door and held it open with one hip while she bent to take the groceries from Fee's lap. Fee looked down into the bag and saw a cardboard carton of brown eggs and a box of sugar-covered doughnuts. Mrs. Sunchana's live black hair brushed his forehead. The world wavered before him, and a trembling electricity filled his head. She drew the bag out of his arms, then quizzed him with a look.

"Coming in?"

"I'm going to the movies pretty soon."

"You don't want to wait inside, where it is warm?"

He shook his head. Mrs. Sunchana tightened her grip on the grocery bag. The expression on her face frightened him, and he turned away to look at the empty sidewalk.

"Is your mother all right, Fee?"

"She's sleeping."

"Oh." Mrs. Sunchana nodded.

"We're letting her sleep until my dad gets home."

Mrs. Sunchana kept nodding as she backed through the door. Fee remembered the eggs and the sugary doughnuts, and turned around again before she could see how hungry he was. "Do you know what time it is?"

She leaned over the bag to look at her watch. "About ten-thirty. Why, Fee?"

A black car moved down the street, its tires swishing through the fallen elm leaves. The front door clicked shut behind him.

A minute later, a window slid upward in its frame. A painful self-consciousness brought him to his feet. He put his hands in his pockets.

Fee walked stiffly and slowly down the path to the sidewalk and turned left toward Livermore Avenue. He remembered the moment when Mrs. Sunchana's electrically alive hair had moved against his forehead, and an extraordinary internal pain sent him gliding over the pavement.

The elms of Livermore Avenue interlocked their branches far overhead. Preoccupied men and women in coats moved up and down past the shop fronts. Fee was away from his block, and no one was going to ask him questions. Fee glanced to his right and experienced a sharp flame of anger and disgrace that somehow seemed connected to Mrs. Sunchana's questions about his mother.

But of course what was across the street had nothing to do with his mother. Beyond the slowly moving vehicles, the high boxy automobiles and the slat-sided trucks, a dark, arched passage led into a narrow alley. In front of the brick passage was a tall gray building with what to Fee looked like a hundred windows, and behind it was the blank facade of a smaller, brown brick building. The gray building was the St. Alwyn Hotel, the smaller building its annex. Fee felt that he was no longer supposed to *look* at the St. Alwyn. The St. Alwyn had done something bad, grievously bad—it had opened a most terrible hole in the world, and from that hole had issued hellish screams and groans.

A pure, terrible ache occurred in the middle of his body. From across the street, the St. Alwyn leered at him. Cold gray air sifted through his clothing. Brilliant leaves packed the gutters; water more transparent than the air streamed over and through the leaves. The ache within Fee threatened to blow him apart. He wanted to lower his face into the water—to dissolve into the transparent stream.

A man in a dark coat had appeared at the end of the tunnel behind the St. Alwyn, and Fee's heart moved with an involuntary constriction of pain and love before he consciously took in that the man was his father.

His father staring at a spot on the tunnel wall.

Why was his father behind the hated St. Alwyn, when he was supposed to be working at the Hotel Hepton?

His father looked from side to side, then moved into the darkness of the tunnel.

Bob Bandolier began fleeing down the alley. A confusion of feelings like voices raised in Fee's chest.

Now the alley was empty. Fee walked a few yards along the sidewalk, looking down at the clear water moving through the brilliant leaves. The sorrow and misery within him threatened to overflow. Without thinking, Fee dropped to his knees and thrust both of his hands into the water. A shock of cold bit into him. His small white hands sank farther than he had expected into the transparent water, and handcuffs made of burning ice formed around his wrists. The leaves drifted apart when he touched them. A brown stain oozed out and drifted, obscuring the leaves. Gasping, Fee pulled his hands from the water and wiped them on his jacket. He leaned over the gutter to watch the brown stain pour from the hole he had made in the leaves. Whatever it was, he had turned it loose, set it free.

4

THE BOX OF popcorn warmed Fee's hands. The Beldame Oriental Theater's luxurious space, with its floating cherubs and robed women raising lamps, its gilded arabesques and swooping curves of plaster, lay all about him. Empty rows of seats extended forward and back, and high up in the darkness hung the huge raft of the balcony. An old woman in a flowerpot hat sat far down in the second row; off to his left a congregation of shapeless men drank from pint bottles in paper bags.

This happened every day, Fee realized.

MOVIETONE NEWS blared from the screen, and a voice like a descending fist spoke over film of soldiers pointing rifles into dark skies, of a black boxer with a knotted forehead knocking down a white boxer in a brilliant spray of sweat. Women in bathing suits and sashes stood in a row and smiled at the camera; a woman in a long gown raised a crown from her head and placed it on the glowing black hair of a woman who looked like Mrs. Sunchana. It *was* Mrs. Sunchana, Fee thought, but then saw that her face was thinner than Mrs. Sunchana's, and his panic calmed.

The grinning heads of a gray cat and a small brown mouse popped onto the screen. Fee laughed in delight. In cartoons the music was loud and relentless, and the animals behaved like bad children. Characters were turned to smoking ruins, pressed flat, dismembered, broken like twigs, consumed by fires, and in seconds were whole again. Cartoons were about not being hurt.

Abruptly, he was running through a cartoon house, alongside a cartoon mouse. The mouse ran upright on his legs, like a human being. Behind him, also on whirling back legs, ran the cat. The mouse scorched a track through the carpet and zoomed into a neat mouse hole seconds before the cat's huge paw filled the hole. Fee brought salty popcorn to his mouth. Jerry Mouse sat at a little table and ate a mouse-sized steak with a knife and a fork. Fee drank in the enormity of his pleasure, the self-delight and swagger of the mouse, and the jealous rage of Tom Cat, rolling his giant bloodshot eye at the mouse hole.

After the cartoon, Fee walked up the aisle to buy a hot dog. Two or three people had taken seats in the vast space behind him. An old woman wrapped in a hairy brown coat mumbled to herself; a teenage boy cutting school cocked his feet on the seat in front of him. Fee saw the outline of a big man's head and shoulders on the other side of the theater, looked away, felt an odd sense of recognition, and looked back at an empty seat. He had been seen, but who had seen him?

Fee pushed through the wide doors into the lobby. A skinny man in a red jacket stood behind the candy counter, and an usher exhaled smoke from a velvet bench. The door to the men's room was just now swinging shut.

Fee bought a steaming hot dog and squirted ketchup onto it, wrapped it in a flimsy paper napkin, and hurried back into the theater. He heard the door of the men's room sliding across the lobby carpet. He rushed down the aisle and took his seat as the titles came up on the screen.

The stars of *From Dangerous Depths* were Robert Ryan and Ida Lupino. It was directed by Robert Siodmak. Fee had never heard of any of these people, nor of any of the supporting actors, and he was disappointed that the movie was not in color.

Charlie Carpenter (Robert Ryan) was a tall, well-dressed accountant who lived alone in a hotel room like those at the St. Alwyn. Charlie Carpenter put a wide-brimmed hat on the floor and flipped cards into it. He wore a necktie at home and, like Bob Bandolier, he peered into the mirror to scowl at his handsome, embittered face, At work he snubbed his office mates, and after work he drank in a bar. On Sundays he attended mass. One day, Charlie Carpenter noticed a discrepancy in the accounts, but when he asked about it, his angry supervisor (William Bendix) said that he had come upon traces of the Elijah Fund—this fund was used for certain investments, it was none of Charlie's business, he should never have discovered it in the first place, a junior clerk had made a mistake, Charlie must forget he'd ever heard of it. When Charlie wondered about the corporate officers in control of the fund, his supervisor reluctantly gave him two names, Fenton Welles and Lily Sheehan, but warned him to leave the matter alone.

Fenton Welles (Ralph Meeker) and Lily Sheehan (Ida Lupino) owned comfortable houses in the wealthy part of town. Charlie Carpenter scanned their lawn parties through field glasses; he followed them to their country houses on opposite sides of Random Lake, fifty miles north of the city.

Lily Sheehan summoned Charlie to her office. He feared that she knew he had been following her, but Lily gave Charlie a cigarette and sat on the edge of her

165

desk and said she had noticed that his reports were unusually perceptive. Charlie was a smart loner, just the sort of man whose help she needed.

Lily had suspicions about Fenton Welles. Charlie didn't have to know more than he *should* know, but Lily thought that Welles had been stealing from the company by manipulating a confidential fund. Was Charlie willing to work for her?

Charlie broke the lock on Fenton Welles's back door and groped through the dark house. Using a flashlight, he found the staircase and worked his way upstairs. He found the master bedroom and went to the desk. Just as he opened the center drawer and found a folder marked ELIJAH, the front door opened downstairs. Holding his breath, he looked in the file and saw photographs of various men, alone and in groups, in military uniform. He put the file back in the drawer, climbed out the window, and scrambled down the roof until he could jump onto the lawn. A dog charged him out of the darkness, and Charlie picked up a heavy stick beneath a tree and battered the dog to death.

Lily Sheehan told Charlie to take a room at the Random Lake Motel, rent a motorboat, and break into Welles's house when he was at a country club dance. Charlie and Lily were both smoking, and Lily prowled around him. She sat on the arm of his chair. Her dress seemed tighter.

In the dark behind him, somebody whistled.

Charlie and Lily kissed.

The music behind Charlie Carpenter announced *doom, ruin, death.* He pulled a carton from a closet in Fenton Welles's lake house and dumped its contents onto the floor. Stacks of bills held together with rubber bands fell out of the carton, along with a big envelope marked ELIJAH. Charlie opened the envelope and pulled out photographs of Fenton Welles and Lily Sheehan shot through window of a restaurant, Fenton Welles and Lily walking down a street arm in arm, Fenton Welles and Lily in the back seat of a taxi, driving away.

"Aha," said a voice from the back of the theater.

An angry, betrayed Charlie shouted at Lily Sheehan, waved a fist in the air, kicked at furniture. These sounds, Fee knew, were those that came before the screams and the sobs.

But the beatings did not come. Lily Sheehan began to cry, and Charlie took her in his arms.

He's evil, Lily said.

A stunned look bloomed in Charlie's dark eyes.

It's the only way I'll ever be free.

"Watch out," the man called, and Fee turned around and squinted into the back of the theater.

In the second row from the back, far under the beam of light from the projectionist's booth, a big man with light hair leaned forward with his hands held up like binoculars. "Peekaboo," he said. Fee whirled around, his face burning.

"I know who you are," the man said.

I'm all the soul you need, Lily said from the screen.

Fenton Welles walked in from a round of golf at the Random Lake Country Club, and Charlie Carpenter came sneering out from behind the staircase with a fireplace poker raised in his right hand. He smashed it down onto Welles's head.

Lily wiped the last trace of blood from Charlie's face with a tiny handkerchief, and for a second Fee *had* it, he knew the name of the man behind him, but this knowledge disappeared into the dread taking place on the screen, where Lily and Charlie lay in a shadowy bed talking about the next thing Charlie must do.

Death death death sang the soundtrack.

Charlie hid in the shadowy corner of William Bendix's office. Slanting shadows of the blinds fell across his suit, his face, his broad-brimmed hat.

A sweet pressure built in Fee's chest.

William Bendix walked into his office, and suddenly Fee knew the identity of the man behind him. Charlie Carpenter stepped out of the shadow-stripes with a knife in his hands. William Bendix smiled and waggled his fat hands—what's going on here, Miss Sheehan told him there wouldn't be any trouble—and Charlie rammed the knife into his chest.

Fee remembered the odor of raw meat the heavy smell of blood in Mr. Stenmitz's shop.

Charlie Carpenter scrubbed his hands and face in the company bathroom until the basin was black with blood. Charlie ripped towel after towel from the dispenser, blotted his face, and threw the damp towels on the floor. Impatient Charlie Carpenter rode a train out of the city, and two girls across the aisle peeked at him, wondering *Who's that handsome guy?* and *Why is he so nervous?* The train pulled past the front of an immense Catholic church with stained-glass windows blazing with light.

Fee turned around to see the big head and wide shoulders of Heinz Stenmitz. In the darkness, he could just make out white teeth shining in a smile. Joking, Mr. Stenmitz put his hands to his eyes again and pretended to peer at Fee through binoculars.

Fee giggled.

Mr. Stenmitz motioned for Fee to join him, and Fee got out of his seat and walked up the long aisle toward the back of the theater. Mr. Stenmitz wound his hand in the air, reeling him in. He patted the seat beside him and leaned over and whispered, "Sit here next to your old friend Heinz." Fee sat down. Mr. Stenmitz's hand swallowed his. "I'm very very glad you're here," he whispered. "This movie is too scary for me to see alone."

Charlie Carpenter piloted a motorboat across Random Lake. It was early morning. Drops of foam spattered across his lapels. Charlie was smiling a dark, funny smile.

"Do you know what?" Mr. Stenmitz asked.

"What?"

"Do you know what?"

Fee giggled. "No, what?"

"You have to guess."

There was blood everywhere on the screen but it was invisible blood, it was the blood scrubbed from the office floor and washed away in the sink.

The boat slid into the reeds, and Charlie jumped out onto marshy ground—the boat will drift away, Charlie doesn't care about the boat, it's nothing but a stolen boat, let it go, let it be gone...

⊪⊪⊪⊪⊪⊪⊪⊪⊪⊪⊪⊪⊪⊪⊪⊪⊪⊪⊪⊪⊪⊪⊪⊪⊪⊪⊪⊪⊪⊪⊪⊪⊪

AN UNIMAGINABLE TIME later Fee found himself standing in the dark outside the Beldame Oriental Theater. The last thing he could remember was Lily Sheehan turning from her stove and saying *Decided to stop off on your way to work, Charlie?* She wore a long white robe, and her hair looked loose and full. *You're full of surprises. I thought you'd be here last night.* His face burned, and his heart was pounding. Smoke and oil filled his stomach.

He felt appallingly, astoundingly dirty.

The world turned spangly and gray. The headlights on Livermore Avenue swung toward him. The smoke in his stomach spilled upward into his throat.

Fee moved a step deeper into the comparative darkness of the street and bent over the curb. Something that looked and tasted like smoke drifted from his mouth. He gagged and wiped his mouth and his eyes. It seemed to him that an enormous arm lay across his shoulders, that a deep low voice was saying—was saying—

No.

Fee fled down Livermore Avenue.

PART TWO

1

HE TURNED INTO his street and saw the neat row of cement blocks bisecting the dead lawn and the concrete steps leading up to the rosebushes and the front door.

Nothing around him was real. The moon had been painted, and the houses had no backs, and everything he saw was a fraction of an inch thick, like paint.

He watched himself sit down on the front steps. The night darkened. Footsteps came down the stairs from the Sunchanas' apartment, and the relief of dread focused his attention. The lock turned, and the door opened.

"Fee, poor child," said Mrs. Sunchana. "I thought I heard you crying."

"I wasn't crying," Fee said in a wobbly voice, but he felt cold tears on his cheeks.

"Won't your mother let you in?" Mrs. Sunchana stepped around him, and he scooted aside to let her pass.

He wiped his face on his sleeve. She was still waiting for an answer. "My mother's sick," he said "I'm waiting for my daddy to come back."

Pretty, dark-haired Mrs. Sunchana wrapped her arms about herself. "It's almost seven," she said. "Why don't you come upstairs? Have some hot chocolate. Maybe you want a bowl of soup? Vegetables, chicken, good thick soup for you. Delicious. I know, I made it myself."

Fee's reason began to slip away beneath the barrage of these seductive words. He saw himself at the Sunchana's table, raising a spoon of intoxicating soup to his mouth. Saliva poured into his mouth, and his stomach growled.

By itself, a sob flexed wide black wings in his throat and flew from his mouth.

And then, like salvation, came his father's voice. "Leave my son alone! Get away from him!" Fee opened his eyes.

Mrs. Sunchana pressed her hands together so tightly her fingers looked flat. Fee saw that she was frightened, and understood that he was safe again—back in the movie of his life.

And here came Bob Bandolier up the walls, his face glowing, his eyes glowing, his mustache riding confidently above his mouth, his coat billowing out behind him.

"Fee was sitting here alone in the cold," Mrs. Sunchana said.

"You will go upstairs, please, Mrs. Sunchana."

"I was just trying to help," persisted Mrs. Sunchana. Only her flattened-out hands betrayed her.

"Well, we don't need your help," bellowed Fee's glorious dad. "Go away and leave us alone."

"There is no need to give me orders."

"Shut up!"

"Or to yell at me."

"LEAVE MY SON ALONE!" Bob Bandolier raised his arms like a madman and stamped his foot. "Go!" He rushed toward the front steps, and Mrs. Sunchana went quickly past Fee into the building.

Bob Bandolier grasped Fee's hand, yanked him upright, and pulled him through the front door. Fee cried out in pain. Mrs. Sunchana had retreated halfway up the stairs, and her husband's face hung like a balloon in the cracked-open door to their apartment. In front of their own door, Bob Bandolier let go of Fee's hand to reach for his key.

"I think you must be crazy," said Mrs. Sunchana. "I was being nice to your little boy. He was locked out of the house in the cold."

Bob Bandolier unlocked the door and turned sideways toward her.

"We live right above you, you know," said Mrs. Sunchana. "We know what you do."

Fee's father pushed him into their apartment, and the smell from the bedroom announced itself like the boom of a bass drum. Fee thought that Mrs. Sunchana must have been able to smell it, too.

"And what do I do?" his father asked. His voice was dangerously calm.

Fee knew that his father was smiling.

He heard Mrs. Sunchana move one step up.

"You know what you do. It is not right."

Her husband whispered her name from the top of the stairs.

"On the contrary," his father said. "Everything I do, Mrs. Sunchana, is precisely right. Everything I do, I do for a reason." He moved away from the door, and Mrs. Sunchana went two steps up.

Fee watched his father with absolute admiration. He had won, He had said the brave right things, and the enemy had fled.

Bob Bandolier came scowling toward him.

Fee backed into the living room. His father strode through the doorway and pushed the door shut. He gave Fee one flat, black-eyed glare, removed his top-coat, and hung it carefully in the closet without seeming to notice the smell from the bedroom. He unbuttoned his suit jacket and the top of his shirt and pulled his necktie down a precise half inch.

"I'm going to tell you something very important. You are never to talk to them again, do you hear me? They might try to get information out of you, but if you say one word to those snoops, I'll whale the stuffing out of you." He patted Fee's cheek. "You won't say anything to them, I know."

Fee shook his head.

"They think they know things—ten generations of keyhole listeners."

His father gave his cheek another astounding pat. He snapped his fingers. At the code for cat food, Jude stalked out from beneath the chaise. Fee followed both of them into the kitchen. His father spooned half a can of cat food into Jude's dish and put the remainder of the can into the refrigerator.

Bob Bandolier was an amazing man, for now he went whirling and dancing across the kitchen floor, startling even Jude. Amazing Bob spun through the living room, not forgetting to smile up at the ceiling and toss a cheery wave to the Sunchanas, clicked open the bedroom door with his hip, and called *Hello, honeybunch* to his wife. Fee followed, wondering at him. His father supped from a brown bottle of Pforzheimer beer, Millhaven's own, winked at Sleeping Beauty, and said, *Darling, don't give up yet.*

"Here she is, Fee," his father said. "She knows, she knows, you know she knows."

Fee nodded: that was right. His mother knew exactly what it was that he himself had forgotten.

"This lady right here, *she* never doubted." He kissed her yellow cheek. "Let's rustle up some grub, what do you say?"

Fee was in the presence of a miracle.

2

AFTER DINNER HIS father washed the dishes, now and then taking a soapy hand from the foam to pick up his beer bottle. Fee marveled at the speed with which his father drank—three long swallows, and the bottle was empty, like a magic trick.

Bob Bandolier filled a plastic bucket with warm tap water, put some dishwashing powder in the bucket, swirled it around with his hand, and dropped in a sponge.

"Well, here goes." He winked at Fee. "The dirty part of the day. Your mother is one of the decent people in this world, and that's why we take care of her." He was swirling the water around in the bucket again, raising a white lather. "Let me tell you something. There's a guy who is not one of the decent people of the world, who thinks all he has to do is sit behind a desk all day and count his money. He even thinks he knows the hotel business." Bob Bandolier laughed out loud. "I have a little plan, and we'll see how fine and dandy Mr. Fine and Dandy really is, when he starts to sweat." His face was red as an apple.

Fee understood—his father was talking about the St. Alwyn.

He squeezed the sponge twice, and water drizzled into the bucket. "Tonight I'm going to tell you about the blue rose of Dachau. Which was the bottom of the

176

world. That was where you saw the things that are real in this world. You come along while I wash your mother."

"Not all the way in," his father said. "You don't have to see the whole thing, just stay in the door. I just want you to be able to hear me."

Bob Bandolier put a hand on Fee's shoulder and showed him where to stand.

"This one's going to be messy," he said.

The smell in the bedroom took root in Fee's nose and invaded the back of his throat. Bob Bandolier set down the bucket, grasped the blanket near his wife's chin, and flipped it down to the end of the bed.

As the blanket moved, his mother's arms jerked up and snapped back into place, elbows bent and the hands curled toward the wrists. Beneath the blanket lay a sheet molded around his mother's body. Watery brown stains covered the parts of the sheet clinging to her waist and hips.

"Anyway," Bob said, and grabbed the sheet with one hand and walked down the length of the bed, pulling it away from his wife's body. At the bottom of the bed, he yanked the end of the sheet from under the mattress and carefully wadded it up.

From his place in the doorway, Fee saw the yellow soles of his mother's feet, from which her long toenails twisted away; the starved undersides of her legs, peaking at her slightly raised knees; her bony thighs, which disappeared like sticks into the big St. Alwyn towel his father had folded around her groin. Once white, this towel was now stained the same watery brown that had leaked through to the sheet. Above the towel was her small swollen belly; two distinct, high-arched rows of ribs; her small flat breasts and brown nipples; shoulders with sunken flesh, from which thin straight bones seemed to want to escape; a lined, deeply hollowed neck; and above all these, propped on a pillow in the limp nest of her hair, his mother's familiar and untroubled face.

"How does stuff still come out, hey, when so damn little goes in? Hold on, honey, we gotta get this *thing* off of you."

Dedicated Bob Bandolier tugged at the folds of the wet towel, managing with the use of only two fingers to pull it free, exposing Anna Bandolier's knifelike hipbones and her astonishingly thick pubic bush—astonishingly, that is, to Fee, who had expected only a smooth pink passage of flesh, like the region between the legs of a doll. Where all the rest of his mother's skin was the color of yellowing milk, the area uncovered by the towel was a riot of color: milk chocolate flecks and smears distributed over the blazing red of the thighs, and the actual crumbling or shredding of blue and green flesh disappearing into the wound where her buttocks should have been. From this wound surrounded by evaporating flesh came the smell that flooded their apartment.

Fee's heart froze, and the breath in his lungs turned to ice.

Deep within the hole of ragged flesh that was his mother's bottom was a stripe of white bone.

His father slid the dripping sponge beneath her arms, over the pubic tangle and the reddish-gray drooping flesh between her legs. After every few passes he squeezed the sponge into the bucket. He dabbed at the enormous bedsores. "This started happening a while ago—figured it would take care of itself long as I kept her clean, but...well, I just do what I can do." He touched the oddly stiff bottom sheet. "See this? Rubber. Sponge it off, it's good as new. Weren't for this baby, we'd have gone through a lot of mattresses by now. Right, honey?"

His father knew he was in a movie.

"Get me another sheet and towel from the linen cabinet."

His father was wiping the rubber sheet with a clean section of the old towel when Fee came back into the bedroom. He dropped the towel on top of the wadded sheet and took the new linen out of Fee's arms.

"Teamwork, that's what we got."

He set the linen on the end of the bed and bent to squeeze out the sponge before lightly, quickly passing it over the rubber sheet.

"I don't know if I ever told you much about my war," he said. "You're old enough now to begin to understand things."

It seemed to Fee that he had no heartbeat all. His mouth was a desert. Everything around him, even the dust in the air, saw what he himself was seeing.

"This war was no damn picnic." Bob Bandolier tilted his wife's body up to wipe beneath her, and Fee raised his eyes to the top of the bedstead.

Bob wiped the fresh towel over the damp sheet, straightened it out, and turned his wife over onto the towel. Her toenails clicked together.

"But I want to tell you about this one thing I did, and it has to do with roses." He gave Fee a humorous look. "You know how I feel about roses."

Fee knew how he felt about roses.

From the bottom of the bed, his father snapped open the clean sheet and sent it sailing over Anna Bandolier's body. "I was crazy about roses even way back then. But the kind of guy I am, I didn't just grow them, I got interested in them. I did research." He tucked the sheet beneath the mattress.

Bob Bandolier smoothed the sheet over his wife's body, and Fee saw him taking a mental picture of the tunnel behind the St. Alwyn hotel.

"There's one kind, one color, of rose no one has ever managed to grow. There has never been a true blue rose. You could call it a Holy Grail."

He lifted first one arm, then the other, to slide the sheet beneath them.

He moved back to appraise the sheet. He gave it a sharp tug, snapping it into alignment. Then he stepped back again, with the air of a painter stepping back from a finished canvas.

"What it is, is an enzyme. An enzyme controls the color of a rose. Over the years, I've managed to teach myself a little bit about enzymes. Basically, an enzyme is a biological catalyst. It speeds up chemical changes without going through any changes itself. Believe it or not, Millhaven, this city right here, is one of the enzyme centers of the world—because of the breweries. You need enzymes to get fermentation, and without fermentation you don't get beer. When they managed to crystallize an enzyme, they discovered that it was protein." He pointed at Fee. "Okay so far, but here's your big problem. Enzymes are picky. They react with only a tiny little group of molecules. Some of them only work with one molecule!"

He pointed the forefinger at the ceiling. "Now, what does that say about roses? It says that you have be a pretty damn good chemist to create your blue rose. Which is the reason that no one has ever done it." He paused for effect.

"Except for one man. I met him in Germany in 1945, and I saw his rose garden. He had four blue rosebushes in that garden. The ones on the first bush were deep, dark blue, the color of the ink in fountain pens. On the second bush the roses grew a rich navy blue; on the third bush, they were the most beautiful pale blue—the color of a nigger's Cadillac. All of these roses were beautiful, but the most beautiful roses grew on the fourth bush. They were all the other shades in stripes and feathers, dark blue against that heaven-sky blue, little brush strokes of heaven-sky blue against that velvety black-blue. The man who grew them was the greatest gardener in the history of rose cultivation. And there are two other things you should know about him. He grew these roses in ten square empty feet of ground in a concentration camp during the war. He was a guard there. And the second thing is, I shot him dead."

He put his hands on his hips. "Let's go get this lady her dinner, okay? Now that she's had her bath, my baby's hungry."

3

FEE'S FATHER BUSIED himself measuring out dry oatmeal into a saucepan, poured in milk, lit a match, and snapped the gas flame into life. He stood beside the stove, holding a long wooden spoon and another bottle of beer, looking as though a spotlight were trained on him.

"We get this job." He gave the oatmeal another twirl of the spoon. "It could have been any company, any unit. It didn't have to be mine, but it was mine. We were going to be the first people into what they called the death camp. I didn't even know what it meant, death camp, I didn't know what it was.

"There were some English soldiers that met us there, sort of a share-the-glory, Allied effort. Let the English grab their share. The officers of the camp will surrender to a joint Anglo-American force, and the prisoners will be identified and assisted in their eventual relocation. Meaning, we ship them off after somebody else decides what to do with them. We liberate them. We're the liberators. What does that mean? Women, music, champagne, right?"

He stirred the oatmeal again, looking down into the saucepan and frowning.

"So we get lined up on the road to the camp. We're outside this little town on some river. From where we're standing, I can see a castle, a real castle on a hill over the river, like something out of a movie. There's us, and there's the British. There's photographers, too, from the news-reels and the papers. This is a big deal, because nobody really knows what we're going to find once we get in. The brass is in front. We start moving in columns toward the camp, and all of a sudden everything looks ugly—even the ground looks ugly. We're going toward barbed wire and guardhouses, and you *know* it's some kind of prison.

"I was wrong about everything, I see that right away. The place is like a factory. Once we go through the gates, we're on a long straight road, everything right angles, with little wooden buildings in rows. Okay, we're ready."

He upturned the pot and spooned oatmeal into a bowl. He added butter, brown sugar, and a dollop of milk. "Perfect. Let's feed your mother, Fee."

In radiant humor, he stood beside the bed and raised a spoonful of oatmeal to his wife's lips. "You have to help me out now, honey, I know you have to be hungry. Here comes some delicious oatmeal—open your mouth." He pushed the spoon into her mouth and slid it back and forth to dislodge the oatmeal. "Attaway. Getting a little better every day, aren't we? Pretty soon we're going to be up on our feet."

Fee remembered what his mother's feet looked like. It was as though a vast dark light surrounded them, a light full of darkness with a greater, deeper darkness all around it, the three of them all alone at its center.

His father slid the spoon from his mother's mouth. A trace of oatmeal remained in the bottom of the spoon. He filled it again and pushed it between her lips. Fee had not seen his mother swallow. He wondered if she could swallow. His father withdrew the spoon again, and a wad of oatmeal the size of a housefly stuck to his mother's top lip.

"Right away I noticed this terrible smell. You couldn't imagine working in a place that smelled that bad. Like a fire in a garbage dump.

"Anyhow, we go marching up this street without seeing anybody, and when we pass this courtyard I see something I can't figure out at all. At first, I don't even know what it is. You know what it was? A giant pile of glasses. Eyeglasses! Must be a thousand of them. Creepy. I mean, that's when I begin to get the idea. They were saving the metal, you did that during the war, but there used to be people that went with those glasses.

"We can see those smokestacks up ahead, big smokestacks on top of the furnaces. We go past buildings that seem like they're full of old clothes, piles and piles of shirts and jackets..."

The spoon went in full and came out half full. Flecks of oatmeal coated his mother's lips.

"Then we get to the main part of the camp, the barracks, and we see what the people are like. We're not even marching in step anymore, we're not marching at all, we're just moving along, because these are *people* out in front of these barracks, but you never saw people like this in your life. They're walking skeletons. Bones and eyes, like monkeys. Big heads and tiny little bodies. You wonder how smart is it to liberate these zombies in the first place. The ones that can talk are whining, whining, whining—man! These people are watching every move we make, and what you think is: they want to eat us alive.

"So I'm walking along with my company. Half of us want to throw up. These things, these zombies are watching us go by, most of them too weak to do anything but prop themselves up, and I actually realize what is going on. This is the earth we live on, I say to myself. This is what we call earth. There was no *pretending* about what was going on in this place. This was it. This was the last stop."

Bob Bandolier absentmindedly ate a spoonful of oatmeal. His eyes shone. He licked the spoon.

"And why do I say that? Even the Nazis, the most efficient organization on earth, couldn't move all these people through the gas chambers and into the ovens. Besides the zombies, they had all these dead bodies left over. You can't imagine. Nobody could. This place, the most horrible place the world has ever seen—it was holy."

Bob Bandolier noticed he was still holding a spoon and a bowl of oatmeal. He smiled at himself, and began again to feed his wife. Oatmeal bubbled out past her lips.

"Finished, honey? Looks like you had enough for today. Good baby."

He ran the edges of the spoon over her mouth and scraped off most of the visible oatmeal. He set the bowl down on the bed and turned to Fee, still smiling.

"And then I knew I was exactly right, because we turned into this square where the Germans were waiting for us, and here was this ordinary little house, a fence, a walk to the front door, and in this little lot beside it was the rose garden. With those four bushes full of blue roses.

"I stepped out of the column and went up to the garden. Nobody said anything. I sort of heard what was going on—the captain was taking over from the commandant, and the two of them and some other brass went to the back of the square and into the commandant's office. What did I care? I was looking at a miracle. In this miserable hell, someone had managed

186

to grow blue roses. It was a sign. I knew one thing, Fee. I was in the only place on earth where a blue rose could grow.

"I wanted to grab people and say, *For God's sake, look at that garden over there,* but why waste my time? They were just staring at the zombies or the guards.

"But everybody felt *something,* Fee.

"I looked each one of those guards in the face. They just stared straight ahead, no expression, nothing in their eyes, no fear....These guys were just doing their jobs like good little cops, they had no more imagination than they were allowed. Except for one man, the one I wanted to find.

"Of course, it was easy. He was the only one who actually looked back at me. He had the moral courage of knowing who he was. Besides that, he saw me standing in front of his roses. Maybe the commandant thought they were *his* roses, maybe some of the zombies even thought they were *their* roses, but they belonged to one man only, their gardener. The goddamned genius who was the right man in the right place at the right time. He knew what he had done, and he knew that *I* knew. He looked straight into my eyes when I stood in front of him.

"You'd never pick him out of a crowd. He was a big bullet-headed guy with a wide nose and little eyes. Big, fat hands and a huge chest. Sort of—sort of like all overgrown dwarf. I would have gone right past him, I almost did go right past him, but then I caught his eye and he caught mine, and I saw that *light*...he was the one. He didn't give a damn about anything else on earth.

"I stood in front of him and I said, *How did you do it?* The guys who heard me thought I was asking how he could have treated people that way, but he knew what I meant.

"Our captain and the commandant come out of the office and the captain gets everybody back into formation and tells my platoon to keep watch on the guards. The captain goes away to take care of business. The guys are loading prisoners on trucks, they're setting up desks and taking down names, *I* don't know, my job is to keep an eye on the guards until someone else shows up to take them away.

"Pretty soon it's just us and the guards in the square. Ten of us; about fifteen, twenty of them. There are Americans running all over the camp by now, the place is organized chaos. I decide to try again, and I go up to the guy, the gardener, and boy oh boy I know I'm right all over again because his eyes light up as soon as I come up to him.

"I ask him again. *How did you do it?* This time he almost smiles. He shakes his head.

"*I want to know about the roses,* I say. I point at them, as if he didn't know what I was talking about.

"*Do any of you people speak English?*

"A guy off to the left, a tall gray-haired character with a scar on his forehead, sort of looks at me, and I tell him to help me or I'll blow his head off. He comes up. I say, I want to know about the roses. He can hardly believe that *this* is what I'm interested in, but he gets the idea, and I hear him say something about *blaue rose.*

"My guard, the genius, the one man on earth who ever managed to create a blue rose, finally starts talking. He's bored—he knows this stuff backwards and forwards, he worked it all out by himself and I'm some American private, I don't deserve to know it. But he's under arrest, he'll tell me, all right? He starts spouting this scientific gobbledygook German full of chemical formulas, and not only do I not have any chance of understanding it, neither does the *other* guy, the other Nazi. The gardener knows we don't get it.

"When he's done talking he shuts up, he came to the end and he stopped, like he read the whole thing off a card. Nobody has the faintest idea what he said. Some of the other guys are giving me funny looks, because the zombies get all worked up, they can't hear what the guard is saying but they're excited anyhow.

"Picture this. There's us and them, and then there's the freak show behind us. On the other side of the guards are the camp offices, two wooden buildings about ten feet apart. Between the offices, you can see walls of barbed wire and an empty guardhouse, maybe fifty yards away. Way off to the left are those chimneys. There's just a muddy field between the offices and the fence.

"So the gardener spits on the ground and starts walking away. He just walks right through the other guards. Now the zombies are going crazy. The guard is going toward the space between the buildings. The other guards sort of watch him out of the corners of their eyes. I figure he's going to take a leak, come back.

"One of our guys says, *Hey, that Kraut's getting away.*

"I tell him to shut up.

"But he doesn't stop when he gets to the offices, he just keeps walking on through.

"The rabble is screaming the place down. Some guy says, *What do we do, what are we supposed to do?*

"The gardener just keeps on walking until he's in the field. Then he turns around and looks at me. He's one ugly fucker. He doesn't smile, he doesn't blink, he just gives me a look. Then he starts running for the fence.

"You know what he thinks? He thinks I'll let him get away, on account of I know how great he is. This is what I know—this bastard is taking advantage of me, and I do know how great he is, but nobody takes advantage of me, Fee.

"I raise my rifle and take aim. I pull the trigger, and I shoot him right in the back. Down he goes, boom. One shot. That's all she wrote. We left him where he dropped. None of the rest of those assholes made a move until the truck came for them, you can bet on that."

His father picked up the bowl of oatmeal and smiled. "I never even knew his name. For two weeks, me and my platoon, all we did was identify corpses. I mean, that's what we tried to do. The survivors who could still get around made the identifications and we wrote them down. In the end, the Corps of Engineers dug these bit trenches and we just plowed 'em in there. Men, women, and children. Poured lime over them and covered them up with dirt. When I went back to see those roses again, the bushes were all pulled up and chopped to pieces. The colonel came in, and he thought they were the ugliest things he'd ever seen in his life. The colonel said: Rip these ugly goddamned blue nightmares out of the ground and chop 'em up, pronto. The guy who cut them down told me that. You know what else he said? He said they gave him the creeps, too. We're in a concentration camp, and *roses* gave him the creeps."

Bob Bandolier shook his head. He leaned over and kissed his wife's waxy forehead.

"We'll let her get some rest."

They returned the bowl and spoon to the kitchen. "I have to go back to the Hepton tomorrow. So you'll get another day at the movies." He was mellow and slow; tonight Bob Bandolier was a satisfied man.

Fee could not remember having seen a movie.

"You know what you are? You're a little blue rose, that's what you are."

Fee brushed his teeth and put himself to bed while his father leaned against the wall with an impatient hand on the light switch. Fee's breathing lengthened; his body seemed to grow mysteriously heavy. The noises of the house, the creaking of boards, the wind moving past his window, the slow chugging of the washing machine carried him to a boat with a prow like an eagle's head before the similarly proud and upright head of his mother, whose silken hair stirred in the sea air. They sailed far and away for many a day, and he found himself bobbing and blooming in a garden. Bob Bandolier moved his hand toward the pocket of his gray suit and took out a pair of shears.

4

FEE CAME AWAKE with no memory of what had happened in the night. His father was leaning against the wall, flipping the light on and off and saying, "Come on, come on." His face was blotchy and white. "If you make me one minute late for work at the Hepton, you are going to be one sorry little boy, is that understood?"

He walked out of the room. Fee's body seemed to be made of ice, of lead, of a substance impossible to move.

"Don't you understand?" His father leaned back into the room. "This is the Hepton. You get out of bed, little boy."

His father's breath still smelled like beer. Fee pushed back his covers and swung his legs over the side of the bed.

"You want oatmeal?"

He nearly threw up on Bob Bandolier's perfect black shoes.

"No? Then that's it, I'm not your personal short-order cook. You can go hungry until you get to the show."

Fee struggled into underpants, socks, yesterday's shirt and pants. His father stood over him, snapping his fingers like a metronome.

"Get in the bathroom and wash up, for God's sake."

Fee scampered down the hall.

"You made a lot of noise last night. What the hell was the matter?"

He looked up from the sink and saw, behind his own dripping face, his father's powerful, scowling face. Pouches of dark flesh hung beneath his eyes.

Into his yellow towel, Fee mumbled that he did not remember. His father batted the side of his head.

"What was wrong with you?"

"I don't know," Fee cried. "I don't *remember.*"

"There will be no more screaming and shouting in the middle of the night. You will make no noise at all from the time you enter your bedroom until the time you leave it in the morning. Is that understood?" His father was pointing at him. "Or else there will be punishment."

"Yes, sir."

His father straightened up. "Okay, we understand each other. Get set to go, and I'll get you a glass of milk or something. You have to have something in your stomach."

When Fee had dried his face and pulled on his coat and zipped it up, when he went down the hall and into the kitchen with Jude winding in and out of his feet, his father, also enclosed in his coat, held out a tall white glass of milk.

"Drink up, drink up."

Fee took the glass from his hand.

"I'll say goodbye to your mother."

His father hurried out of the kitchen, and Fee looked at the glass in his hand. He raised it to his mouth. An image blazed in his mind and was banished before he had even a glimpse of it. His hand started shaking. In order to keep from spilling the milk, Fee swung the glass toward the counter with both hands and set it down. He moaned to see a pattern of little white drops on the counter.

"God damn, *God damn, GOD DAMN,*" his father shouted.

Fee wiped the dots of milk with his hand. They turned to white streaks, then smears, then nothing. He was panting, and his face was hot.

Bob Bandolier raged back into the kitchen, and Fee quailed back against the cabinets. His father seemed hardly to notice him as he turned on the water and passed a dishtowel back and forth beneath the stream. His face was tight with impatience and disgust.

"Go outside and wait for me."

He hurried back toward the bedroom. Fee poured the milk into the sink, his heart beating as if he had committed a crime.

Jude followed him to the front door, crying for food. He bent over to stroke the cat, and Jude arched her back and made a noise like fat sizzling in a pan. Still hissing, she moved back several steps. Her huge eyes gleamed, but not at Fee.

Fee groped for the doorknob. Through the open bedroom door, he saw his father's back, bent over the bed. He turned around and pulled the door open.

Standing before him were the Sunchanas, he in a suit, she two, steps behind him in a checked robe. Both of them looked startled.

"Oh!" said Mr. Sunchana. His wife clasped both hands in front of her chest. "Fee," she said, and then looked past her husband into the apartment. The cat sizzled and spat.

"David," said Mrs. Sunchana.

David took his eyes from Fee and looked over his head toward whatever his wife had seen. His eyes changed.

Slowly, Fee turned around.

Bob Bandolier was stepping away from the bed, holding stretched out between his hands a dish towel blotched with brilliant red. The usual odor floated from the bedroom.

Something black and wet covered his mother's chin.

Bob Bandolier dropped one end of the cloth and began moving toward the bedroom door. He did not shout, although he looked as though he wanted to yell the house down. He slammed the door.

"Last night—" said Mr. Sunchana.

"We heard you last night," said Mrs. Sunchana.

"You were making a lot of noise."

"And we were worried for you. Are you all right, Fee?"

Fee swallowed and nodded.

"Really?"

"Yes," he said. "Really."

The bedroom door burst open, and Bob Bandolier stepped out and immediately closed the door behind him. He was not holding the dish towel. "Haven't we had enough violations of our privacy from you two? Get away from our apartment or I'll throw you out of this house. I mean it."

Mr. Sunchana backed away and bumped into his wife.

"Out, out, out."

"What is wrong with your wife?" asked Mrs. Sunchana.

Fee's father stopped moving a few feet from the door. "My wife had a nosebleed. She has been unwell. I am in danger of being late for work, and I cannot allow you to delay me any longer."

"You call that a nosebleed?" Mrs. Sunchana's wide face had grown pale. Her hands were shaking.

Bob Bandolier shut the door and waited for them to retreat up the stairs.

Outside, white breath steamed from his father's mouth. "You'll need money." He gave Fee a dollar bill. "This is for today and tomorrow. I hope I don't have to tell you not to talk to the Sunchanas. If they won't leave you alone, just tell them to go away."

Fee put the bill in his jacket pocket.

His father patted his head before striding down South Seventh Street to Livermore Avenue and the bus to the Hotel Hepton.

5

FEE PAUSED AGAIN on his way to the Beldame Oriental, feeling dazed, as if caught between two worlds, and stared down into the moving water.

A huge man with warm hands was waiting to pull him into a movie.

6

MOST OF THE seats are empty. The big man with kind eyes and a flaring mustache looms beside you. He puts his arm around your shoulders. A Negro boxer knits his forehead and batters another man. Mrs. Sunchana accepts her crown. She looks at him, and he whispers *nosebleed*. God's arm tightens around his shoulders and God whispers *nice boy*. The cat chased the mouse on whirling legs. I know you're glad to see me. God's hand is huge and hot, and the gray slab of his face weighs a thousand pounds. You came back to see me. With Robert Ryan, Ida Lupino, and William Bendix. You could hear Jerry's ghost sobbing in the black-and-white shadows. Charlie Carpenter sat in a long quiet church and turned his attention to God, who chuckled and took your hand. Candles flared and sputtered. Mrs. Sunchana bowed her head at the edge of the frame. You don't remember what we did? You liked it, and I liked it. Why did God make lonely people? Answer: He was lonely, too. Some of my special friends come to visit and we go into my basement. You're the special friend I go to visit, so you're the most special of all the special friends. There is a toy you have to play with now. Lily Sheehan takes Charlie Carpenter's hand. Here it is, here's the toy. Lily smiles and places Charlie's hand on her toy. Unzip it, God says. Come on. Lucky Strike Means Pine Tobacco. I'd Walk a Mile for a Camel. You see it, here it is, it's all yours. You know what to do with it. Little dear one. God is so stern and tender. Have a cigarette, Charlie. It likes you, can't you see how much it likes you? Random Lake is a pretty nice lake. I need you to help me. Here we are, on Fenton Welles's long lawn. If you stop now, I'll kill you. Hah hah. That's a joke. I'll cut you up and turn you into lamb chops, sweetie-pie, I know how to do that. But here is the envelope marked ELIJAH, here are the photographs. Every one of those soldiers has one like mine, a big thick one that likes to come out and play.

The dog jumps up from Fenton Welles's lawn and you smash its head in with a stick. You are kissing a long kiss. Smoke from his mouth fills the air. God placed both hands on the sides of your head and pushed your head down toward the other little mouth. Hello, Duffy's Tavern, Duffy speaking. Jack Armstrong, the all-American boy. Welcome to the Adventures of. The roaring in his ears. He pushed the big thing into his cheek so he would not gag, but God's hands raised his head and lowered it again. Charlie and Lily kissed and Lily's penis threshed out like a snake. A woman should put your mouth on her breast, and milk should flow. I'm all the soul you need. The second you take it in your mouth, it moves—it twitches and shoves itself upward. God's pleasure makes Him sigh. His hand around yours. Now kiss. They are burning photographs, the smell is harsh. The taste is sour burning. Wait for it, the music says. Mrs. Sunchana covers her face. The world bursts into flame. From up out of that long thing, all the way up from its bottom, from the deep bottom of the well, it rushes. God presses His hands against your head. You open your mouth and smoke and drool leak out. If he wanted, God could drown the world. Maxwell House Coffee Is Good to the Very Last Drop. The tiny Arab man on the lip of the huge tilted cup. What is in your mouth is the taste of bread. The taste of bread is warm and silky. To be loved. Charlie in his good suit rides the train, and the girls stare. Bunny is good bread. A normal girl is attracted by a handsome man. Invisible blood, God's blood, washes through the world. Charlie Carpenter rides across the lake and water mists his lapels. You can lean back against God's giant chest. His hand strokes your cheek. Jack Armstrong eats Wheaties every day. The boat slides into the reeds. Water-music, death-music. God rubs your chest, and His hand is rough. Make big money selling Christmas cards to all your neighbors. The hotel business is America's business. Don't you think that they all take towels, the big guys? The best hamburgers come with the works. Charlie shoved the boat into the reeds, and now he strides across the lawn to Lily's house. Oh the face of Charlie Carpenter, oh the anger in his stride. You could be crushed to death. This man is holding on. The little Arab clings to his giant cup. What grows out of him is not human, that thing is not human. His arms surrounding you, blue rose, little blue rose.

7

THE STORY OF THE LEAVES

His mother had a nosebleed from her mouth. The boy put his hand in the water to stop her from going, and a cloud swarmed out of the leaves and darkened all the water like a stain.

THE STORY OF THE MOVIE

Charlie Carpenter and Lily Sheehan held hands and looked out of the screen. Kiss me, Lily said, and the dead boy leaned over and kissed it by taking it into his mouth. Every day the same thing happened in the seats of the Beldame Oriental. The end of the movie was so terrible that you could never remember it, not even if you tried.

THE STORY OF THE NOSEBLEED

When Mrs. Sunchana saw it, she said, "Do you call that a nosebleed?" His father said, "What else could you call it?"

THE STORY OF THE MOVIE

Lily Sheehan wrapped her arms around Charlie Carpenter the way Someone wrapped his arms around the dead boy. Something grew between her legs and from that Something Charlie Carpenter did take suck. We remember folds of gray flesh. Whenever the warm silky fluid shuddered out, it tasted like bread.

The Juniper Tree |||||||||||||||||||||||||||||||||||||||||||||||||||||||||||||||||||||||||||||
AND OTHER BLUE ROSE STORIES

THE STORY OF THE BLUE ROSE

Charlie Carpenter rang Lily Sheehan's hell, and when she opened the door he gave her a blue rose. This stands for dying, for death. My daddy met the man who grew them, and when the man tried to run away my daddy shot him in the back.

THE STORY OF THE MOVIE

After a long time, the movie ended. Robert Ryan lay in a pool of blood, and a rank, feral odor filled the air. Lily Sheehan closed her front door and a little boat drifted away across Random Lake. A few people left their seats and walked up the aisle and swung open the doors to the lobby. My entire body is buzzing, with what feelings I do not know. In my hands I can feel the weight of plums in a coarse sack, my fingers retain the heat of—my hands tingle. No other world exists but this, with its empty seats and the enormous body beside mine. I am doubly dead, I am buried beneath the carpet, strewn with flecks of popcorn, of the Beldame Oriental. My heart buzzes when the enormous man pulls me tight into his chest. The story of the movie was too terrible to remember. I say, yes, I will be back tomorrow. I have forgotten everything. Words from the radio gong through my mind. Jack Armstrong, Lucky Strikes, the Irish songs on Saint Patrick's Day when I was sick and stayed in bed all day and heard my mother humming and talking to herself while she cleaned the rooms we lived in.

THE STORY OF MY FIRST VICTIM

The first person I ever killed was a six-year-old boy named Lance Torkelson. I was thirteen. We were in a quarry in Tangent, Ohio, and I made Lance hold my erection in his hand and put the tip against his face. Amazed by sensation, I cried out, and the semen shot out like ropes and clung to his face. If I had kept my mouth shut he would have been all right, but my yelling frightened him and he began to wail. I was still shooting and pumping—some of it hit Lance's throat and slid down inside his collar. He screamed. I picked up a rock and hit Lance as hard as I could on the side of his head. He fell right down. Then I hit him until something broke and his head felt soft. My cock was still hard, but there was nothing left inside me. I tossed aside the rock and watched myself stay so stiff and alive, so ready. I could hardly believe what had happened. I never knew that was how it worked.

8

A SUDDEN CHANGE in air pressure brought him groaning out of the movie. His entire body felt taut with misery. *She's dead,* he thought, *she just died.* Into his bedroom floated the odors of beer and garbage. The darkness above his bed whirled itself into a pattern as meaningless as an oil slick. He tossed back his covers and swung his feet over the edge of the bed. The shape in the darkness above him shifted and rolled.

Everything in his room, his bed and dresser, the toys and clothes on the floor, had been thrown into unfamiliarity by the white light that filtered in through the gauze curtains. His room seemed larger than in the daytime. A deep sound had been reaching him since he had thrown off his blankets, a deep mechanical rasp that poured up from the floor and through the walls. This sound flowed up from the earth—it was the earth itself at work, the great machine at the heart of the earth.

He came into the living room. Pale moonlight covered the carpet and chaise. Sleeping Jude had curled into a dark knot, from which only the points of her ears protruded. All the furniture looked as if it would float away if he touched it. The bedroom door had been closed. The earth's great chugging machinelike noise went on.

The sound grew louder as he approached the bedroom door. A great confusion went through him like a fog.

204

He stood in the moonlight-flooded room with his hand frozen to the knob and gulped down fire. A certain terrible knowledge had come to him: the rasping sound that had awakened him was the sound of his mother's breathing, a relentless struggle to draw in air and then force it out again. Fee nearly passed out on the spot—the cloud of confusion had left him so swiftly that it was as if he had been stripped. He had thought his mother was dead, but now she was going to have to die all over again.

He turned the knob and opened the door, and the rattling sounds not only became louder but *increased in size and mass.* Inside the Beldame Oriental, you paused while your eyes adjusted to the darkness. Lightly counterpointing the noises of his mother's body attempting to keep itself alive came the milder sounds of his father's snores.

He stepped into the bedroom, and the shapes before him gradually coalesced and solidified. His mother lay with her hands on her chest, her face pointed to the ceiling. It sounded as if, length by length, something long and rough and reluctantly surrendered were being torn out of her. Faceup on the mattress to the right of the bed, clad only in white boxer shorts, lay his father's pale, muscular body, an arm curved over the top of his head, a leg bent at the knee. A constellation of beer bottles fanned out beside his mattress.

Fee wiped his hands over his eyes and finally saw that his mother's hands shook up and down with the rapid regular quiver of a small animal's heartbeat. He reached out and lay his fingers on her forearm. It moved with the same quick pulse as her hands. Another ragged inhalation negotiated air into his mother, and when he tightened his hold on her arm, invisible hands tore the breath out of her. The little boat his mother rowed was now only the tiniest speck on the black water.

His mother's body seemed as long as a city block. How could he do anything to affect what was happening to that body? The hands curling into her chest were as big as his head. The nails that sprouted from those hands were longer than his fingers. Her chin separated volumes of darkness. His mother's face was as wide as a map. All of this size and power shrank him—her struggle erased him, breath by breath.

The hands on her breasts jittered on. The sounds of taking in and releasing air no longer seemed to have anything to do with breathing. They were the sounds of combat, of scores of men dying at either hand, of heavy feet thudding into the earth, of shells destroying ancient trees, of aircraft moving through the sky. Men groaned on a battlefield. The air was pink with shell-burst. Garish yellow tracers ripped across it.

Fee opened his eyes. His mother's body *was* a battlefield. Her feet trembled beneath the sheet; her breathing settled into a raspy inhuman chug. He reached out to touch her arm again, and the arm danced away from his fingers. He wailed in loneliness and terror, but the sounds coming from her mouth obliterated his cry. Her arms shot up three or four inches and slammed down onto her body. Two fingernails cracked off with sharp popping sounds like the snapping of chicken hones. The long yellow fingernails rolled down the sheet and clicked together at the side of the bed. Fee felt that whatever was happening inside his mother was also happening to him. He could feel the great hands reaching down inside him, grasping his essence and tearing it out.

For an instant, she stopped moving. Her hands hung in the air with their fingernails intertwined; her feet were planted flat on the mattress; her hips floated up. Her feet skidded out, and her hips collapsed back to the bed. The sheet drifted down to her waist. The smell of blood filled the room. His mother's hands fell back on her breasts, and the rumpled sheet turned a deep red which soaked down to her knees. At her waist, blood darkened and rose through the gathered sheet.

Something inside his mother made a soft ripping sound.

Her breathing began again in midbeat, softer than before. Fee could feel the enormous hands within him pulling harder at some limp, exhausted thing. Groans rose from the ruined earth. Her breathing moved in and out like a freight train. His own breath pounded in and out with hers.

Her hands settled into the sides of her chest. The long nails clicked. He looked for, but did not see, the broken fingernails that had rolled toward him—he was afraid to look down and see them curling beside his naked feet. If he had stepped on them, he would have screeched like an owl.

He pulled in a searing rush of air. Blood and death dragged themselves far into his body and snagged on his flesh so that they stayed behind when he exhaled in time with his mother. Somehow blood had coated his hands, and he left dark prints on the bed.

The rhythm of their breathing halted. His heart halted, too. The giant hands damped down inside his mother's body. A breath caught in her throat and pushed itself out with a sharp exclamation. He and his mother drew in a ragged lungful of blood and death and released a mouthful of steam.

The little rower on the black lake trembled on the horizon.

Sips of air entered her mouth, paused, and got lost. She took in two, waited, waited, and released one. A long time passed. Amazed, he noticed feeble daylight leaking into the room. Her mouth was furry with labor and dehydration. His mother took another sip of air and lost it inside herself. She did not take another.

Fee observed that he had left his body and could see himself standing by the bed.

He waited, not breathing, for what would happen next. He saw that he was smaller than he had imagined, and that beneath the streaks of blood on his face, he looked blank with fear. Bruises covered his chest, arms, and back. He saw himself gripping his mother's arm—he had not known he was doing that.

A ripple moved through his mother's body, beginning near her ankles and passing up her legs and into her hips. It rolled through her belly and entered her chest. Those powerful hands had found what they wanted, and now they would never let go of it.

Her face tightened as if around a bad taste. Both of them, his body and himself standing beside his body, leaned over the bed. The movement made its way into her throat, then moved like a current up into her head. Something inside him grabbed his essential substance and squeezed. His feet left the ground. A silent explosion transformed the shape and pressure of the air, transformed color, transformed everything. A final twitch cleared her forehead of lines, her head came to rest on the pillow, and it was over. For a moment he saw or thought he saw some small white thing move rapidly toward the ceiling. Fee was back in his body. He reeled back from the bed.

His father said, "Hey? Huh?"

Fee screamed—he had forgotten that his father was on the other side of the bed.

Bob Bandolier's puffy face appeared above the midpoint of the body on the bed. He rubbed his eyes, then took in the bloody sheet. He staggered to his feet. "Get out of here, Fee. This is no place for you."

"Mom is dead," Fee said.

His father moved around the bed so quickly that Fee did not see him move at all—he simply appeared beside him and pushed him toward the door. "Do what I say, right now."

Fee walked out of the bedroom.

His father yelled, "She's going to be okay!"

Fee moved on damp, cold feet to the chaise and lay down.

"Close your eyes," his lather said.

Obediently, Fee closed his eyes. When he heard the bedroom door close, he opened them again. The sheet made a wet, sloppy sound when it hit the floor. Fee let himself revisit what had happened. He heard the inhuman, chugging noise come out of his throat. He drummed his feet against the back of the chaise. Something in his stomach flipped into the back of his throat and filled his mouth with the taste of vomit. In his mind, he leaned over and smoothed the wrinkles from his mother's forehead.

The bedroom door banged open, and he closed his eyes.

Bob Bandolier came walking fast through the living room. "You ought to be in bed," he said, but without heat. Fee kept his eyes shut. His father went into the kitchen. Water gushed from the tap: a drawer opened, an object rustled against other objects, the drawer closed. All this had happened before, therefore it was comforting. In Fee's mind Charlie Carpenter stood at the wheel of his motorboat and sped across the glossy lake. A bearded man in Arab dress lifted his head and took into his mouth the last drop from an enormous cup. The warm liquid fell on his tongue like bread, but burned as he swallowed it. His father carried a sloshing pail past him, and the pail exuded the surpassing sweetness and cleanliness of the dishwashing soap. The bedroom door slammed shut, and Fee opened his eyes again.

They were still open when Bob Bandolier walked out with the bucket and sponge in one hand, a huge red wad wrapped in the dripping rubber sheet under the other arm. "I have to talk to you," he said to Fee. "After I get this stuff downstairs."

Fee nodded. His father walked toward the kitchen and the basement stairs.

Downstairs, the washing machine gurgled and hummed. Footsteps came up the stairs, the door closed. There came the sound of cupboard doors, of liquid gurgling from a bottle. Bob Bandolier came back into the living room. He was wearing a stretched-out T-shirt and striped boxer shorts, and he was carrying a glass half full of whiskey. His hair stood up on the crown of his head, and his face was still puffy.

"This isn't easy, kid." He looked around for somewhere to sit, and moved backward three or four feet to lower himself into a chair. He swung his eyes up at Fee and sipped from the glass. "We did our best, we did everything we could, but it just didn't pan out. This is going to be hard on both of us, but we can help each other out. We can be buddies." He drank without taking his eyes from Fee.

"Okay?"

"Okay."

"All that help and love we gave your mother—it didn't do the job." He took a swallow of his drink, and this time lowered his eyes before raising them again to Fee's. "She passed away last night. It was very peaceful She did not suffer, Fee."

"Oh," Fee said.

"When you were trying to get her attention in there, before I chased you out, she was already gone. She was already in heaven."

"Uh-huh," Fee said.

Bob Bandolier dropped his head and looked down for a little time. He scratched his head. He swallowed more whiskey. "It's hard to believe." He shook his head. "That it could end like this. That woman." He looked away, then turned back to Fee with tears in his eyes. "That woman, she loved me. She was the best. Lots of people think they know me, but your mother knew what I was really capable of—for good and bad." Another shake of the head. He wiped his eyes. "Anna, Anna was what a wife should be. She was what *people* should be. She was *obedient*. She knew the meaning of *duty*. She didn't question my decisions more than three, four times in all the years we spent together, she was *clean*, she could *cook*..." He raised his wet eyes. "And she was one hell of a mother to you, Fee. Never forget that. There was never a dirty floor in this house."

He put down his glass and covered his face with his hands. Suffocated sobs leaked through his fingers.

"This isn't over," his father said. "This isn't over by a long shot."

Fee sighed.

"I know who's to blame," his father said to the floor. "Then he raised his head. "How do you think this all started?"

Fee said nothing.

"A hotshot at the St. Alwyn Hotel decided that he didn't need me anymore. *That* is when the trouble started. And why did I miss some time at the job? Because I had to take care of my wife."

He grinned at nothing. "They didn't have the simple decency to understand that a man has to take care of his wife." His ghastly smile was like a convulsion. "But my campaign has started, sonny boy. I have fired the first shot. Let them pay heed." He leaned forward. "And the next time *I won't be interrupted.*

"She didn't only die," Bob Bandolier said. "The St. Alwyn killed her." He finished his whiskey, and his face convulsed again. "They didn't *get* it. In sickness as in health, you know? And they think someone else can do Bob Bandolier's job. You think they asked the guests? They did not. They could have asked that nigger saxophone player—even *him*. Glenroy Breakstone. Every night that man said, 'Good evening, Mr. Bandolier,'

when he wouldn't waste two words on anyone else—
thought he was too important. But he paid his respects
to me, he did. Did they want to know? Well, now
they're going to find out. Things are going to happen."
He composed his face. "It's my whole life—like that
woman in there."

He stood up. "Now there's things to do. Your mom
is dead, but the world goes on."

All of a sudden the truth came to Fee. He was one-
half dead himself; half of him belonged to his dead
mother. His father went to the telephone. "We're going
to be all right. Everybody else, watch out." He peered
at the telephone for a second, trying to remember a
number, then dialed.

The Sunchanas began walking around their bedroom.

"Dr. Hudson, this is Bob Bandolier." His imitation of a smile appeared and disappeared. "I know it's
early, Hudson. I'm not calling to pass the time of day.
Do you know where I live?...Because....Yes, I'm serious.
You better believe I'm serious."

Fee got off the chaise. He bent down and picked
up fat black Jude, who began purring. His hands and
arms were still covered with drying blood, and his fingers showed red against the black fur.

"Because I need you here right now, old pal. My
wife died during the night, and I need a death certifi-
cate so I can take care of her."

Long individual cat hairs adhered to the backs of
Fee's fingers.

"Hudson."

Overhead, a toilet flushed.

Fee carried Jude to the window.

"Hudson, listen to me. Remember how I covered your ass? I was the *night manager,* I know what goes on."

Fee wiped his eyes and looked out the window. Some invisible person was out there, looking in.

"I'd say you were a busy boy, that's what was going on."

"Call it heart disease," his father said.

Jude could see the invisible person. Jude had always seen the invisible people—they were nothing new to her. The Sunchanas moved around in their bedroom, getting dressed.

"We'll cremate," his father said.

For some reason, Fee blushed.

"Hello, give me Mr. Ledwell," his father said. "I'm Bob Bandolier. Mr. Ledwell? Bob Bandolier. I'm sorry to have to say that my wife passed away during the night and unless I am *absolutely* required, I'd like to stay home today. There are many arrangements to make, and I have a young son....She'd been ill, yes, sir, gravely ill, but it's still a great tragedy for the two of us...."

Fee's eyes filled, and a tear slipped down his cheek. Held too tightly, Jude uttered a high-pitched cry of irritation and sank a claw into Fee's forearm.

"That is much appreciated, sir," said Bob Bandolier. He put down the phone and in a different voice said, "That old lush of a doctor will be here as soon as he can find a whole suit from the clothes on the floor. We have work to do, so stop crying and get dressed. Hear me?"

9

BOB BANDOLIER OPENED the door as Mr. Sunchana was leaving for work, and Fee saw their upstairs neighbors take in their undistinguished-looking visitor: the black bag, the wrinkled suit, the cigarette burned down to his lips. Dr. Hudson was shown to the bedroom and escorted in.

When Dr. Hudson came back out of the bedroom, he looked at his watch and began filling out a printed form at the dining room table. Bob Bandolier supplied his wife's maiden name (Dymczeck), date of birth (August 16, 1928), place if birth (Azure, Ohio). The cause of death was respiratory failure.

Half an hour after the doctor left, two men in dark suits arrived to wrap Fee's mother in the sheet that covered her and carry her away on a stretcher.

Bob Bandolier shaved twice, giving his face a military glaze. He dressed in a dark blue suit. He took a shot of whiskey while he looked through the knife drawer. Finally he slipped a black-handled paring knife into the pocket of his suit jacket. He put on his dark overcoat and told Fee that he would be home soon. He let himself out of the apartment and locked the door behind him.

An hour later, he returned in a mood so foul that when he struck Fee, his son could tell that he was being beaten simply because he was within reach. It had nothing to do with him. To keep the Sunchanas from hearing, he tried to keep silent. Anger made Bob Bandolier so clumsy that he cut himself taking the paring knife out of his pocket. Bob Bandolier raged and stamped his feet and wrapped his finger in tissue paper—another outburst when he could not find bandages, I can't find any bandages, don't we even have any god-damned *bandages*? He opened a fresh bottle and poured drink after drink after drink.

In the morning, Bob Bandolier dressed in the same blue suit and returned to the Hotel Hepton. Fee, who had said he was too sick to go to the movies, spent the day waiting to see the invisible people.

Some nights later, Bob remembered to cook dinner, and long after the moon had risen and his son lay in a semiconscious stupor on the living room rug, sucking on his pain as if on a piece of candy, he returned to the knife drawer in ruminating, well-fed, well-exercised fashion, and selected a six-inch blade with a carved wooden handle. Many hours later, Fee came awake long enough to register that his father was actually carrying him to bed, and knew at once from the exultant triumph he saw in his father's handsome face that late at night, when no one had

seen him, Bob Bandolier had gone back to the St.
Alwyn Hotel.

Their life became regular again. Bob Bandolier left
sandwiches on the table and locked the door behind
him—he seemed to have forgotten about the Beldame
Oriental, or to have decided that going to and from
the theater exposed his son to unwelcome attention
from the neighbors: better to lock him up and leave
him alone.

One night Fee awakened when his father picked
him up from the chaise, and when he saw the gleeful
face burning over his, he knew again that his father
had been to the hotel he hated: that his father hated
the St. Alwyn because he loved it, and that this time at
least he had managed to get inside it.

Sometimes it was as if Fee had never had a mother
at all. Now and then he saw the cat staring at empty air,
and knew that Jude could see one of the people from
the invisible world. *From Dangerous Depths* returned
to him, and alone in the empty room he played at being
Charlie Carpenter—Charlie killing the big dog, Charlie
stepping away from the wall to batter William Bendix
to death, Charlie dying while Lily Sheehan smiled.

After his father gave him a box of crayons and a
pad of paper left behind by a guest at the Hepton, Fee
spent days drawing pictures of enormous feet smashing
houses, feet crushing men and women, crushing whole
cities, of people sprawled dead in bomb craters and
encampments as a pair of giant feet walked away. He

hid these drawings beneath his bed. Once he lowered a drawing of a naked foot onto his exposed penis and nearly fainted from a combination of bliss and terror. He was Charlie Carpenter, living out Charlie Carpenter's secret history.

Whenever he saw the Sunchanas, either alone or with his father, they fled behind their front door. Bob Bandolier said: "Never uttered a word about your mother, never dropped a card or paid her the honor of making a telephone call. People like that are no better than animals."

On the night of October twenty-fifth, Bob Bandolier came home from work restless and impatient despite the two steaks and the bottle of whiskey he had in a big brown bag, and he slapped his son almost as soon as he took off his coat. He fried the steaks and drank the whiskey from the bottle. Every ten minutes he left the table to check on the state of his collar, the perfection of the knot in his necktie, the gloss of his mustache. The Hotel Hepton, once second only to the Pforzheimer, was a "sewer," a "sty." He could see it now. They thought they knew what it was all about, but the penny-pinching assholes didn't have the first idea. They get a first-class hotel man, and what do they do to him? Give him lectures. Suggest he say less to the guests. Even the St. Alwyn, even the *St. Alwyn,* the hotel that had done the greatest damage to him, the hotel that had *insulted and injured* him, had *actually managed to kill his wife,* hadn't been so stupid. Maybe he ought to "switch operations," "change the battle-field," "carry the fight into another theater." You give and give, and *this*—this humiliation—was how they repaid you.

|||||||||||||||||||||||||||||||||||||||||||||

STARING THROUGH THE window the next morning, Fee finally glimpsed one of the invisible people. He nearly fainted. She was a pale, unhappy-looking blond woman, a woman who had seemed ghostly even when she had been alive. She had come to see him, Fee knew. She was looking for him—as if his lost mother were trying to find him. The second that the tears came into his eyes, the woman on the sidewalk vanished. Hurriedly, almost guiltily, he wiped the tears off his face. If he could, he would have gone through the door and followed her—straight to the St. Alwyn Hotel, for that was where she was going.

|||||||||||||||||||||||||||||||||||||||||||||

THE NEXT GREAT change in Fee's life began after his father discovered his drawings. In the midst of the whirlwind caused by this next change, for the second time an inhabitant of the invisible world appeared before Fee, in a form and manner suggesting that he had caused a death.

It BEGAN AS a calm dinner. There was the "hypocritical lowlife" who gave orders to Bob Bandolier, there was an "untrustworthy and corrupt" colleague, there were mentions of the fine Christian woman Anna Bandolier had been—Fee warmed his hands at the fire of his father's loves and hates. In the midst of the pleasure he took from this warmth, he realized that his father had asked him a question. He asked to hear it again.

"Whatever happened to the drawing paper and those crayons I gave you? That stuff costs money, you know."

It had not cost Bob Bandolier any money, but that was secondary: the loss or waste of the precious materials would be a crime. You did not have to want to be bad to succeed in being as bad as possible.

"I don't know," Fee said, but his eyes shifted sideways.

"Oh, you don't know," said Bob Bandolier, his manner transformed in an instant. Fee was very close now to being beaten, but a beating was preferable to having his father see his drawings.

"You expect me to believe that?"

Again Fee glanced toward the hallway and his bedroom. His father jumped out of his chair, leaned across the table, and pushed him over in his chair.

Bob Bandolier rushed around the table and pulled him up by his collar. "Are you so goddamned stupid you think you can get away with lying to me?"

Fee blubbered and whined, and his father pulled him into the hallway.

"You could have made it easy for yourself, but you made it hard. What did you do? Break the crayons? Tear up the paper?"

Fee shook his head, trying to work out how much truth he could give his father without showing him the drawings.

"Then show me." His father pulled him into his room and pushed him toward the bed. "Where are they?"

Again Fee could not avoid self-betrayal: he looked beneath his bed.

"I see."

Fee wailed *nooo,* and scrambled under the bed in a crazy attempt to protect the drawings with his own body.

Swearing, his father got down on the floor, reached beneath the bed, grabbed Fee's arm, and pulled him out. Sweating, struggling Fee threw his armful of drawings into the room and feebly struck his father. He tried to charge out of his arms to destroy the drawings—he wanted to cram them into his mouth, rip them to confetti, escape through the front door and run down the block.

For a time they were both roaring and screaming. Fee ran out of breath, but he continued to writhe.

His father hit him on the ear and said, "I should rip your heart out."

Fee went limp—the drawings lay all about them, waiting to be seen. Bob Bandolier's attention went out to the images on the big pieces of paper. Then he put Fee down and bent to pick up the two drawings closest to him.

Fee hid his face in his arms.

"Feet," his father said. "What the hell? I don't get it."

He moved around the room, turning over the pictures. He flipped one over and displayed it to Fee: the giant's feet striding away from a flattened movie theater.

"You are going to tell me what this is about, right now."

An absolutely unprecedented thing happened to Fee Bandolier: he opened his mouth and spoke words over which he had no control at all. Someone else inside him spoke these words. Fee heard them as they proceeded from his mouth, but forgot them as soon as they were uttered.

FINALLY HE HAD said it all, though he could not have repeated a single word if he had been held over a fire. His father's face had turned red. Troubled in some absolutely new way, Bob Bandolier seemed uncertain whether to comfort Fee or to beat him up. He could no longer meet Fee's eyes. He wandered around the room, picking up scattered drawings. After a few seconds he dropped them back onto the floor.

"Pick these up. Then get rid of them. I never want to see any of this ever again."

The first sign of the change was in Bob Bandolier's new attitude toward his son. For Fee, the new attitude suggested that he had simultaneously become both much better and much worse. His father never struck him anymore, but Fee felt that his father did not want to touch him in any way. Days and nights passed almost wordlessly. Fee began to feel that he too had become invisible, at least to his father. Bob Bandolier drank, but instead of talking he read and reread that morning's copy of the *Ledger*.

On the night of November seventh, the closing of the front door awakened Fee. From the perfect quiet in the apartment, he knew his father had just gone out. He was sleeping again when his father returned.

The following morning, Fee turned toward his bedroom window as he zipped up his pants, and all the breath seemed to leave his body. A dark-haired boy roughly his own age stood looking in from the little front lawn. He had been waiting for Fee to notice him, but made no effort to communicate. He did not have to. The boy's plaid shirt was too large for him, as if he had stolen or scrounged it. His dirty tan trousers ended above his ankles. On a cold November morning in Millhaven, his feet were bare. The dark eyes beneath the scrappy black hair burned angrily, and the sallow face was frozen with rage. He seemed to quiver with feeling, but Fee had the oddest conviction that all this feeling was not about him—it concerned someone else. The boy had come because of a complicity, an understanding, between them. Dirty, battered-looking, he stared in to find his emotions matched by Fielding Bandolier. But Fielding Bandolier could not match the feelings that came streaming from the boy: he could only remember the sensation of speaking without willing to speak. Something inside him was weeping and gnashing its teeth, but Fee could scarcely hear it.

If you forgot you were in a movie, your own feelings would tear you into bloody rags.

Fee looked down to fasten the button on his waistband. When he looked back through the window, he saw the boy growing fainter and fainter, like a drawing being erased. Traces of the lawn and sidewalk shone through him. All at once it seemed to Fee that something vastly important, an absolutely precious quantity, was fading from his world. Once this quantity was gone, it would be lost forever. Fee moved toward the window, but by now he could not see the blazing dark eyes, and when he touched the glass the boy had disappeared.

That was all right, he told himself: really, he had lost nothing.

Bob Bandolier spent another evening poring over the *Ledger*, which had a large photograph of Heinz Stenmitz on its front page. He ordered Fee to bed early, and Fee felt that he was being dismissed because his father did not want to have a witness to his anxiety.

For he was anxious—he was nervous. His leg jittered when he sat at the table, and he jumped whenever the telephone rang. The calls that came were never the call that his father feared, but their innocence did not quiet his anxiety. For something like a week, Fee's few attempts to talk to his father met either angry silence or a command to shut up, and Fee knew that only his father's reluctance to touch him saved him from a blow.

Over the following days, Bob Bandolier relaxed. He would forget who was in the room with him, and lapse back into the old talk of the "hypocritical low-life" and the "corrupt gang" that worked with him. Then he would look up from his plate or his newspaper, see his son, and blush with a feeling for which he refused to find words. Fee witnessed the old anger only once, when he walked into Bob Bandolier's bedroom and found him sitting on the bed, leafing through a small stack of papers from the shoe box beside him. His father's face darkened, and his eyes darkened, and for a second Fee knew the sick, familiar thrill of knowing he was to be beaten. The beating did not happen. His father slipped the papers into the shoe box and told him to find something to do in the other room, fast.

|||||||||||||||||||||||||||||||||||||||||||||

BOB BANDOLIER CAME home with the news that the Hepton had let him go—the hypocritical lowlife had finally managed to catch him in the meat locker, and the bastard would not listen to any explanation. It was okay, though. The St. Alwyn was taking him back. After everything he had been through, he wouldn't mind going back to the old St. Alwyn. He had settled his score, and now they could go forward.

He and Fee could not go forward together, however, at least not for a while. It wasn't working. He needed quiet, he had to work things out. Fee needed to have a woman around, he needed to play with other kids. Anna's sister Judy in Azure had written, saying that she and her husband, Arnold, would be willing to take the boy in, if Bob was finding it difficult to raise the boy by himself.

His father stared at his hands as he said all this to Fee, and looked up only when he had reached this point.

"It's all arranged."

Bob Bandolier turned his head to look at the window, the porcelain figures, the sleeping cat, anything but his son. Bob Bandolier detested Judy and Arnold, exactly as he detested Anna's brother, Hank, and his wife, Wilda. Fee understood that his father detested him, too.

Bob Bandolier took Fee to the train station in downtown Millhaven, and in a confusion of color and noise passed him and his cardboard suitcase, along with a five-dollar bill, into the hands of a conductor. Fee rode all the way from Millhaven to Chicago by himself, and in Chicago the pitying conductor made sure he boarded the train to Cleveland. He followed his father's orders and talked to no one during the long journey through Illinois and Ohio, though several people, chiefly elderly women, spoke to him. At Cleveland,

Judy and Arnold Leatherwood were waiting for him, and drove the sleeping boy the remaining two hundred miles to Azure.

10

THE REST CAN be told quickly. Though nothing frightening or truly upsetting ever happened—nothing *overt*—the Leatherwoods, who had expected to love their nephew unreservedly and had been overjoyed to claim him from the peculiar and unpleasant man who had married Judy Leatherwood's sister, found that Fee Bandolier made them more uncomfortable with every month he lived in their house. He screamed himself awake two or three nights a week, but could not describe what frightened him. The boy refused to talk about his mother. Not long after Christmas, Judy Leatherwood found a pile of disturbing drawings beneath Fee's bed, but the boy denied having drawn them. He insisted that *someone had sneaked them into his room,* and he became so wild-eyed and terrified that Judy dropped the subject. In February, a neighbor's dog was found stabbed to death in an empty lot down the street. A month later, a neighborhood cat was discovered with its throat slashed open in a ditch two blocks away. Fee spent most of his time sitting quietly in a chair in a corner of the living room, looking into space. At night,

sometimes the Leatherwoods could hear him breathing in a loud, desperate way that made them want to
put the pillows over their heads. When Judy discovered
that she was pregnant that April, she and Arnold came
to a silent agreement and asked Hank and Wilda in
Tangent if they could take Fee in for a while.

Fee moved to Tangent and lived in Hank and Wilda
Dymczeck's drafty old house with their fifteen-year-
old son, Hank Junior, who regularly beat him up but
otherwise paid little attention to him. Hank was the
vice principal of Tangent's Lawrence B. Freeman High
School and Wilda was a nurse, so they spent less time
with Fee than the Leatherwoods had. If he was a little
quiet, a little reserved, he was still "getting over" his
mother's death. Because he had nowhere else to go,
Fee made an effort to behave in ways other people expected and understood. In time, his nightmares went
away. He found a safe secret place for the things he
wrote and drew. Whenever anyone asked him what he
wanted to be when he grew up, he said he wanted to
be a policeman.

Fee passed through grade school and his uncle's
high school with average grades. A few animals
were found killed (and a few more were not), but Fee
Bandolier was so inconspicuous that no one imagined
that he might be responsible for their deaths. Lance
Torkelson's murder horrified the community, but
Tangent decided that an outsider had killed the boy.
At the end of Fee's senior year, a young woman named

Margaret Loewy disappeared after dropping her two children off at a public swimming pool. Six months later, her mutilated body was discovered buried in the woods beside a remote section of farmland. By that time, Fielding Bandolier had enlisted in the army under another name. Margaret Loewy's breasts, vagina, and cheeks had been sliced off, along with sections of her thighs and buttocks; her womb and ovaries had been removed; traces of semen could still be found in her throat, anus, and abdominal wounds.

Far more successful in basic training than he had ever been in high school, Fee applied for Special Forces training. He dialed his father's telephone number when he learned of his acceptance, and when Bob Bandolier answered by saying "Yes?" Fee held on to the telephone without speaking, without even breathing, until his father cursed and hung up.

The Ghost Village

1

IN VIETNAM I KNEW a man who went quietly and purposefully crazy because his wife wrote him that his son had been sexually abused—"messed with"—by the leader of their church choir. This man was a black six-foot-six grunt named Leonard Hamnet, from a small town in Tennessee named Archibald. Before writing, his wife had waited until she had endured the entire business of going to the police, talking to other parents, returning to the police with another accusation, and finally succeeding in having the man charged. He was up for trial in two months. Leonard Hamnet was no happier about that than he was about the original injury.

"I got to murder him, you know, but I'm seriously thinking on murdering her too," he said. He still held the letter in his hands, and he was speaking to Spanky Burrage, Michael Poole, Conor Linklater, SP4 Cotton, Calvin Hill, Tina Pumo, the magnificent M. O. Dengler, and myself. "All this is going on, my boy needs help, this here Mr. Brewster needs to be dismantled, needs to be *racked* and *stacked,* and she don't tell me! Makes me want to put her *down,* man. Take her damn head off and put it up on a stake in the yard, man. With a sign saying: *Here is one stupid woman.*"

We were in the unofficial part of Camp Crandall known as No Man's Land, located between the wire perimeter and a shack, also unofficial, where a cunning little weasel named Wilson Manly sold contraband beer and liquor. No Man's Land, so called because the C.O. pretended it did not exist, contained a mound of old tires, a piss tube, and a lot of dusty red ground. Leonard Hamnet gave the letter in his hand a dispirited look, folded it into the pocket of his fatigues, and began to roam around the heap of tires, aiming kicks at the ones that stuck out farthest. "One stupid woman," he repeated. Dust exploded up from a burst, worn-down wheel of rubber.

I wanted to make sure Hamnet knew he was angry with Mr. Brewster, not his wife, and said, "She was trying—"

Hamnet's great glistening bull's head turned toward me.

"Look at what the woman did. She nailed that bastard. She got other people to admit that he messed with their kids too. That must be almost impossible. And she had the guy arrested. He's going to be put away for a long time."

"I'll put that bitch away, too," Hamnet said, and kicked an old gray tire hard enough to push it nearly a foot back into the heap. All the other tires shuddered and moved. For a second it seemed that the entire mound might collapse.

"This is my *boy* I'm talking about here," Hamnet said. "This shit has gone far enough."

"The important thing," Dengler said, "is to take care of your boy. You have to see he gets help."

"How'm I gonna do that from here?" Hamnet shouted.

"Write him a letter," Dengler said. "Tell him you love him. Tell him he did right to go to his mother. Tell him you think about him all the time."

Hamnet took the letter from his pocket and stared at it. It was already stained and wrinkled. I did not think it could survive many more of Hamnet's readings. His face seemed to get heavier, no easy trick with a face like Hamnet's. "I got to get home," he said. "I got to get back home and take care of these people."

Hamnet began putting in requests for compassionate leave relentlessly—one request a day. When we were out on patrol, sometimes I saw him unfold the tattered sheet of notepaper from his shirt pocket and read it two or three times, concentrating intensely. When the letter began to shred along the folds, Hamnet taped it together.

We were going out on four- and five-day patrols during that period, taking a lot of casualties. Hamnet performed well in the field, but he had retreated so far within himself that he spoke in mono-syllables. He wore a dull, glazed look, and moved like a man who had just eaten a heavy dinner. I thought he looked like a man who had given up, and when people gave up they did not last long—they were already very close to death, and other people avoided them.

We were camped in a stand of trees at the edge of a paddy. That day we had lost two men so new that I had already forgotten their names. We had to eat cold C rations because heating them with C-4 would have been like putting up billboards and arc lights. We couldn't smoke, and we were not supposed to talk. Hamnet's C rations consisted of an old can of Spam that dated from an earlier war and a can of peaches. He saw Spanky staring at the peaches and tossed him the can. Then he dropped the Spam between his legs. Death was almost visible around him. He fingered the note out of his pocket and tried to read it in the damp gray twilight.

At that moment someone started shooting at us, and the Lieutenant yelled *"Shit!"* and we dropped our food and returned fire at the invisible people trying to kill us. When they kept shooting back, we had to go through the paddy.

The warm water came up to our chests. At the dikes, we scrambled over and splashed down into the muck on the other side. A boy from Santa Cruz, California, named Thomas Blevins got a round in the back of his neck and dropped dead into the water just short of the first dike, and another boy named Tyrell Budd coughed and dropped down right beside him. The F.O. called in an artillery strike. We leaned against the backs of the last two dikes when the big shells came thudding in. The ground shook and the water rippled, and the edge of the forest went up in a series of fireballs. We could hear the monkeys screaming.

One by one we crawled over the last dike onto the damp but solid ground on the other side of the paddy. Here the trees were much sparser, and a little group of thatched huts was visible through them.

Then two things I did not understand happened, one after the other. Someone off in the forest fired a mortar round at us—just one. One mortar, one round. That was the first thing. I fell down and shoved my face in the muck, and everybody around me did the same. I considered that this might be my last second on earth, and greedily inhaled whatever life might be left to me. Whoever fired the mortar should have had an excellent idea of our location, and I experienced that endless moment of pure, terrifying helplessness—a moment in which the soul simultaneously clings to the body and readies itself to let go of it—until the shell landed on top of the last dike and blew it to bits. Dirt, mud, and water slopped down around us, and shell fragments whizzed through the air. One of the fragments sailed over us, sliced a hamburger-size wad of bark and wood from a tree, and clanged into Spanky Burrage's helmet with a sound like a brick hitting a garbage can. The fragment fell to the ground, and a little smoke drifted up from it.

We picked ourselves up. Spanky looked dead, except that he was breathing. Hamnet shouldered his pack and picked up Spanky and slung him over his shoulder. He saw me looking at him.

"I gotta take *care* of these people," he said.

The other thing I did not understand—apart from why there had been only one mortar round—came when we entered the village.

Lieutenant Harry Beevers had yet to join us, and we were nearly a year away from the events at Ia Thuc, when everything, the world and ourselves within the world, went crazy. I have to explain what happened. Lieutenant Harry Beevers killed thirty children in a cave at Ia Thuc and their bodies disappeared, but Michael Poole and I went into that cave and knew that something obscene had happened in there. We smelled evil, we touched its wings with our hands. A pitiful character named Victor Spitalny ran into the cave when he heard gunfire, and came pinwheeling out right away, screaming, covered with welts or hives that vanished almost as soon as he came out into the air. Poor Spitalny had touched it too. Because I was twenty and already writing books in my head, I thought that the cave was the place where the other *Tom Sawyer* ended, where Injun Joe raped Becky Thatcher and slit Tom's throat.

THE GHOST VILLAGE

When we walked into the little village in the woods on the other side of the rice paddy, I experienced a kind of foretaste of Ia Thuc. If I can say this without setting off all the Gothic bells, the place seemed intrinsically, inherently wrong—it was too quiet, too still, completely without noise or movement. There were no chickens, dogs, or pigs; no old women came out to look us over, no old men offered conciliatory smiles. The little huts, still inhabitable, were empty—something I had never seen before in Vietnam, and never saw again. It was a ghost village, in a country where people thought the earth was sanctified by their ancestors' bodies.

Poole's map said that the place was named Bong To.

Hamnet lowered Spanky into the long grass as soon as we reached the center of the empty village. I bawled out a few words in my poor Vietnamese.

Spanky groaned. He gently touched the sides of his helmet. "I caught a head wound," he said.

"You wouldn't have a head at all, you was only wearing your liner," Hamnet said.

Spanky bit his lips and pushed the helmet up off his head. He groaned. A finger of blood ran down beside his ear. Finally the helmet passed over a lump the size of an apple that rose up from under his hair. Wincing, Spanky fingered this enormous knot. "I see double," he said. "I'll never get that helmet back on."

The medic said, "Take it easy, we'll get you out of here."

"Out of *here?*" Spanky brightened up.

"Back to Crandall," the medic said.

Spitalny sidled up, and Spanky frowned at him. "There ain't nobody here," Spitalny said. "What the fuck is going on?" He took the emptiness of the village as a personal affront.

Leonard Hamnet turned his back and spat.

"Spitalny, Tiano," the Lieutenant said. "Go into the paddy and get Tyrell and Blevins. Now."

Tattoo Tiano, who was due to die six and a half months later and was Spitalny's only friend, said, "You do it this time, Lieutenant."

Hamnet turned around and began moving toward Tiano and Spitalny. He looked as if he had grown two sizes larger, as if his hands could pick up boulders. I had forgotten how big he was. His head was lowered, and a rim of clear white showed above the irises. I wouldn't have been surprised if he had blown smoke from his nostrils.

"Hey, I'm gone, I'm already there," Tiano said. He and Spitalny began moving quickly through the sparse trees. Whoever had fired the mortar had packed up and gone. By now it was nearly dark, and the mosquitoes had found us.

"So?" Poole said.

Hamnet sat down heavily enough for me to feel the shock in my boots. He said, "I have to go home, Lieutenant. I don't mean no disrespect, but I cannot take this shit much longer."

The Lieutenant said he was working on it.

Poole, Hamnet, and I looked around at the village.

Spanky Burrage said, "Good quiet place for Ham to catch up on his reading."

"Maybe I better take a look," the Lieutenant said. He flicked the lighter a couple of times and walked off toward the nearest hut. The rest of us stood around like fools, listening to the mosquitoes and the sounds of Tiano and Spitalny pulling the dead men up over the dikes. Every now and then Spanky groaned and shook his head. Too much time passed.

The Lieutenant said something almost inaudible from inside the hut. He came back outside in a hurry, looking disturbed and puzzled even in the darkness.

"Underhill, Poole," he said, "I want you to see this."

Poole and I glanced at each other. I wondered if I looked as bad as he did. Poole seemed to be a couple of psychic inches from either taking a poke at the Lieutenant or exploding altogether. In his muddy face his eyes were the size of hen's eggs. He was wound up like a cheap watch. I thought that I probably looked pretty much the same.

"What is it, Lieutenant?" he asked.

The Lieutenant gestured for us to come to the hut, then turned around and went back inside. There was no reason for us not to follow him. The Lieutenant was a jerk, but Harry Beevers, our next lieutenant, was a baron, an earl among jerks, and we nearly always did whatever dumb thing he told us to do. Poole was so ragged and edgy that he looked as if he felt like shooting the Lieutenant in the back. *I* felt like shooting the Lieutenant in the back, I realized a second later. I didn't have an idea in the world what was going on in Poole's mind. I grumbled something and moved toward the hut. Poole followed.

The Lieutenant was standing in the doorway, looking over his shoulder and fingering his sidearm. He frowned at us to let us know we had been slow to obey him, then flicked on the lighter. The sudden hollows and shadows in his face made him resemble one of the corpses I had opened up when I was in graves registration at Camp White Star.

"You want to know what it is, Poole? Okay, you tell me what it is."

He held the lighter before him like a torch and marched into the hut. I imagined the entire dry, flimsy structure bursting into heat and flame. This Lieutenant was not destined to get home walking and breathing, and I pitied and hated him about equally, but I did not want to turn into toast because he had found an American body inside a hut and didn't know what to do about it. I'd heard of platoons finding the mutilated corpses of American prisoners, and hoped that this was not our turn.

And then, in the instant before I smelled blood and saw the Lieutenant stoop to lift a panel on the floor, I thought that what had spooked him was not the body of an American POW but of a child who had been murdered and left behind in this empty place. The

Lieutenant had probably not seen any dead children yet. Some part of the Lieutenant was still worrying about what a girl named Becky Roddenburger was getting up to back at Idaho State, and a dead child would be too much reality for him.

He pulled up the wooden panel in the floor, and I caught the smell of blood. The Zippo died, and darkness closed down on us. The Lieutenant yanked the panel back on its hinges. The smell of blood floated up from whatever was beneath the floor. The Lieutenant flicked the Zippo, and his face jumped out of the darkness. "Now. Tell me what this is."

"It's where they hide the kids when people like us show up," I said. "Smells like something went wrong. Did you take a look?"

I saw in his tight cheeks and almost lipless mouth that he had not. He wasn't about to go down there and get killed by the Minotaur while his platoon stood around outside.

"Taking a look is your job, Underhill," he said.

For a second we both looked at the ladder, made of peeled branches leashed together with rags, that led down into the pit.

"Give me the lighter," Poole said, and grabbed it away from the Lieutenant. He sat on the edge of the hole and leaned over, bringing the flame beneath the level of the floor. He grunted at whatever he saw, and surprised both the Lieutenant and myself by pushing himself off the ledge into the opening. The light went out. The Lieutenant and I looked down into the dark open rectangle in the floor.

The lighter flared again. I could see Poole's extended arm, the jittering little fire, a packed-earth floor. The top of the concealed room was less than an inch above the top of Poole's head. He moved away from the opening.

"What is it? Are there any—" The Lieutenant's voice made a creaky sound. "Any bodies?"

"Come down here, Tim," Poole called up.

I sat on the floor and swung my legs into the pit. Then I jumped down.

Beneath the floor, the smell of blood was almost sickeningly strong.

"What do you see?" the Lieutenant shouted. He was trying to sound like a leader, and his voice squeaked on the last word.

I saw an empty room shaped like a giant grave. The walls were covered by some kind of thick paper held in place by wooden struts sunk into the earth. Both the thick brown paper and two of the struts showed old bloodstains.

"Hot," Poole said, and closed the lighter.

"Come *on*, damn it," came the Lieutenant's voice. "Get out of there."

"Yes, sir," Poole said. He flicked the lighter back on. Many layers of thick paper formed an absorbent pad between the earth and the room, and the topmost, thinnest layer had been covered with vertical lines of Vietnamese writing. The writing looked like poetry, like the left-hand pages of Kenneth Rexroth's translations of Tu Fu and Li Po.

"Well, well," Poole said, and I turned to see him pointing at what first looked like intricately woven strands of rope fixed to the blood-stained wooden uprights. Poole stepped forward and the weave jumped into sharp relief. About four feet off the ground, iron chains had been screwed to the uprights. The thick pad between the two lengths of chain had been soaked with blood. The three feet of ground between the posts looked rusty. Poole moved the lighter closer to the chains, and we saw dried blood on the metal links.

"I want you guys out of there, and I mean *now*," whined the Lieutenant.

Poole slapped the lighter shut.

"I just changed my mind," I said softly. "I'm putting twenty bucks into the Elijah fund. For two weeks from today. That's what, June twentieth?"

"Tell it to Spanky," he said. Spanky Burrage had invented the pool we called the Elijah fund, and he held the money. Michael had not put any money into the pool. He thought that a new lieutenant might be even worse than the one we had. Of course he was right. Harry Beevers was our next lieutenant. Elijah Joys, Lieutenant Elijah Joys of New Utrecht, Idaho, a graduate of the University of Idaho and basic training at Fort Benning, Georgia, was an inept, weak lieutenant, not a disastrous one. If Spanky could have seen what was coming, he would have given back the money and prayed for the safety of Lieutenant Joys.

Poole and I moved back toward the opening. I felt as if I had seen a shrine to an obscene deity. The Lieutenant leaned over and stuck out his hand— uselessly, because he did not bend down far enough for us to reach him. We levered ourselves up out of the hole stiff-armed, as if we were leaving a swimming pool. The Lieutenant stepped back. He had a thin face and thick, fleshy nose, and his Adam's apple danced around in his neck like a jumping bean. He might not have been Harry Beevers, but he was no prize. "Well, how many?"

"How many what?" I asked.

"How many are there?" He wanted to go back to Camp Crandall with a good body count.

"There weren't exactly any bodies, Lieutenant," said Poole, trying to let him down easily. He described what we had seen.

"Well, what's that good for?" he meant, *How is that going to help me?*

"Interrogations, probably," Poole said. "If you questioned someone down there, no one outside the hut would hear anything. At night, you could just drag the body into the woods."

Lieutenant Joys nodded. "Field Interrogation Post," he said, trying out the phrase. "Torture, Use of, Highly Indicated." He nodded again. "Right?"

"Highly," Poole said.

"Shows you what kind of enemy we're dealing with in this conflict."

I could no longer stand being in the same three square feet of space with Elijah Joys, and I took a step toward the door of the hut. I did not know what Poole and I had seen, but I knew it was not a Field Interrogation Post, Torture, Use of, Highly Indicated, unless the Vietnamese had begun to interrogate monkeys. It occurred to me that the writing on the wall might have been names instead of poetry—I thought that we had stumbled into a mystery that had nothing to do with the war, a Vietnamese mystery.

For a second, music from my old life, music too beautiful to be endurable, started playing in my head. Finally I recognized it: "The Walk to the Paradise Garden," from *A Village Romeo and Juliet* by Frederick Delius. Back in Berkeley, I had listened to it hundreds of times.

If nothing else had happened, I think I could have replayed the whole piece in my head. Tears filled my eyes, and I stepped toward the door of the hut. Then I froze. A ragged Vietnamese boy of seven or eight was regarding me with great seriousness from the far corner of the hut. I knew he was not there—I knew he was a spirit. I had no belief in spirits, but that's what he was. Some part of my mind as detached as a crime reporter reminded me that "The Walls to the Paradise Garden" was about two children who were about to die, and that in a sense the music *was* their death. I wiped my eyes with my hand, and when I lowered my arm, the

245

boy was still there. He was beautiful, beautiful in the ordinary way, as Vietnamese children nearly always seemed beautiful to me. Then he vanished all at once, like the flickering light of the Zippo. I nearly groaned aloud. That child had been murdered in the hut: he had not just died, he had been murdered.

I said something to the other two men and went through the door into the growing darkness. I was very dimly aware of the Lieutenant asking Poole to repeat his description of the uprights and the bloody chain. Hamnet and Burrage and Calvin Hill were sitting down and leaning against a tree. Victor Spitalny was wiping his hands on his filthy shirt. White smoke curled up from Hill's cigarette, and Tina Pumo exhaled a long white stream of vapor. The unhinged thought came to me with an absolute conviction that this was the Paradise Garden. The men lounging in the darkness; the pattern of the cigarette smoke, and the patterns they made, sitting or standing; the in-drawing darkness, as physical as a blanket; the frame of the trees and the flat gray-green background of the paddy.

My soul had come back to life.

Then I became aware that there was something wrong about the men arranged before me, and again it tools a moment for my intelligence to catch up to my intuition. Every member of a combat unit makes unconscious adjustments as members of the unit go down in the field; survival sometimes depends on the number of people you know are with you, and you keep count

without being quite aware of doing it. I had registered
that two men too many were in front of me. Instead of
seven, there were nine, and the two men that made up
the nine of us left were still behind me in the hut. M.
O. Dengler was looking at me with growing curiosity,
and I thought to he knew exactly what I was thinking.
A sick chill went through me. I saw Tom Blevins and
Tyrell Budd standing together at the far right of the
platoon, a little muddier than the others but otherwise
different from the rest only in that, like Dengler, they
were looking directly at me.

Hill tossed his cigarette away in an arc of light.
Poole and Lieutenant Joys came out of the hut behind
me. Leonard Hamnet patted his pocket to reassure
himself that he still had his letter. I looked back at the
right of the group, and the two dead men were gone.

"Let's saddle up," the Lieutenant said. "We aren't
doing any good around here."

"Tim?" Dengler asked. He had not taken his eyes
off me since I had come out of the hut. I shook my head.

"Well, what was it?" asked Tina Pumo. "Was it
juicy?"

Spanky and Calvin Hill laughed and slapped hands.

"Aren't we gonna torch this place?" asked Spitalny.

The Lieutenant ignored him. "Juicy enough, Pumo.
Interrogation Post. Field Interrogation Post."

"No shit," said Pumo.

"These people are into torture, Pumo. It's just
another indication."

"Gotcha." Pumo glanced at me and his eyes grew curious. Dengler moved closer.

"I was just remembering something," I said. "Something from the world."

"You better forget about the world while you're over here, Underhill," the Lieutenant told me. "I'm trying to keep you alive, in case you hadn't noticed, but you have to cooperate with me." His Adam's apple jumped like a begging puppy.

As soon as he went ahead to lead us out of the village, I gave twenty dollars to Spanky and said, "Two weeks from today."

"My man," Spanky said.

The rest of the patrol was uneventful.

The next night we had showers, real food, alcohol, cots to sleep in. Sheets and pillows. Two new guys replaced Tyrell Budd and Thomas Blevins, whose names were never mentioned again, at least by me, until long after the war was over and Poole, Linklater, Pumo, and I looked them up, along with the rest of our dead, on the Wall in Washington. I wanted to forget the patrol, especially what I had seen and experienced inside the hut. I wanted the oblivion that came in powdered form.

I remember that it was raining. I remember the steam lifting off the ground, and the condensation dripping down the metal poles in the tents. Moisture shone on the faces around me. I was sitting in the brothers' tent, listening to the music Spanky Burrage

played on the big reel-to-reel recorder he had bought
on R&R in Taipei. Spanky Burrage never played
Delius, but what he played was paradisal: great jazz
from Armstrong to Coltrane, on reels recorded for him
by his friends back in Little Rock and that he knew so
well he could find individual tracks and performances
without bothering to look at the counter. Spanky
liked to play disc jockey during these long sessions,
changing reels and speeding past thousands of feet of
tape to play the same songs by different musicians,
even the same song hiding under different names—
"Cherokee" and "KoKo," "Indiana" and "Donna
Lee"—or long series of songs connected by titles that
used the same words—"I Thought About You" (Art
Tatum), "You and the Night and the Music" (Sonny
Rollins), "I Love You" (Bill Evans), "If I Could Be with
You" (Ike Quebec), " You Leave Me Breathless" (Milt
Jackson), even, for the sake of the joke, "Thou Swell,"
by Glenroy Breakstone. In his single-artist mode on
this day, Spanky was ranging through the work of a
great trumpet player named Clifford Brown.

On this sweltering, rainy day, Clifford Brown's
music sounded regal and unearthly. Clifford Brown
was walking to the Paradise Garden. Listening to him
was like watching a smiling man shouldering open an
enormous door to let in great dazzling rays of light.
We were out of the war. The world we were in tran-
scended pain and loss, and imagination had banished
fear. Even SP4 Cotton and Calvin Hill, who preferred

James Brown to Clifford Brown, lay on their bunks listening as Spanky followed his instincts from one track to another.

After he had played disc jockey for something like two hours, Spanky rewound the long tape and said, "Enough." The end of the tape slapped against the reel. I looked at Dengler, who seemed dazed, as if awakening from a long sleep. The memory of the music was still all around us: light still poured in through the crack in the great door.

"I'm gonna have a smoke *and* a drink," Hill announced, and pushed himself up off his cot. He walked to the door of the tent and pulled the flap aside to expose the green wet drizzle. That dazzling light, the light from another world, began to fade. Hill sighed, plopped a wide-brimmed hat on his head, and slipped outside. Before the stiff flap fell shut, I saw him jumping through the puddles on the way to Wilson Manly's shack. I felt as though I had returned from a long journey.

Spanky finished patting the Clifford Brown reel back into its cardboard box. Someone in the rear of the tent switched on Armed Forces Radio. Spanky looked at me and shrugged. Leonard Hamnet took his letter out of his pocket, unfolded it, and read it through very slowly.

"Leonard," I said, and he swung his big buffalo's head toward me. "You still putting in for compassionate leave?"

He nodded. "You know what I gotta do."

"Yes," Dengler said, in a slow, quiet voice.

"They gonna let me take care of my people. They gonna send me back."

He spoke with a complete absence of nuance, like a man who had learned to get what he wanted by parroting words without knowing what they meant.

Dengler looked at me and smiled. For a second he seemed as alien as Hamnet. "What do you think is going to happen? To us, I mean. Do you think it'll just go on like this day after day until some of us get killed and the rest of us go home, or do you think it's going to get stranger and stranger?" He did not wait for me to answer. "I think it'll always sort of look the same, but it won't be—I think the edges are starting to melt. I think that's what happens when you're out here long enough. The edges melt."

"Your edges melted a long time ago, Dengler," Spanky said, and applauded his own joke.

Dengler was still staring at me. He always resembled a serious, dark-haired child, and never looked as though he belonged in uniform. "Here's what I mean, kind of," he said. "When we were listening to that trumpet player—"

"*Brownie,* Clifford *Brown,*" Spanky whispered.

"—I could see the notes in the air. Like they were written out on a long scroll. And after he played them, they stayed in the air for a long time."

"Sweetie-*pie,*" Spanky said softly. "You pretty hip, for a little ofay square."

"When we were back in that village, last week," Dengler said. "Tell me about that."

I said that I had been there too.

"But something happened to you. Something special."

"I put twenty bucks in the Elijah fund," I said.

"Only twenty?" Cotton asked.

"What was in that hut?" Dengler asked.

I shook my head.

"All right," Dengler said. "But it's happening, isn't it? Things are changing."

I could not speak. I could not tell Dengler in front of Cotton and Spanky Burrage that I had imagined seeing the ghosts of Blevins, Budd, and a murdered child. I smiled and shook my head.

"Fine," Dengler said.

"What the fuck you sayin' is *fine?*" Cotton said. "I don't mind listening to that music, but I do draw the line at this bullshit." He flipped himself off his bunk and pointed a finger at me. "What date you give Spanky?"

"Twentieth."

"He last longer than that." Cotton tilted his head as the song on the radio ended. Armed Forces' Radio began playing a song by Moby Grape. Disgusted, he turned back to me. "Check it out. End of August. He be so tired, he be *sleepwalkin'*. Be halfway through his tour. The fool will go to pieces, and that's when he'll get it."

Cotton had put thirty dollars on August thirty-first, exactly the midpoint of Lieutenant Joys's tour of duty.

He had a long time to adjust to the loss of the money, because he himself stayed alive until a sniper killed him at the beginning of February. Then he became a member of the ghost platoon that followed us wherever we went. I think this ghost platoon, filled with men I had loved and detested, whose names I could or could not remember, disbanded only when I went to the Wall in Washington, D.C., and by then I felt that I was a member of it myself.

2

I LEFT THE tent with a vague notion of getting outside and enjoying the slight coolness that followed the rain. The packet of Si Van Vo's white powder rested at the bottom of my right front pocket, which was so deep that my fingers just brushed its top. I decided that what I needed was a beer.

Wilson Manly's shack was all the way on the other side of camp. I never liked going to the enlisted men's club, where they were rumored to serve cheap Vietnamese beer in American bottles. Certainly the bottles had often been stripped of their labels, and to a suspicious eye the caps looked dented; also, the beer there never quite tasted like the stuff Manly sold.

One other place remained, farther away than the enlisted men's club but closer than Manly's shack and somewhere between them in official status. About twenty minutes' walk from where I stood, just at the curve in the steeply descending road to the airfield and the motor pool, stood an isolated wooden structure called Billy's. Billy himself, supposedly a Green Beret captain who had installed a handful of bar girls in an old French command post, had gone home long ago, but his club had endured. There were no more girls, if there ever had been, and the brand-name liquor was about as reliable as the enlisted men's club's beer. When it was open, a succession of slender Montagnard boys who slept in the nearly empty upstairs rooms served drinks. I visited these rooms two or three times, but I never learned where the boys went when Billy's was closed. They spoke almost no English. Billy's did not look anything like a French command post, even one that had been transformed into a bordello: it looked like a roadhouse.

A long time ago, the building had been painted brown. The wood was soft with rot. Someone had once boarded up the two front windows on the lower floor, and someone else had torn off a narrow band of boards across each of the windows, so that light entered in two flat white bands that traveled across the floor during the day. Around six-thirty the light bounced off the long foxed mirror that stood behind the row of bottles. After five minutes of blinding light, the sun disappeared beneath the pine boards, and for ten or fifteen minutes a shadowy pink glow filled the barroom. There was no electricity and no ice. Fingerprints covered the glasses. When you needed a toilet, you went to a cubicle with inverted metal boot prints on either side of a hole in the floor.

The building stood in a little grove of trees in the curve of the descending road, and as I walked toward it in the diffuse reddish light of the sunset, a mud-spattered jeep painted in the colors of camouflage gradually came into view to the right of the bar, emerging from invisibility like an optical illusion. The jeep seemed to have floated out of the trees behind it, to be a part of them.

I heard low male voices, which stopped when I stepped onto the soft boards of the front porch. I glanced at the jeep, looking for insignia or identification, but the mud covered the door panels. Something white gleamed dully from the back seat. When I looked more closely, I saw in a coil of rope an oval of bone that it took me a moment to recognize as the top of a painstakingly cleaned and bleached human skull.

Before I could reach the handle, the door opened. A boy named Mike stood before me, in loose khaki shorts and a dirty white shirt much too large for him. Then he saw who I was. "Oh," he said. "Yes. Tim. Okay. You come in." His real name was not Mike, but Mike was what it sounded like. He carried himself with an odd defensive alertness, and he shot me a tight, uncomfortable smile. "Far table, right side."

"It's okay?" I asked, because everything about him told me that it wasn't.

"*Yesss.*" He stepped back to let me in.

I smelled cordite before I saw the other men. The bar looked empty, and the band of light coming in through the opening over the windows had already reached the long mirror, creating a bright dazzle, a white fire. I took a couple of steps inside, and Mike moved around me to return to his post.

"Oh, hell," someone said from off to my left. "We have to put up with *this?*"

I turned my head to look into the murk of that side of the bar, and saw three men sitting against the wall at a round table. None of the kerosene lamps had been lighted yet, and the dazzle from the mirror made the far reaches of the bar even less distinct.

"Is okay, is okay," said Mike. "Old customer. Old friend."

"I bet he is," the voice said. "Just don't let any women in here."

"No women," Mike said. "No problem."

I went through the tables to the farthest one on the right.

"You want whiskey, Tim?" Mike asked.

"Tim?" the man said. "*Tim?*"

"Beer," I said, and sat down.

A nearly empty bottle of Johnnie Walker Black, three glasses, and about a dozen cans of beer covered the table before them. The soldier with his back against the wall shoved aside some of the beer cans so that I could see the .45 next to the Johnnie Walker bottle. He leaned forward with a drunk's guarded coordination. The sleeves had been ripped off his shirt, and dirt darkened his skin as if he had not bathed in years. His hair had been cut with a knife, and had once been blond.

"I just want to make sure about this," he said. "You're not a woman, right? You swear to that?"

"Anything you say," I said.

"No woman walks into this place." He put his hand on the gun. "No nurse. No wife. No *anything*. You got that?"

"Got it," I said. Mike hurried around the bar with my beer.

"Tim. Funny name. Tom, now—that's a name. Tim sounds like a little guy—like him." He pointed at Mike with his left hand, the whole hand and not merely the index finger, while his right still rested on the .45. "Little fucker ought to be wearing a dress. Hell, he practically *is* wearing a dress."

"Don't you like women?" I asked. Mike put a can of Budweiser on my table and shook his head rapidly, twice. He had wanted me in the club because he was afraid the drunken soldier was going to shoot him, and now I was just making things worse.

I looked at the two men with the drunken officer. They were dirty and exhausted—whatever had happened to the drunk had also happened to them. The difference was that they were not drunk yet.

"That is a complicated question," the drunk said. "There are questions of responsibility. You can be responsible for yourself. You can be responsible for your children and your tribe. You are responsible for anyone you want to protect. But can you be responsible for women? If so, how responsible?"

Mike quietly moved behind the bar and sat on a stool with his hands out of sight. I knew he had a shotgun under there.

"You don't have any idea what I'm talking about, do you, Tim, you rear-echelon dipshit?"

"You're afraid you'll shoot any women who come in here, so you told the bartender to keep them out."

"This wise-ass sergeant is personally interfering with my state of mind," the drunk said to the burly man on his right. "Tell him to get out of here, or a certain degree of unpleasantness will ensue."

"Leave him alone," the other man said. Stripes of dried mud lay across his lean, haggard face.

The drunken officer startled me by leaning toward the other man and speaking in a clear, carrying Vietnamese. It was an old-fashioned, almost literary Vietnamese, and he must have thought and dreamed in it to speak it so well. He assumed that neither I nor the Montagnand boy would understand him.

This is serious, he said, *and I am serious. If you wish to see how serious, just sit in your chair and do nothing. Do you not know of what I am capable by now? Have you learned nothing? You know what I know. I know what you know. A great heaviness is between us. Of all the people in the world at this moment, the*

*only ones I do not despise are already dead, or should
be. At this moment, murder is weightless.*

There was more, and I cannot swear that this was
exactly what he said, but it's pretty close. He may have
said that murder was *empty.*

Then he said, in that same flowing Vietnamese that
even to my ears sounded as stilted as the language of
a third-rate Victorian novel: *Recall what is in our ve-
hicle* [carriage]; *you should remember what we have
brought with us, because I shall never forget it. Is it so
easy for you to forget?*

It takes a long time and a lot of patience to clean
and bleach bone. A skull would be more difficult than
most of a skeleton.

Your leader requires more of this nectar, he said,
and rolled back in his chair, looking at me with his
hand on his gun.

"Whiskey," said the burly soldier. Mike was already pulling the bottle off the shelf. He understood
that the officer was trying to knock himself out before
he would find it necessary to shoot someone.

For a moment I thought that the burly soldier to
his right looked familiar. His head had been shaved
so close he looked bald, and his eyes were enormous
above the streaks of dirt. A stainless-steel watch hung
from a slot in his collar. He extended a muscular arm
for the bottle Mike passed him while keeping as far
from the table as he could. The soldier twisted off the
cap and poured into all three glasses. The man in the

center immediately drank all the whiskey in his glass and banged the glass down on the table for a refill.

The haggard soldier who had been silent until now said, "Something is gonna happen here." He looked straight at me. "Pal?"

"That man is nobody's pal," the drunk said. Before anyone could stop him, he snatched up the gun, pointed it across the room, and fired. There was a flash of fire, a huge explosion, and the reek of cordite. The bullet went straight through the soft wooden wall, about eight feet to my left. A stray bit of light slanted through the hole it made.

For a moment I was deaf. I swallowed the last of my beer and stood up. My head was ringing.

"Is it clear that I hate the necessity for this kind of shit?" said the drunk. "Is that much understood?"

The soldier who had called me *pal* laughed, and the burly soldier poured more whiskey into the drunk's glass. Then he stood up and started coming toward me. Beneath the exhaustion and the stripes of dirt, his face was taut with anxiety. He put himself between me and the man with the gun.

"I am not a rear-echelon dipshit," I said. "I don't want any trouble, but people like him do not own this war."

"Will you maybe let me save your ass, Sergeant?" he whispered. "Major Bachelor hasn't been anywhere near white men in three years, and he's having a little trouble readjusting. Compared to him, we're all rear-echelon dipshits."

I looked at his tattered shirt. "Are you his baby-sitter, Captain?"

He gave me an exasperated look and glanced over his shoulder at the major. "Major, put down your damn weapon. The sergeant is a combat soldier. He is on his way back to camp."

I don't care what he is, the major said in Vietnamese.

The captain began pulling me toward the door, keeping his body between me and the other table. I motioned for Mike to come out with me.

"Don't worry, the major won't shoot him. Major Bachelor loves the Yards," the captain said. He gave me an impatient glance because I had refused to move at his pace. Then I saw him notice my pupils. "God damn," he said, and then he stopped moving altogether and said "God damn" again, but in a different tone of voice.

I started laughing.

"Oh, this is—" He shook his head. "This is really—"

"Where have you *been?*" I asked him.

John Ransom turned to the table. "Hey, I know this guy. He's an old football friend of mine."

Major Bachelor shrugged and put the .45 back on the table. His eyelids had nearly closed. "I don't care about football," he said, but he kept his hand off the weapon.

"Buy the sergeant a drink," said the haggard officer.

"Buy the fucking sergeant a drink," the major chimed in.

John Ransom quickly moved to the bar and reached for a glass, which the confused Mike put into his hand. Ransom went through the tables, filled his glass and mine, and carried both back to join me.

We watched the major's head slip down by notches toward his chest. When his chin finally reached the unbuttoned top of his ruined shirt, Ransom said, "All right, Bob," and the other man slid the .45 out from under the major's hand. He pushed it beneath his belt.

"The man is out," Bob said.

Ransom turned back to me. "He was up three days straight with us, God knows how long before that." Ransom did not specify who *he* was. "Bob and I got some sleep, trading off, but he just kept on talking." He fell into one of the chairs at my table and tilted his glass to his mouth. I sat down beside him.

For a moment no one in the bar spoke. The line of light from the open space across the windows had already left the mirror, and was now approaching the place on the wall that meant it would soon disappear. Mike lifted the cover from one of the lamps and began trimming the wick.

"How come you're always fucked up when I see you?"

"You have to ask?"

He smiled. He looked very different from when I had seen him preparing to give a sales pitch to Senator Burrman at Camp White Star. His body had thickened and hardened, and his eyes had retreated far back into his head. He seemed to me to have moved a long step nearer the goal I had always seen in him than when he had given me the zealot's word about stopping the spread of communism. This man had taken in more of the war, and that much more of the war was inside him now.

"I got you off graves registration at White Star, didn't I?"

I agreed that he had.

"What did you call it, the body squad? It wasn't even a real graves registration unit, was it?" He smiled and shook his head. "I took care of your Captain McCue, too—he was using it as a kind of dumping ground. I don't know how he got away with it as long as he did. The only one with any training was that sergeant, what's-his-name. Italian."

"DiMaestro."

Ransom nodded. "The whole operation was going off the rails." Mike lit a big kitchen match and touched it to the wick of the kerosene lamp. "I heard some things—" He slumped against the wall and swallowed whiskey. He closed his eyes. "Some crazy stuff went on back there."

I asked if he was still stationed in the highlands up around the Laotian border. He almost sighed when he shook his head.

"You're not with the tribesmen anymore? What were they, Khatu?"

He opened his eyes. "You have a good memory. No, I'm not there anymore." He considered saying more, but decided not to. He had failed himself. "I'm kind of on hold until they send me up around Khe Sahn. It'll be better up there—the Bru are tremendous. But right now, all I want to do is take a bath and get into bed. Any bed. Actually, I'd settle for a dry level place on the ground."

"Where did you come from now?"

"In-country." His face creased and he showed his teeth. The effect was so unsettling that I did not immediately realize that he was smiling. "Way in-country. We had to get the major out."

"Looks more like you had to pull him out, like a tooth."

My ignorance made him sit up straight. "You mean you never heard of him? Franklin Bachelor?"

And then I thought I had, that someone had mentioned him to me a long time ago.

"In the bush for years. Bachelor did stuff that ordinary people don't even *dream* of—he's a legend."

A legend, I thought. Like the Green Berets Ransom had mentioned a lifetime ago at White Star.

"Ran what amounted to a private army, did a lot of good work in Darlac Province. He was out there on his own. The man was a hero. that's straight. Bachelor got to places we couldn't even get close to—he got *inside* an NVA encampment, you hear me, *inside* the encampment and *silently* killed about an entire division."

Of all the people in the world at this minute, I remembered, the only ones he did not detest were already dead. I thought I must have heard it wrong.

"He was absorbed right into Rhade life," Ransom said. I could hear the awe in his voice. "The man even got married. Rhade ceremony. His wife went with him on missions. I hear she was beautiful."

Then I knew where I had heard of Franklin Bachelor before. He had been a captain when Ratman and his platoon had run into him after a private named Bobby Swett had been blown to pieces on a trail in Darlac Province. Ratman had thought his wife was a black-haired angel.

And then I knew whose skull lay wound in rope in the back seat of the jeep.

"I did hear of him," I said. "I knew someone who met him. The Rhade woman, too."

"His *wife*," Ransom said.

I asked him where they were taking Bachelor.

"We're stopping overnight at Crandall for some rest. Then we hope to Tan Son Nhut and bring him back to the States—Langley. I thought we might have to strap him down, but I guess we'll just keep pouring whiskey into him."

"He's going to want his gun back."

Maybe I'll give it to him." His look told me what he thought Major Bachelor would do with his .45, if he was left alone with it long enough. "He's in for a rough time at Langley. There'll be a some heat."

"Why Langley?"

"Don't ask. But don't be naive, either. Don't you think they're..." He would not finish that sentence.

"Why do you think we had to bring him out in the first place?"

"Because something went wrong."

"Oh, everything went wrong. Bachelor went totally out of control. He had his own war. Ran a lot of sidelines, some of which were supposed to be under, shall we say, tighter controls?"

He had lost me.

"Ventures into Laos. Business trips to Cambodia. Sometimes he wound up in control of airfields Air America was using, and that meant he was in control of the cargo."

When I shook my head, he said, "Don't you have a little something in your pocket? A little package?"

A secret world—inside this world, another, secret world.

"You understand, I don't care what he did any more than I care about what *you* do. I think Langley can go fuck itself. Bachelor wrote the book. In spite of his sidelines. In spite of whatever *trouble* he got into. The man was effective. He stepped over a boundary, maybe a lot of boundaries—but tell me that you can do what we're supposed to do without stepping over boundaries."

I wondered why he seemed to be defending himself, and asked if he would have to testify at Langley.

"It's not a trial."

"A debriefing."

"Sure, a debriefing. They can ask me anything they want. All I can tell them is what I saw. That's *my* evidence, right? What I saw? They don't have any evidence, except maybe this, uh, these human remains the major insisted on bringing out."

For a second, I wished that I could see the sober shadowy gentlemen of Langley, Virginia, the gentlemen with slicked-back hair and pin-striped suits, question Major Bachelor. They thought *they* were serious men.

"It was like Bong To, in a funny way." Ransom waited for me to ask. When I did not, he said, "A ghost town, I mean. I don't suppose you've ever heard of Bong To."

"My unit was just there." His head jerked up. "A mortar round scared us into the village."

"You saw the place?"

I nodded.

"Funny story." Now he was sorry he had ever mentioned it. "Well, think about Bachelor, now. I think he must have been in Cambodia or someplace, doing what he does, when his village was overrun. He comes back and finds everybody dead, his wife included. I mean, I don't think *Bachelor* killed those people—they weren't just dead, they'd been made to beg for it. So Bachelor wasn't there, and his assistant, a Captain Bennington, must have just run off—we never did find him. Officially, Bennington's MIA. It's simple. You can't find the main guy, so you make sure he can see how mad you are when he gets back. You do a little grievous bodily harm on his people. They were not nice to his wife, Tim, to her they were especially not nice. What does he do? He buries all the bodies in the village graveyard, because that's a sacred responsibility. Don't ask me what else he does, because you don't have to know this, okay? But the bodies are buried. Generally speaking. Captain Bennington never does show up. We arrive and take Bachelor away. But sooner or later, some of the people who escaped are going to come back to that village. They're going to go on living there. The worst thing in the world happened to them in that place, but they won't leave. Eventually, other people in their family will join them, if they're still alive, and the terrible thing will be a part of their lives. Because it is not thinkable to leave your dead."

"But they did in Bong To," I said.

"In Bong To, they did."

I saw the look of regret on his face again, and said that I wasn't asking him to tell me any secrets.

"It's not a secret. It's not even military."

"It's just a ghost town."

Ransom was still uncomfortable. He turned his glass around and around in his hands before he drank. "I have to get the major into camp."

"A real ghost town," I said. "Complete with ghosts."

"I honestly wouldn't be surprised." He drank what was left in his glass and stood up. He had decided not to say any more about it. "Let's take care of Major Bachelor, Bob," he said.

"Right."

Ransom carried our bottle to the bar and paid Mike. I stepped toward him to do the same, and Ransom said, "Taken care of."

There was that phrase again—it seemed I had been hearing it all day, and that its meaning would not stay still.

Ransom and Bob picked up the major between them. They were strong enough to lift him easily. Bachelor's greasy head rolled forward. Bob put the .45 into his pocket, and Ransom put the bottle into his own pocket. Together they carried the major to the door.

I followed them outside. Artillery pounded hills a long way off. It was dark now, and light from the lanterns spilled out through the gaps in the windows.

All of us went down the rotting steps, the major bobbing between the other two.

Ransom opened the jeep, and they took a while to maneuver the major into the back seat. Bob squeezed in beside him and pulled him upright.

John Ransom got in behind the wheel and sighed. He had no taste for the next part of his job.

"I'll give you a ride back to camp," he said. "We don't want an M.P. to get a close look at you."

I took the seat beside him. Ransom started the engine and turned on the lights. He jerked the gearshift into reverse and rolled backward. "You know why that mortar round came in, don't you?" he asked me. He grinned at me, and we bounced onto the road back to the main part of camp. "He was trying to chase you away from Bong To, and your fool of a lieutenant went straight for the place instead." He was still grinning. "It must have steamed him, seeing a bunch of round-eyes going in there."

"He didn't send in any more fire."

"No. He didn't want to damage the place. It's supposed to stay the way it is. I don't think they'd use the word, but that village is supposed to be like a kind of monument." He glanced at me again. "To shame."

For some reason, all I could think of was the drunken major in the seat behind me, who had said that you were responsible for the people you wanted to protect. Ransom said, "Did you go into any of the huts? Did you see anything unusual there?"

"I went into a hut. I saw something unusual."

"A list of names?"

"I thought that's what they were."

"Okay," Ransom said. "You know a little Vietnamese?"

"A little."

"You notice anything about those names?"

I could not remember. My Vietnamese had been picked up in bars and markets, and was almost completely oral.

"Four of them were from a family named Trang. Trang was the village chief, like his father before him, and his grandfather before him. Trang had four daughters. As each one got to the age of six or seven, he took them down into that underground room and chained them to the posts and raped them. A lot of those huts have hidden storage areas, but Trang must have modified his after his first daughter was born. The funny thing is, I think everybody in the village knew what he was doing. I'm not saying they thought it was okay, but they let it happen. They could pretend they didn't know: the girls never complained, and nobody ever heard any screams. I guess Trang was a good enough chief. When the daughters got to sixteen, they left for the cities. Sent back money, too. So maybe they thought it was okay, but I don't think they did, myself, do you?"

"How would I know? But there's a man in my platoon, a guy from—"

"I think there's a difference between private and public shame. Between what's acknowledged and what is not acknowledged. That's what Bachelor has to cope with, when he gets to Langley. Some things are acceptable, as long as you don't talk about them—" He looked sideways at me as we began to approach the northern end of the camp proper. He wiped his face, and flakes of dried mud fell off his cheek. The exposed skin looked red, and so did his eyes. "Because the way I see it, this is a whole general issue. The issue is: what is *expressible?* This goes way beyond the tendency of people to tolerate thoughts, actions, or behavior they would otherwise find unacceptable."

I had never heard a soldier speak this way before. It was a little bit like being back in Berkeley.

"I'm talking about the difference between what is expressed and what is described," Ransom said. "A lot of experience is unacknowledged. Religion lets us handle some of the unacknowledged stuff in an acceptable way. But suppose—just suppose—that you were forced to confront extreme experience directly, without any mediation?"

"I have," I said. "You have, too."

"More extreme than combat, more extreme than terror. Something like that happened to the major: he *encountered* God. Demands were made upon him. He had to move out of the ordinary, even as *he* defined it."

Ransom was telling me how Major Bachelor had wound up being brought to Camp Crandall with his wife's skull, but none of it was clear to me.

"I've been learning things," Ransom told me. He was almost whispering. "Think about what would make all the people of a village pick up and leave, when sacred obligation ties them to that village."

"I don't know the answer," I said.

"An even more sacred obligation, created by a really spectacular sense of shame. When a crime is too great to live with, the memory of it becomes sacred. Becomes the crime itself—"

I remembered thinking that the arrangement in the hut's basement had been a shrine to an obscene deity.

"Here we have this village and its chief. The village knows but does not know what the chief has been

272

doing. They are used to consulting and obeying him. Then—one day, a little boy disappears."

My heart gave a thud.

"A little boy. Say: three. Old enough to talk and get into trouble, but too young to take care of himself. He's just gone—*poof*. Well, this is Vietnam, right? You turn your back, your kid wanders away, some animal gets him. He could get lost in the jungle and wander into a claymore. Someone like you might even shoot him. He could fall into a booby trap and never be seen again. It could happen.

"A couple of months later, it happens again. Mom turns her back, where the hell did Junior go? This time they really look, not just Mom and Grandma, all their friends. They scour the village. The *villagers* scour the village, every square foot of that place, and then they do the same to the rice paddy, and then they look through the forest.

"And guess what happens next. This is the interesting part. An old woman goes out one morning to fetch water from the well, and she sees a ghost. This old lady is part of the extended family of the first lost kid, but the ghost she sees isn't the kid's—it's the ghost of a disreputable old man from another village, a drunkard, in fact. A local no-good, in fact. He's just standing near the well with his hands together, he's hungry—that's what these people know about ghosts. The skinny old bastard wants *more*. He wants to be *fed*. The old lady gives a squawk and passes out. When she comes to again, the ghost is gone.

"Well, the old lady tells everybody what she saw, and the whole village gets in a panic. Evil forces have been set loose. Next thing you know, two thirteen-year-old girls are working in the paddy, they look up and see an old woman who died when they were ten—she's about six feet away from them. Her hair is stringy and gray and her fingernails are about a foot long. She used to be a friendly old lady, but she doesn't look too friendly now. She's hungry too, like all ghosts. They start screaming and crying, but no one else can see her, and she comes closer and closer, and they try to get away but one of them falls down, and the old woman is on her like a cat. And do you know what she does? She rubs her filthy hands over the screaming girl's face, and licks the tears and slobber off her fingers.

"The next night, another little boy disappears. Two men go looking around the village latrine behind the houses, and they see two ghosts down in the pit, shoving excrement into their mouths. They rush back into the village, and then they both see half a dozen ghosts around the chief's hut. Among them are a sister who died during the war with the French and a twenty-year-old first wife who died of dengue fever. They want to eat. One of the men screeches, because not only did he see his dead wife, who looks something like what we could call a vampire, he saw her pass into the chief's hut without the benefit of the door.

"These people believe in ghosts, Underhill, they know ghosts exist , but it is extremely rare for them

274

to see these ghosts. And these people are like psycho-
analysts, because they do not believe in accidents.
Every event contains meaning.

"The dead twenty-year-old wife comes back out
through the wall of the chiefs hut. Her hands are empty
but dripping with red, and she is licking them like a
starving cat.

"The former husband stands there pointing and
jabbering, and the mothers and grandmothers of the
missing boys come out of their huts. They are as afraid
of what they're thinking as they are of all the ghosts
moving around them. The ghosts are part of what they
know they know, even though most of them have never
seen one until now. What is going through their minds
is something new: new because it was hidden.

"The mothers and grandmothers go to the chief's
door and begin howling like dogs. When the chief
comes out, they push past him and they take the hut
apart. And you know what they find. They find the end
of Bong To."

Ransom had parked the jeep near my battalion
headquarters five minutes before, and now he smiled
as if he had explained everything.

"But what *happened?*" I asked. "How did you hear
about it?"

He shrugged. "We learned all this in interrogation.
When the women found the underground room, they
knew the chief had forced the boys into sex, and then
killed them. They didn't know what he had done with

the bodies, but they knew he had killed the boys. The next time the V.C. paid one of their courtesy calls, they told the cadre leader what they knew. The V.C. did the rest. They were disgusted—Trang had betrayed *them*, too—betrayed everything he was supposed to represent. One of the V.C. we captured took the chief downstairs into his underground room and chained the man to the posts, wrote the names of the dead boys and Trang's daughters on the padding that covered the walls, and then...then they did what they did to him. They probably carried out the pieces and threw them into the excrement pit. And over months, bit by bit, not all at once but slowly, everybody in the village moved out. By that time, they were seeing ghosts all the time. They had crossed a kind of border."

"Do you think they really saw ghosts?" I asked him. "I mean, do you think they were real ghosts?"

"If you want an expert opinion, you'd have to ask Major Bachelor. He has a lot to say about ghosts." He hesitated for a moment, and then leaned over to open my door. "But if you ask me, sure they did."

I got out of the jeep and closed the door.

Ransom peered at me. "Take better care of yourself."

"Good luck with your Bru."

"The Bru are fantastic." he slammed the jeep into gear and shot away, cranking the wheel to turn the jeep around in a giant circle in front of the battalion head-quarters before he jammed it into second and took off to wherever he was going.

Two weeks later Leonard Hamnet managed to get the Lutheran chaplain at Crandall to write a letter to the Tin Man for him, and two days after that he was in a clean uniform, packing up his kit for an overnight flight to an air force base in California. From there he was connecting to a Memphis flight, and from there the army had booked him onto a six-passenger puddle jumper to Lookout Mountain.

When I came into Hamnet's tent he was zipping his bag shut in a zone of quiet afforded him by the other men. He did not want to talk about where he was going or the reason he was going there, and instead of answering my questions about his flights, he unzipped a pocket on the side of his bag and handed me a thick folder of airline tickets.

I looked through them and gave them back. "Hard travel," I said.

"From now on, everything is easy," Hamnet said. He seemed rigid and constrained as he zipped the precious tickets back into the bag. By this time his wife's letter was a rag held together with Scotch tape. I could picture him reading and rereading it, for the thousandth or two thousandth time, on the long flight over the Pacific.

"They need your help," I said. "I'm glad they're going to get it."

"That's right." Hamnet waited for me to leave him alone.

Because his bag seemed heavy, I asked about the length of his leave. He wanted to get the tickets back out of the bag rather than answer me directly, but he forced himself to speak. "They gave me seven days. Plus travel time."

"Good," I said, meaninglessly, and then there was nothing left to say, and we both knew it. Hamnet hoisted his bag off his bunk and turned to the door without any of the usual farewells and embraces. Some of the other men called to him, but he seemed to hear nothing but his own thoughts. I followed him outside and stood beside him in the heat. Hamnet was wearing a tie and his boots had a high polish. He was already sweating through his stiff khaki shirt. He would not meet my eyes. In a minute a jeep pulled up before us. The Lutheran chaplain had surpassed himself.

"Good-bye, Leonard," I said, and Hamnet tossed his bag in back and got into the jeep. He sat up straight as a statue. The private driving the jeep said something to him as they drove off, but Hamnet did not reply. I bet he did not say a word to the stewardesses, either, or to the cabdrivers or baggage handlers or anyone else who witnessed his long journey home.

3

ON THE DAY after Leonard Hamnet was scheduled to return, Lieutenant Joys called Michael Poole and myself into his quarters to tell us what had happened back in Tennessee. He held a sheaf of papers in his hand, and he seemed both angry and embarrassed. Hamnet would not be returning to the platoon. It was a little funny. Well, of course it wasn't funny at all. The whole thing was terrible—that was what it was. Someone was to blame, too. Irresponsible decisions had been made, and we'd all be lucky if there wasn't an investigation. We were closest to the man, hadn't we seen what was likely to happen? If not, what the hell was our excuse?

Didn't we have any inkling of what the man was planning to do?

Well, yes, at the beginning, Poole and I said. But he seemed to have adjusted.

We have stupidity and incompetence all the way down the line here, said Lieutenant Elijah Joys. Here is a man who manages to carry a semiautomatic weapon through security at three different airports, bring it into a courthouse, and carry out threats he made months before, without anybody stopping him.

I remembered the bag Hamnet had tossed into the back of the jeep; I remembered the reluctance with which he had zipped it open to show me his tickets. Hamnet had not carried his weapon through airport security. He had just shipped it home in his bag and walked straight through customs in his clean uniform and shiny boots.

As soon as the foreman had announced the guilty verdict, Leonard Hamnet had gotten to his feet, pulled the semiautomatic pistol from inside his jacket, and executed Mr. Brewster where he was sitting at the defense table. While people shouted and screamed and dove for cover, while the courthouse officer tried to unsnap his gun, Hamnet killed his wife and his son. By the time he raised the pistol to his own head, the security officer had shot him twice in the chest. He died on the operating table at Lookout Mountain Lutheran Hospital, and his mother had requested that his remains receive burial at Arlington National Cemetery.

His mother. Arlington. I ask you.

That was what the Lieutenant said. *His mother. Arlington. I ask you.*

A private from Indianapolis named E. W. Burroughs won the six hundred and twenty dollars in the Elijah fund when Lieutenant Joys was killed by a fragmentation bomb thirty-two days before the end of his tour. After that we were delivered unsuspecting into the hands of Harry Beevers, the Lost Boss, the worst lieutenant in the world. Private Burroughs died a week later, down in Dragon Valley along with Tiano and Calvin Hill and lots of others, when Lieutenant Beevers walked us into a mined field, where we spent forty-eight hours under fire between two companies of NVA. I suppose Burroughs's mother back in Indianapolis got the six hundred and twenty dollars.

Interview with
Peter Straub
Conducted by Bill Sheehan

Bill Sheehan: I'd like to begin by asking about the specific connections between these stories and the group of novels—*Koko, Mystery*, and *The Throat*—now known as the Blue Rose trilogy. In what ways were these stories inspired by, or connected to, the larger works?

Peter Straub: The first, "Blue Rose," was my entry into all of this material: I saw it as a very compelling story, also as a way to work out a few things about Harry Beevers before I began *Koko*. "The Ghost Village" was originally a section of *Koko* I realized that I could beef up by putting it into a frame and adding some extra material. "Bunny is Good Bread" was written as a section of *The Throat* intended to explain and dramatize the forces that made Fielding Bandolier turn out the way he did. When the book was finished, it

281

was the only section not in the first person and seemed perfectly capable of standing on its own, so I took it out and eventually sent it to Tom Monteleone for a Borderlands anthology. "The Juniper Tree" will be discussed a little further down.

BS: I've often thought that Maryrose Beevers, mother of Harry Beevers, resembled one of Tennessee Williams's delusional matriarchs, such as Amanda Wingfield of *The Glass Menagerie*. Oddly, Laura Wingfield, from that same play, was given the nickname "Blue Roses" because she once suffered from pleurosis. Did Williams exert any kind of influence on you, or is this just sheerest coincidence? And if that's the case, where did the phrase "Blue Rose" come from?

PS: Williams had no influence at all on me. The last time I read his plays was when I was a teenager. The phrase "Blue Rose" came, just as in the story, from the book about hypnotism I read at 15 or 16 and used to hypnotize my brother John, my cousin Judy and about half the neighborhood. As in the story, it was used to plant a post-hypnotic suggestion. It always worked, too, though by now I trust it has lost its potency.

BS: One of the common threads running through these novels and stories is the Vietnam War. You never served in the military, but the scenes set in

Vietnam all have enormous authority. Can you talk a bit about how you approached this material and how you brought it so vividly to life?

PS: Basically, I read everything I could find about the Vietnam war, including publications put out by the army (these were very helpful), books of photos, and fiction. A lot of veterans kindly shared their experiences with me. Though not a vet, I felt very close to these men; I thought I understood certain central truths about them. There was a time when at a party or some other social gathering, I could unerringly pick out which of the men around me had been in Vietnam and which had not. The childhood traumas referred to in the question immediately below, and my long-delayed understanding of them, seemed to have affected me in much the same way that extended experiences of fear, the whole experience of combat, had affected them, in both cases permanently and irrevocably. All trauma, I began to think, was the same trauma. Like all great disorders and damages, in the end it becomes a gift.

BS: Another common thread, a hugely important one, is that of childhood trauma. There are moments, particularly in "The Juniper Tree" and "Bunny is Good Bread," that are almost too raw and painful to read. Was the process of creating these stories a difficult or painful one for you?

The Juniper Tree |||||||||||||||||||||||||||||||||||||||||||||||||||||||||||||||||||||||||||||||||||||||||||||||
AND OTHER BLUE ROSE STORIES

PS: "The Juniper Tree" felt like something I *had* to write. It did not seem to have any connection to my actual life. I was caught by the odd ambiguous ambivalent ratio of power between the abuser and the abused, and it seemed of crucial importance to me that I get the actual deed itself down as clearly, as transparently as possible. This necessity befell me in the middle of writing *Koko*, and I took the summer off — the summer I spent mainly alone in my brownstone while the carpenters put in many enormous bookshelves—to see the story through to the end. After I'd finished, I put it on a shelf and did not look at it again for nearly two years. A kind of archaic power seemed to inhabit it, a force too great to mess with. (This should have told me something.)

"Bunny is Good Bread," a kind of replay of the other story, was much more difficult. It came along initially as a section of *The Throat*, and writing it was like going to hell every day, like walking into a blazing furnace.

BS: On a related note, these stories and novels spend a great deal of time investigating the sources of deranged or irrational behavior. Did your experience with psychoanalysis play a significant role in your approach to this volatile material?

PS: My analysis helped me in a great many ways, but probably not in this one. I looked inward and exaggerated some of the less socialized stuff, and I read a lot about the topic itself—the sources of irrational and destructive behaviors. The teenaged Harry Beevers is practically a text book case in one aspect of the formation of a monstrous human being: a weak father, a mother who feels that she has married into a lower class and never lets her family forget it.

BS: In the Blue Rose sequence, you moved from the sort of supernatural horror you were famous for to fiction marked by greater realism and psychological complexity. Did your style, your actual use of language, change significantly as a result of this transition?

PS: I think my style did change at that point, partly because in "Blue Rose" and "The Juniper Tree" I revised and revised to attain a real transparency of language that would let the terrible events present themselves with absolute clarity. This renewed attention to language was enormously helpful in the multiple revisions of *Koko*, where I was trying to create a language that would surprise and delight and allow for insights without getting in the way. Once you go through that process, which is always very demanding and can be quite painful, it becomes a part of you, always alert and questioning and ready to pounce.

BS: Before the publication of "Blue Rose," most of your work took the form of big, complex novels.

What sort of difficulties and satisfactions did you experience in scaling down to these smaller fictional canvases?

PS: There is the pleasure, the joy even, of working on something so small that you have at least a dim chance of making it more or less perfect; the satisfaction of going through the whole cycle of creation, revision and completion in a couple of weeks, or over a single summer; the fun of realizing that everything in one's life is not riding on the project-at-hand, so that you can take risks that might otherwise be daunting.

BS: In a sense, the world of the Blue Rose has continued through the character of Tim Underhill, who appeared most recently in the novel *In the Night Room*. What is it about Underhill that keeps drawing you back to him? Do you have any plans to use him again in the future?

PS: Tim Underhill became very useful to me—I understood him pretty well, and I respected him, since it was clear that he could do all kinds of things that are beyond me. Sometimes I felt that I simply was not done with him, that he still had important things to yield up to me, at other times that he amounted to a wonderful convenience, like a well-known, deeply familiar tool lying close at hand. A lot of history, of emotion, of lessons learned, came with him.

BS: Finally, I have to remark on how well these stories have held up. I've read them many times, and they still generate a powerful emotional impact. There is a sense of genuine permanence about them, at least to my mind. Looking back at them from your present vantage point, how well do they hold up for you? How well, or poorly, do they seem to reflect your original intentions?

PS: I am still proud of these stories. They helped me reach a new, more ambitious stage in my work. Writing them, I was able, even when I was not conscious of doing so, to confront some of the most ugly, painful and horrifying moments of my life and render them available to the powers of imagination. As far as I know, they do not too much betray the intentions I originally had for them. Usually, those "intentions" were pretty cloudy, therefore full of possibility and promise.